Pay Days

The Harpur & Iles Series

PAY DAYS

Bill James

W. W. Norton & Company

New York   London

First published in Great Britain 2001 by Constable,
an imprint of Constable & Robinson Ltd
Copyright © 2001 by Bill James
First American edition 2001

For information about permission to reproduce selections from this book,
write to Permissions, W. W. Norton & Company, Inc.,
500 Fifth Avenue, New York, NY 10110

Manufacturing by Quebecor Fairfield

Library of Congress Cataloging-in-Publication Data

James, Bill, 1929–
    Pay days / Bill James.—1st American ed.
        p. cm.
    ISBN 0-393-04214-6
    1. Harpur, Colin (Fictitious character)—Fiction. 2. Iles, Desmond (Fictitious
character)—Fiction. 3. Police—England—Fiction. 4. Police corruption—
Fiction. 5. Drug traffic—Fiction. 6. England—Fiction. I. Title.

PR6070.U23 P39 2001

                                                            2001030911

W. W. Norton & Company, Inc.
500 Fifth Avenue, New York, N.Y. 10110
www.wwnorton.com

W. W. Norton & Company Ltd.
Castle House, 75/76 Wells Street, London W1T 3QT

1 2 3 4 5 6 7 8 9 0

I misbehaved once at a funeral.
Charles Lamb

Chapter One

Iles said: 'Col, I honestly don't think anyone would suggest I'm the sort who might kill a brother officer merely because he's on the take.'

Iles liked answers to his questions and, as Assistant Chief Constable, was entitled to answers to his questions, but this wasn't quite a question and Harpur said nothing.

'In any case, proof that Dick Nivette takes is shaky. Around 65–35. There aren't many officers one couldn't say the same about, or even worse, Col, including you.'

They were in Harpur's room at headquarters. As he sometimes liked to do, Iles had stretched out on the desk, the back of his head in the Out-tray, resting on an Overnight Offences Summary. Half his legs and his feet in fine black lace-ups hung over the edge at the opposite end like lessons in stress relief.

Standing at the window, Colin Harpur gazed down. It was early summer and things looked good, wholesome: the business buildings, St John's spire and the bright white stone of North Bridge. Anyone might want a piece of this city. Dick Nivette might. One way was backhanders from some villain team who already had a piece.

Iles said: 'Grand girls jiggling unrestrictedly out there this morning, Col?'

This *was* a question and Harpur replied: 'Nivette? Problematical. He might be genuinely taking or only pretending to, as cover for some private undercover ploys. You know, sir – *seeming* to double-cross us, but only as a means of getting into a villain firm and double-crossing *them*, eventually with a prosecution when he's found out enough. Double-double. You've heard of it.'

'Nothing better than liberated summer chests in filmy garments after winter, even glimpsed from the altitude of this office,' the ACC replied. 'And how's Denise, the undergrad girlfriend, Col? Hale? Good. Nivette's doing *private* undercover? You mean, unofficial, unknown to us, maverick, freelance, no stand-by back-up, no protection, no headquarters Controller for his operation, no system?'

'Along those lines, sir. Fast-track detectives sometimes do. They love playing solo. None but the lonely heart. They want total, unshared *gloire*. They see the system as a hindrance.'

Iles turned his head slightly to stare at Harpur and the ACC's head rustled on stationery. 'And you sympathise, don't you? Once you did something like it yourself, of course, Col. At least once.'

'Oh, I doubt that, sir.'

'You did, you fucker. Nobody knew you were under-cover. It was –'

'I don't have a watch on Nivette, in case he *is* only playing at the take. Someone working like that can't operate if he thinks we're spying. Nivette's bright enough to spot surveillance.'

'Remind me, did we put *you* under surveillance?'

'We'll deal with him, sir,' Harpur replied. He grieved a little for Nivette, corrupt or not, dangerous or not, double-double-crossing or not. Harpur would have grieved at least a little for anyone the ACC took the trouble to deny wanting to kill.

Iles crooned something quietly, but the song seemed feverish, madly hurried. Harpur failed to make out the words. They might have been Mexican or Portuguese or Erse. When it was over the ACC said with something close to genuine feeling: 'As you probably realise, Col, my main wish is to guard our Chief from further hurt, the dear eminent mouse.'

Harpur did not need to respond to this.

'That man's health and well-being, a non-stop anxiety to me.' Iles turned on to his side and brought his legs up to the crouch position, a grey-haired foetus in one of his £1500 grey-flannel suits. 'One knows the Chief dotes on Nivette,' he said. 'Has really brought him on – only twenty-seven and Chief Inspector. Better even than you did, Col? And I'm sure the sod won't be well stuck as Detective Chief Super at, what are you now – thirty-seven, eight? Should he live.'

'Mr Lane sees extraordinary organisational flair in Nivette, sir,' Harpur replied.

Iles sang a bit more, still very quietly, maybe a Tonton Macoute fraternity jingle. The ACC said: 'Myself, I made Chief Inspector at just turned twenty-six, and damn pretty with it. Oh, you'll say fluke and brown-nosing, so piss off, Harpur.'

'And the Chief was very impressed with Nivette's handling of the Capel-Nelmes case. Seven convictions, wonderful Press.'

Iles groaned. 'I don't say anything fleshly between the Chief and Nivette. Just professional. Mark Lane's invested his soul in that lad. If we come along now and tell him this trusted minion might be dirty right through, what's it going to do to the Chief's flimsy self-belief? Justifiably flimsy. Lane would blame himself – guilt's his hobby, Col – he'd blame himself for nurturing a piece of rottenness whose taint touches the whole Force. We must shield the Chief from that. Hasn't our sweet, wife-run relic slid into clinical breakdown at least twice before? Do you know what I believe, Harpur?'

'That because of –'

'I believe some would take quite an extreme view.'

'Yes, sir?'

'Some might even argue that the kindest, surest thing

is kill Nivette in circumstances made to look as if he died valiantly on police business – say get him into the forefront of an ambush, knock him over with an untraceable and duly inscribe his memorial on the Halo Wall downstairs. We'd be rid of the treacherous shit, if that's what he is – possible, possible – and at the same time the Chief could feel his devotion to the shit he wouldn't know was a shit was far-sighted and noble – Nivette a nicely corpsed hero, no suggestion of two-timing. You'll remember Bogart in *Casablanca* talking about the murdered Jerry couriers: "Yesterday they were just two German clerks. Today, the honoured dead."'

'Are you asking me to fix his death for you, you mad jerk, sir?' Harpur replied. 'If so you can –'

'The caption under his name could read, "Much missed, but not on this occasion." It's almost impossible to prove malpractice by an officer, and even more impossible to get him chucked out for it, especially when people like you concoct defences for him. However, as I've said, Col, although I might see the charm, even rightness, in an execution it's not something to appeal to me, personally, is it? A tactic like that could never rate as law and order – correct me if I'm wrong. I mean, if an Assistant Chief doesn't know what law and order is, who, I ask, does?'

Harpur was trying to whistle up an answer to this when someone knocked the door and the Chief pushed it gently open a few inches and peered in. The moment seemed to sum up his standing these days. Even when only part on view in the gap, Lane's big doughy face looked as almost always, benign, twitchy and gamely – hopelessly – intent on displaying resolve. Iles was lying with his back to the door but, hearing the knock, had raised his head a little and turned. 'Oh, you, sir,' he cried over his shoulder. 'I know I speak for Col when I say this is a fine treat. Isn't it a treat, Col?'

Harpur said: 'As a matter of fact, Mr Lane, we were just discussing –'

10

'Yes, Harpur and 1 reminisced about that seminal talk you gave to the accelerated promotion course at Bramshill on "The Inevitability of Ethics", published in *Police Today*, and lucky they were to get it. This was a mind getting to grips, if I may say. I wish I could have heard it in the as it were flesh.' Iles remained in his position on the desk.

The Chief came slowly into the room. 'Targeting,' he said.

'Ah,' Iles replied.

'It's time.' There was a rasp of almost decisiveness in the Chief's words. He must have rehearsed. Oh, God, Harpur longed for him not to get reannihilated by Iles. Oh, God, Harpur longed for Lane to retire or move up to the Inspectorate of Constabulary while he still often made sense. The Chief sat down in a straight-backed wooden chair beneath a big street map of the inner city. He was in uniform today for some function later, the buttons badly in need of a clean: this would be part of his endearing, radiantly successful campaign always to look scruffy and unmilitary. 'My dread, Desmond, Colin – well, do I need to bore you again with that central terror of my life – the terror that we will come to tolerate evil on our patch for the sake of a kind of peace?'

'Bore us, sir?' Iles cried. He gave a brilliant amazed chuckle. 'To bore is not within your nature, as it is not in the nature of a pekinese to climb trees. Would you think the Chief could conceivably bore, Col?'

Lane said: 'But perhaps we have this situation already – a state of tolerated evil.' The Chief shuddered and lowered his head for a moment. Abruptly he straightened and made his voice hiss like a whip: 'An end to the appeasing blind eye, Desmond, Colin. Instead, targeting. We select one, perhaps two, major criminal operators on our ground – people who have come to feel their massive but discreet drugs trading is acceptable to us for the sake of stability and the quiet life – and we build a case – no matter how long it takes – we build

11

and build and eventually show them and show the
public – yes, show the public, this also is crucial – show
everyone that these fine, smart, loaded crooked figures
are not in fact above prosecution, any more than back
alley muggers and small-time thieves are above prosecution.' He smiled minutely. 'Forgive a little rhetoric, but
I speak of my eternal mission.'

Iles sat up on the desk, his body tense, as though he
saw a vision. 'I believe I recognise your thinking, sir,' he
said. 'This is top drawer theology. This is your fear of
that ultimate, unforgivable sin, despair – the state of
mind which says evil is so strong it must prevail, and
therefore should be accepted. Col was brought up
Gospel Hall, and he'd know in detail about all the sins,
not just the flesh ones. Yes, Col?'

'Which criminal, criminals, would you want targeted,
Chief?' Harpur replied.

At once Lane said: 'People who think they have achieved a kind of business respectability, even business
sainthood, yet whose illegal empires thrive beneath such
cover. They've come to believe they have a right to work
cheek-by-jowl with us.'

'Panicking Ralphy Ember?' Iles asked. 'Manse
Shale?'

Lane's body arched forward suddenly in the chair,
like a strychnine spasm. 'Right, Desmond! Those two
above all . . . Grubby emblems. Their very names sicken
me – the familiarity with which you speak of them.
Ralphy Ember. Mansel – Manse – Shale.'

'Oh, they not bad old entities, sir,' Iles said. 'Ember
and Shale try to stick to the rules.'

'Rules? Which damn rules?' Lane cried. 'That is what
I mean. The rules, Desmond, are unspoken permissions
for Ember and Shale to carry on their deplorable trade in
exchange for forswearing violence. Nod-nod, wink-
wink.' The slang seemed wrong coming from him:
déclassé, flippant. Harpur wanted the Chief dignified. A
couple of scarlet nodules gleamed for a moment on a

vein in his right cheek. These would appear now and then and were the only signs of rage Harpur had ever seen him show. Lane said: 'I don't imply blame against you, Desmond, Colin. How could I? Who's in charge here? I. I.' He struck himself with the tips of his fingers on the chest. Occasionally, Lane was obviously appalled by his responsibilities. Iles said it was a notorious management phenomenon: people promoted a fatal stage beyond their skills, like Kennedy and St Peter. Once, Lane had been a great detective on the neighbouring patch, but Chiefdom and Iles had murderously sapped him. Now, Lane fretted that moral decay would grow rampant in his realm and from here infect the cosmos, like the spread of TV.

The Chief said: 'If there has been apathy that apathy has been mine. You were entitled to look to me for a different kind of leadership. I have failed you.'

Iles leaned forward and stared at Lane. Harpur saw for a second real, motherly anguish in the ACC's eyes. Harpur never fully understood Iles. Who did? The ACC would hound and defeat and ignore Lane, yet now and then – now – it became touchingly clear he did not want him altogether flattened. Ultimately there was a kind of tenderness in Iles, an Iles kind. Ultimately there was a kind of reverence for hierarchy and proper process in Iles, an Iles kind. And the Chief still represented these, however ramshackle he had grown. The ACC said: 'Oh, you are painfully unjust to yourself, sir. I know I speak for Harpur, also, when I –'

'Colin, I'd like to see someone young given the job of bringing such people as Ember and Mansel Shale to trial and conviction through a long-term targeting operation,' the Chief replied. 'Targeting has worked in the Met and many other Forces. I want someone with hope and resolve and stamina to run this. Someone still free from that odious, enfeebling willingness to compromise which has disgracefully crippled myself and Desmond and . . . yes, even you.'

'Did you have anyone specific in mind, I wonder, sir?' Iles asked.

'Oh, not for me – not for me to intrude upon Colin's operational decisions,' Lane said. He gave a tiny lost laugh. 'I hope I know my place, Desmond.'

Harpur said: 'I suppose that someone like –'

'There's Richard Nivette, for instance,' the Chief replied.

Iles said: 'Nivette has certainly –'

'Yes, someone like Richard Nivette,' Lane said, that hiss of command in his voice again.

Chapter Two

Harpur had one of those phone calls at home. 'It's super-fink,' his daughter yelled, holding out the receiver. 'I recognise the creepy tone: "Would Detective Chief Superintendent Colin Harpur be there I wonder, dear?"' She did not cover the mouthpiece – never did when rubbishing an informant. Both his daughters hated almost all police work and liked everyone to know it, particularly Harpur and particularly Harpur's tipsters. But then all kids were keen to look gift horses in the mouth and kick their teeth down their throats, given a chance.

When the telephone rang he had been in the kitchen getting quite a supper ready for them and himself, something extensive and fried. Harpur craved a reputation as a damn conscientious single parent and tried to be around at least two or three times a week to cook breakfast and the evening meal. It unnerved the girls and they sometimes called him Earthmother. He took the phone and Jack Lamb asked: 'Which one was that, Col?'

'Jill.'

'Age now?'

'Going on fourteen.'

'Lovely time of life – things look so simple and positive, and the larynx grows strong. We need to go on a journey, you and I. Obviously a death matter.'

'Right.'

'Tonight.'

'Right.'

Harpur waited. Lamb was possibly the greatest informant in the world, and certainly the greatest never to have been jailed. He informed only to Harpur, and when Jack made a suggestion Harpur always agreed, always agreed and asked nothing. You let an informant make the pace. It was his or her skin. And you especially let Jack Lamb make the pace, not just because he had a lot of skin but because he preferred to deliver slowly, so that what he brought could be properly savoured, properly valued.

'Don't they realise it would all stop, Col?'

'Who?'

'Your daughters. And, I have to say – looking back – your wonderful late wife, Megan.'

'What would all stop?' Harpur asked, knowing the answer, but also knowing he could get into this script only as little boy lost.

'Detection would stop, Col. If it wasn't for voices like me.'

'There aren't any voices like you.'

'Some try. That's what I mean, a death matter. Tonight I want to take you to one who might have tried, or threatened to try, poor sod. Where do they learn these words, Col?'

'Who?'

'Your daughters.'

'Which words?'

'Fink.'

'I'll speak to her.'

'It's American TV,' Lamb said. 'Rendezvous 3?'

'Right.' They had a list of spots where they would meet, supposedly remote and secret. Lamb did not like to speak their locations by phone, so this code. Number 3 was a defence blockhouse built at the beginning of the Second World War to protect the coast from Hitler. It must have put him off. Harpur had the idea the concrete hut was used these days by all sorts for confidential meetings, villains included. But he accepted Jack's suggestion. Always he accepted Jack's suggestions.

'I hear some targeting's under way from your side,' Lamb said.

'Targeting?'

'New term to you, Col? You know – an educated focus on one or two prime crooks. The Chief's own project as I understand.'

'I hope we focus all the time on prime crooks. We call it policing.'

'Led by Nivette. By Nivette! Have I really got that right, in the circs? In the problematical circs.'

'Where do you pick up such things?' Harpur replied.

It was the sort of question Harpur often put and which Lamb or any other informant never heard. 'I can drive you from Rendezvous 3 to where you need to be, Col,' he said.

'Right.'

'This will be a boat trip.'

'Right,' Harpur said.

'You can manage a rope ladder in the dark?' Lamb asked.

'In the dark, in the light, rope ladders are my thing. Will you be with me?'

'Yes. You might need protection. Are they there now, in the room, listening?'

'Who?'

'Your daughters. Jill. The other one. Hazel? Older?'

They were but Harpur said: 'Of course not. Into homework.'

'Occasionally I wish I had children – to inherit and keep up the name and business like Jane Fonda, if something goes wrong.'

'Oh, we make sure it doesn't.'

'Yes, we do, Col. We do. That's why I'm coming as protection. And who protects *me*, you'll ask.'

No, he wouldn't have asked. But now he said: 'Who?'

'Too self-effacing, Col. Grand reciprocity. I know you'd do it, if something went wrong.'

'We make sure it doesn't,' Harpur replied.

When he had replaced the receiver, Hazel said: 'A rope ladder at your age, dad? In the dark?'

'You'd trust your safety to the hands of a fink?' Jill asked. She was reading *The Sweet Science*, a boxing book, but put it down now. 'Do you ever think what would happen to . . . well, to Denise if you were . . . But I suppose she'd be all right. Yea, she smokes but she's young, and pretty, with boobs, *and* clever, so there'd soon be another boyfriend, more her own age, less coarse than you, probably, and going to be a merchant banker or quantity surveyor, something high.'

'What rope ladder?' Hazel asked. 'A vessel?'

Jill did an imitation of him, but whining: '"Will you be with me?" Sounds feeble, dad – like, "Hold my hand."'

'I wish you wouldn't use that word,' Harpur replied.

'Fink?' Jill said.

'And in any case not shouted,' Harpur said.

'I could say nark or grass or snout or snitch,' Jill said.

Harpur finished preparing the meal and they sat down to eat at the kitchen table. He loved the sense of ordinariness and peace. 'Does it upset them when I say fink?' Jill asked.

'Naturally,' Harpur said.

'Does it upset *you*?' Jill asked.

'Of course it does, dreg,' Hazel told her. 'Look at his face when you do it. It's already deadbeat but – These are people he has to keep sweet and you're bellowing down the phone they're slime.'

'Does it upset *you*, dad?' Jill asked, baked bean juice neat and bubbly along her lower lip like effluent at the sea's edge.

'Yes,' Harpur replied.

She chewed and thought and slowly pulled a length of bacon rind from her mouth. 'Perhaps I'll stop doing it, then,' she said.

'Thanks, Jill. The informants' livery company will be grateful, too.'

'Dumbo kid. Do you have to have everything said straight out before you see it?' Hazel asked her.

'I'll be working tonight,' Harpur said.

'No, *honestly*?' Hazel replied.

'You said "targeting", dad. Who? Do you realise if you make somebody a target they might turn around and make one of you?'

'Thus spake the prophet,' Hazel muttered. 'What do we say if Denise or some other woman rings up for you or comes around here sniffing the way they do?'

'That I'll be back shortly,' Harpur replied.

'Unless you're a target on a rope ladder,' Jill said. 'Marriage is just not wanted by you, is it, dad? I mean with Denise. You like things as they are – casual. But is that . . . well, grown-up? Is it . . . right, even for a cop?'

'Would someone such as Denise – college girl, own motor, soon with a degree – I mean would she want to marry him?' Hazel asked. 'His age and the job and us around his neck and his Day Centre music.'

'Of course she would, of course she would,' Jill said. 'I've heard of much older people than dad. Think of George Foreman making a comeback.'

'Wipe your gob,' Hazel replied. 'If Denise turns up here in the night and you're out she'll think you're dallying with someone else, dad, she always does. She's very bright.'

'He will be. His fink,' Jill replied.

* * *

When Harpur arrived, Jack Lamb was already at the blockhouse, standing massive and slightly hunched outside in the shadows. They left Harpur's old Renault from the police pool there and Lamb drove towards the docks. 'This is a death by long-drawn-out savagery,' he said. 'As I hear.'

'Oh, God. Who? Who told you about it, Jack?'

'Maybe just torture for the sake of it or maybe to get a conversation going or maybe to warn others.'

Jack did not usually speak in maybes. It was worrying to know even he suffered doubts.

'Are you carrying anything?' Lamb asked.

'My notebook,' Harpur replied.

'You won't call the cops if I tell you I've got a Mustang Colt?'

'That a gun?'

'Not a fucking horse. We've got a dark situation here. But I can't say at this stage that the Chief's friend is involved.'

'Which friend's that, Jack?' he asked, again knowing the answer, and this time wishing he didn't.

'Nivette. Possibly.' Jack drove on to what remained of the docks. He seemed to be making for the Invet Basin, one of only two docks active now. In these last few years marina development and new bijou housing had colonised much of the area and would colonise more. The Chief loved the marina. To him it said rebirth. Lamb's voice grew heavy: 'As you know, Col, I inform only as and when.'

Harpur had frequently been given Lamb's gospel of grassing, but always listened properly: informants were despised, might hear contempt from children, and naturally needed to explain now and then why they did it.

Lamb parked behind some sheds. They walked. It was just after midnight. 'When your daughter calls me fink, Col, she –'

20

'She's an infant, crude.'

'In a way, Jill's obviously right. But I think you'll agree I don't talk to you unless I see something especially filthy and chaotic, something that could ruin the whole system.'

'Absolutely.'

'And not for gain.'

'Not for simple gain.' Harpur saw three middle-sized vessels moored against one another, the first along the quay wall, then the next tied to her and the third out towards the middle of the dock fixed to the second. They called it stacking. You could probably step from ship to ship. Jack said: 'We're going on to the far one, the *Dion.*'

They looked like freighters all from one line, each showing a D inside a red circle on the funnel and with names starting with D. The company must have laid them up here waiting for cargoes. The ships were not properly mothballed yet, but that could be the next stage, or the breaker's. Even the working docks were not really working. Change and decay all round. The Chief might have a point about the marina.

The vessel against the dockside had a gangplank but it was raised high now on davits for security. Lamb said: 'There's a boat at the steps. We row out to the far side of the third. She's got a ladder down there to a platform. They've had a diver looking at her hull.'

'If the docks police see us pulling out at this time of night they'll –'

'That will be all right,' Jack replied.

'Who says?'

'That will be all right.'

'How is it there's a boat at the steps?' Harpur asked.

'I'll row,' Jack replied.

Harpur was brought up around docks. Ships did nothing for him. The buggers always looked so brave and top-heavy and doomed and the steering was damned approximate. They spoke tragedy. These three also spoke redundancy and made the wide, otherwise empty dock seem an ante-room to extinction. Harpur's father used to say that when he was growing up in the war he knew ten or a dozen neighbours at sea in merchant ships and not one survived. Lamb led down the steps to the rowing boat and took the oars. Harpur cast off. They moved out on black water under the stern of the first ship. The quayside cranes stood thin and high in the moonlight behind Jack, probably as underused as the ships.

'You won't be able to report this death, Col,' Lamb said. He rowed easily and spoke without effort.

'I'm a senior police officer, Jack. I'll be duty bound to.'

'Of course. But don't.'

'Right,' Harpur replied.

'You report it and it points to me. Then where are we?'

'Right,' Harpur replied. They passed the second ship and started to round the back of the third. Lamb had on what he might consider typical boatman's gear – not yachtsman's smartarse stuff, but the kind of outfit worn by freighter crews. This was like Jack. He loved to garb himself in tune with the meeting place they used. At the blockhouse he would often turn up in bits of army uniform bought at a surplus store, once with the epaulettes of a field marshal. Tonight, he wore a roll-necked navy sweater under heavy, full-length black oilskins, although the night was cloudless and warm. On Jack full-length meant full-length and full-breadth as well. He was six foot five and weighed 260 pounds. People thought of informants as small and furtive like Toothpick Charlie in *Some Like It Hot*. Not Jack. Fink would never be the word for him.

'I think Nivette's all right,' Harpur said. 'Charading in a worthy cause.'

'Ah, there *is* a ladder,' Lamb replied, as they came

around to the starboard side of the *Dion*. *'Something* I got right.'

'Like the boat at the steps and no bother from the docks police. Laid on?'

'God, but you're lucky to get this kind of aid,' Lamb replied.

'Have you been out here for a look already?'

'And all for free.'

More or less. Lamb certainly required no dabs in the hand. He owned a brilliantly lucrative art business, lived in a lovely manor house, ran a turbo Lancia and could go mad on army surplus. But sometimes there might be worrying doubts over where pictures he sold came from. Harpur hardly ever inquired. This was give and take, the unsolid rock on which detection survived, when it did. There was a name for the kind of relationship where a detective became so tied to an informant that the officer might blind-eye big law breaking by the grass, even take part. It was called the Stockholm Syndrome, though Harpur did not know why Stockholm. He never participated in Lamb's business, but did little to discover how it worked. Of course, he knew it would be useless to ask Jack.

Lamb brought them alongside the *Dion*. 'I'll go up first,' he said. 'Wait for my word. If there's any bother you ought to get into the water and swim back. *Can* you swim? Too easy to pick you off from above sitting in a boat.' Harpur fixed their painter to the diver's platform and Lamb immediately began to climb the rope ladder expertly and fast. When he reached the deck he paused and looked about. Harpur saw him draw the pistol from a pocket in his oilskin. He went aboard and disappeared. After seven or eight minutes he came back and called down, 'OK, admiral.' Harpur followed him up the ladder, less expertly, less fast. At the top, Lamb gave him his hand and said: 'I've found our lad.' He pulled Harpur on to the *Dion*. Jack had put the pistol away but was carrying a small flashlight now.

'Who is he?' Harpur asked.

'My information says someone called Goussard.'

'Victor Goussard – Slow Victor? Gay. Known too as All Passion Bent?'

'Not someone I recognise. You might,' Lamb replied.

'Facially he's still all right.'

'Low-level pusher. Gets his supplies from Shale or Ralph Ember.'

'So does everyone, as you know, Col. Victor was earning some extra as watchman on these three. Or he had reasons to lie low.'

Because they were afloat, Harpur expected a death in some special way to do with ships. But as watchman Slow Victor had been given the captain's cabin, and he was strung up with cord by wrists and ankles from the double wardrobe crossbeam used for hanging clothes, like a leopard on a pole between safari porters. The room could have been the Savoy, except there was no electricity and Lamb had lit two big gas lamps. Harpur saw a line of blood beneath Victor and some hefty splashes on the back wall of the wardrobe and several small calibre bullet holes there. His body was scarred by gunshot wounds for what seemed its whole length – feet, legs, arms, chest, head. It looked as if someone or more than one had fired at him from the other side of the cabin, the first rounds probably deliberately non-lethal. There would be nobody about to hear, and the weapon, weapons, were most likely silenced anyway.

'Don't touch anything, Col. Well, hark at me telling basics to a detective! All right, maybe not Nivette. But someone wanting a lot of silence.'

'So, why the brutalising?'

'Perhaps he'd asked for money as fee to stay quiet. People can get ratty. And they'd want to discourage others from talking, if others know. Whatever it is.'

'How discourage others when he's hidden here?'

'Not hidden for ever, Col. The diving party could be back some day soon, I expect. Or the *Dion* will get herself chartered. But for the present, private to you and me.'

'And to who told you. Someone trying to do a bit of thieving around the boats but runs into a corpse instead? And so a whisper to Jack Lamb and maybe to others. You went straight to the body when you came aboard? *Have* you been before?'

Lamb closed the wardrobe doors, wiped around the cabin with a handkerchief, and put out the lights. He switched on his torch.

Harpur said: 'If you don't want anything done about it why bring me out for the show?'

'I didn't say you couldn't do anything about it. I said you mustn't report it, tell your people. Not yet.'

'What else can I do, for God's sake?' Harpur said. He saw at least a few things he could do, of course, and, of course, knew Jack would see them, too.

'Some find going down a rope ladder worse than the ascent,' Lamb replied. 'I'll lead again, shall I? I can catch you if you tumble. Well, my eternal role.'

On the way back to Rendezvous 3, Lamb drove to a street near where Harpur knew from dossier memories Slow Victor lived alone, and pulled up. Harpur left the car, walked around the corner and broke into the terraced house. Harpur and Lamb had not discussed this, but Jack's instincts would be the same as Harpur's. It was crucial to look for anything in Victor's home that might prove he'd come into some rare knowledge. As soon as the body was found detectives would tooth-comb the house. Harpur had no idea what he would do with it if he did find something. In fact, he had no clear notion what his motives were for searching, but that did not make it any less necessary to get in ahead of colleagues. This was policing. Perhaps he wanted to protect the Chief, that lifelong, worthwhile mission. Protect him from what? The truth? From disintegration? Yes, always that.

Still without saying anything, Lamb had handed him

the flashlight and his Mustang Colt pistol just before Harpur climbed out of the Lancia. After all, there might be others interested already in possible disclosures of whatever it was Slow Victor had known.

Harpur loved this kind of work: digging alone and clandestinely into the domestic banalities of someone's life and forming a profile. But he found he could not relax tonight and his probe was skimped. It would be at least very bad to be found here, and possibly hazardous. He must leave no signs and so worked too delicately – found nothing of use. Most of the time he spent going through Slow Victor's desk. In the drawers were some minor-sum accounts, and a bundle of well-phrased love letters from a man called Bernie, tied together with a bit of electricity wire. It was a big, roll-top desk, possibly Edwardian or earlier. Sitting at it, Harpur felt a kind of grandeur despite his edginess: a sort of fine, respectable dignity. His daughters should have seen him foursquare at this desk, except, of course, they would ask, and go on asking, whether it wasn't criminal for him to have broken in. He hoped Lamb was keeping an eye outside.

This desk was so right for Slow Victor. He had always been keen on style and weight. A couple of years ago it had looked briefly as if he might get himself a drugs career near the top, with its own style and weight – and wealth. That had never happened, though, or even nearly happened. Harpur was not sure what went wrong. Some gays had such demanding emotional lives that they were distracted from career paths. Victor had stayed in the trade but stayed in the trade very near the base: mostly grass to kids, occasionally crack and Ecstasy. Perhaps the accounts recorded some of those tiny deals in code. It must have been a tonic for Victor to come back from a pub toilet sales mission and do some thinking and paperwork at this grand desk, or relax on his re-covered red leather chesterfield, the frame also Edwardian or Victorian. All the furniture in

26

Victor's small comfortable property was solid and worthwhile. Harpur tried to imagine him moving in that graceful way of his among so many good possessions, but found he could only see him as he had just seen him, an aunt sally, slung-up afloat like a sagging hammock.

Lamb had waited. 'In vain?' he asked when Harpur returned. 'Oh, someone's been there before you I should think.'

'No evidence of entry.'

'There are folk who don't leave evidence of entry, Col. I hope you're one of them.'

Chapter Three

'I've been to look for him, Mr Harpur. No luck,' he said. It was spoken gently, offhandedly, but Harpur heard feeling there. Oh, Christ, he heard agony. 'And so I come to you. I want him found, and found safe. But not the intrusiveness and heaviness of an all-out police search. Victor would loathe that, resent that. There has to be tact. And also, I suppose, tact as far as one is concerned personally. I am, after all, political agent to a Government Minister. One hears that you, personally, sometimes act with a certain independence and know about subtlety. I do realise my self-interest is showing, as well as concern for Vic. Victor.'

'Been to look for him where?' Harpur replied.

'At the docks. I remember his mentioning a possible job there, but no details. Victor can be very cagey, even with me. It's hurtful to a degree, a professional instinct in him.'

'Did you meet him first through a habit? Victor Goussard supplied you?'

To this he went a bit stone-faced. 'No, I've no habit. One met him. This is all that counts.'

'I'd like to know how you looked for him, Mr Finnane,' Harpur said.

'Well, quite. Not very efficiently, I'm afraid.'

'But you know the area. The docks are in the Minister's constituency, aren't they?'

'Still not very efficiently. I drove around the quays a few times, different days, different nights, hoping to spot him. He's dear to me, Mr Harpur. I don't know whether you can understand that, sympathise.' His round, bright face grew peaky for a second as he said this, a kind of plea. He was about fifty but on good days would probably look less. Not now.

And, yes, naturally Harpur could sympathise. Sex was sex, love was love, whether between man and woman, man and man, woman and woman. He *did* believe this, didn't he? 'Talk to anyone, ask folk about him at the docks?' Harpur asked.

'A mistake, you think? I realise I'm into danger regions. One is of course aware that Victor's life was always very near to peril.'

A bit of rough, a bit of hazardous rough – his turn-on? 'You'd have to ask questions,' Harpur replied. 'How else could you search?'

'But just the same you believe it might have been an error – drawing attention to myself and to Victor? I was off balance from worry. Still am. I don't know whether you can understand this kind of . . . bond.'

'You said.'

'Look, do you think he might be in difficulty somewhere, Mr Harpur, real difficulty? Am I exposed, through asking people if they'd seen him? I don't much care about myself. There's the Minister to think about, of course.' But he spoke as though the Minister and Ministerial matters rated pretty low with him for now. 'Above all, it's Victor. Do you think something bad could have happened? Sometimes I did feel he knew too much about too many people.'

Harpur's daughters were at judo, thank God. He could do without their help in speaking to Slow Victor's sad, political, fretful lover: but not sad or fretful enough, because he did not know enough and wouldn't, not from Harpur. They were drinking tea in Harpur's good, big sitting room, homely now he'd had all his late wife's lumpy, high-calibre books taken away and the shelves removed.

'I believe Victor had picked up a lot of information, sensitive information, Mr Harpur. At least, this is what I *want* to think – that he's merely keeping out of sight somewhere, afraid.' Mystification and terror touched his face: 'Suddenly he's not in touch. It's been many days. He was so reliable, always on time, always came – always turned up, I mean.'

'When you asked around what kind of response did –?'

'Nothing. Blank. It could be genuine. Perhaps they truly did not know. But more as if people *did* know – knew Victor was an unsafe item to discuss. So I decided I needed help, looked your address up in the phone book. Rang your front door bell. Thank you for welcoming me in. But is it wise to have your name in the book?'

'I have to be available. I'm not like your Minister, Mr Finnane. People of Victor Goussard's sort are always liable to disappear for spells, often suddenly, no announcement, even to intimates. They come back. They have crisis business trips, crisis love trips – but obviously not that in this case.'

'Oh, thank you.'

'They have –'

'I'm not ashamed of this relationship, you understand,' he said with great levelness. 'All right, I'm married, passably happily married, family, but this with Victor is . . . well, I'm not ashamed. And then, of course, my job makes matters a bit delicate.'

'Does the Minister know?' Harpur replied.

'Know? Know about Victor?'

'Know about Victor. Know Victor is apparently missing.'

'Not just apparently.'

No, Harpur would buy that. 'Does he?'

'That this Home Office Minister's agent has a homosexual affair with a small-time pusher who's connected with people like Shale and Ember? No, the Minister

30

does not know, or not as far as I can tell. And, so, neither does he know Vic is missing.'

'Information, you say – Victor has information. About what sort of people?'

'He hears a lot – that kind of work. Mixing. And across class, of course. As Victor puts it, "All sorts need a fix."'

'The pusher's logo.'

'He has a lovely way with him – people talk to Vic.'

'If you've been asking around –'

'People may think he talked to me? Bed talk?'

Harpur said: 'Well, I'd take a little care. Things are strained among the firms just now. People can be intemperate.'

Finnane swallowed some tea and used the moment to get a question together. 'You know something about him – about what's happened to him?' Harpur heard the politician then: the steady suspicion in his voice that someone was trying to fool you, was ahead of you.

'I can do some fairly quiet inquiries,' Harpur replied.

'Yes, but – There's more to this, isn't there? You *know* something.' The words came very hesitantly. He was afraid to ask and get an answer. There would be *no* answer. This was ordained by Jack. What Jack ordained, Harpur always kowtowed to. Your grass's safety was your first concern. First and second.

'This would be without activating the full missing persons programme,' Harpur said.

Finnane sat forward and gazed at Harpur, his eyes hard, like a selection grilling for prospective candidates. 'My God, Harpur, I almost think you know what's happened to him, even where he is.' He had to force the words.

'Tell me when you were last in touch,' Harpur replied. 'What was said.'

But he seemed to have clammed. Finnane stared about the room, as if he feared that to come here had been an absurd lapse – that police were police and some police had all kinds of outside interests.

'If he spoke any names,' Harpur said.

'Have you been threatening me?' he replied. '"I'd be a little careful," you said. Damn gangster movie talk. I didn't realise the significance.' He sounded sickeningly shocked, at his own dimness. Finnane wore an oldish but very good green-brown tweed suit, a squire's suit. Slow might have liked the county flavour.

'I need a starting point,' Harpur said.

'Some of the information that Victor has – I know this as fact – in outline only, but as *fact* – some of it is about very inflluential business people who might have clout.'

'Clout with whom?'

'Oh, the police, obviously.' Finnane was dogged and worldly now. 'Mr Harpur, I have to ask you, are you in on – well, in on whatever has happened to Victor?'

The kids arrived with their boyfriends and a few other teenagers from an après judo visit to the rap café, all of them possibly highish and definitely intense. Harpur sniffed for grass. 'We fancied Monopoly,' Jill said.

'Here's Mr Finnane, our MP's agent,' Harpur replied. 'This is Jill, Hazel, Darren, Scott, Elvira, Barnaby and Jake.'

'I've done you in Civics, Mr Finnane,' Jill said. 'Our MP's Government post is to do with the police, yes? Also drugs et cetera. Is your boss dad's boss? Dad keeps his nose pretty clean, don't you, dad – if that's why you're here, Mr Finnane. It's a political matter? Dad doesn't know much about that. He's strong on the Bible.'

'I wanted help,' Finnane said.

'Dad's often quite good at that,' Hazel replied. 'Could he do anything for you?'

'I'm not sure.'

'We get many different types here, or on the phone,' Jill said. 'In some ways it's a pain – I don't mean *you*, Mr Finnane, but some of the others. But dad's a one for duty. Now and then.'

'Dad can play things quite close,' Hazel said. 'It's a nasty side to him, but professional. Police business has dark regions, as you'd expect.'

'Can you help him, dad?' Jill asked.

'That sounds to me like you're poking into police business, Jill,' Darren said. 'This could be grave and to do with the whole drugs business, the firms, which the Home Office must fight.'

'Some people do regret coming to see him,' Hazel said. 'He can be a problem. Sometimes not dad's fault. All sorts twisting his arm.'

'Mr Finnane looks really desperate, dad,' Jill said.

'Yes, I'm desperate,' Finnane replied.

'Look – being frank now, Mr Finnane,' Hazel said, 'it's not a love matter, is it? Dad hasn't been getting among someone dear to you, woman friend, even wife? This can happen. He's got a great relationship going – I mean steady and decent, a great girl – an undergrad in the university here – called Denise – but some straying does occur, all the same.'

'I don't know how you can speak about your father like that,' Scott told her.

'No, it's crude of you, Haze,' Jill said.

'*Is* it a love thing, Mr Finnane?' Hazel asked.

'Someone's missing,' he said.

'Would this be someone whose life is in a grey area?' Jill asked.

'Dad probably knows who and where but there might be reasons for staying silent,' Hazel said. 'It could even be for your own safety. Or that would be *his* story.'

Finnane stood up, ready to leave. 'You *will* help, search, Mr Harpur?'

Hazel stared at him, then at Harpur. 'This is a question that seems to say so much more than it seems to say.'

Yes, it did. It asked where Harpur stood. It asked if Harpur was uncorrupt. And, talking of threats, could this be one? Was Finnane in his despair and pain saying that if Victor had been hurt or killed Harpur might have done or connived at the hurting and killing and would pay? There was a priority promise to Jack Lamb that stopped Harpur from saying Victor *had* been hurt and killed, even if he had wanted to say it. All promises to Jack were priorities. 'Let me know how I can reach you,' Harpur said.

Finnane handed him a card and went. The card said Bernard Finnane and gave an address uptown.

'No, not to do with dad and a woman,' Jill said. 'I wonder if he's gay. Don't know why I think so. Just a feeling. Has he lost his boyfriend? That might place him in a kind of dilemma – his sort of job and those clothes. If he hasn't come out.'

'Do you think he might be in a bad way, dad?' Hazel asked. 'Shall I go see? I haven't heard a car drive off.'

'No, I'll go,' Harpur replied. He had not helped Finnane and could not help him. That troubled Harpur a bit. He went out to the street. Finnane was sitting behind the wheel of his Mondeo, head hanging slightly forward. He had not started the engine. Harpur walked to the car and pulled the passenger door open. 'Shall we look at the docks together?' he asked. Finnane did not answer, but turned the key in the ignition. Harpur climbed aboard.

As they entered the docks, Finnane said: 'Is this mad – being seen together, after I've been around asking questions? People know you, I expect.'

'Some. Yes, a little mad.' More than a little, of course, since Harpur could have taken him straight to Victor, without all this conspicuous driving: could have, but couldn't. 'I felt you needed company,' Harpur replied. 'Reassurance.'

'About?'

'That I'm no part of it,' Harpur replied.

'That you know nothing about it?'

'That I'm no part of it.'

Finnane took that in, then nodded. 'Right. And you wanted another chance to ask which big people Victor had information on.'

'No. You said he gave no names.'

'Not yours. Not anyone's.'

They slowly toured the docks. The three D vessels were dark and the gangway to the quayside remained up. Finnane hardly glanced towards them. They saw nobody.

Finnane said: 'Thanks for coming. Yes, I needed company. Perhaps I panic, imagine the worst, because the relationship with Victor has always been fragile.'

It's often best to imagine the worst. Harpur thought this, but did not speak it. 'I'd get some sleep,' he replied.

Chapter Four

'He's like any other officer who takes, or like *seems* to take,' Mansel Shale said. 'You got to ask, is it a ploy, the oldest ploy? Is he double-double-crossing?'

'Double-double-crossing, Manse?' Ivis said.

'Someone like that makes himself look bought by pocketing the sweeteners. He gets inside a firm such as ours, Alfred, and pretends to be helping us for the bribes, big bribes. But really he's only *playing* bent. He penetrates the organisation, learns the lot. Then one day, when he knows enough, wham, he's the main witness for the prosecution and we find he been putting the dab-in-the-palm money into a special account so it can be handed over full of fucking virtue like treasure trove to the forces of right and no shadow on his career. I seen it done before. Now you got this Nivette at it. Or *might* have this Nivette. Or then again he might be absolutely honest. That is, I mean honest corrupt – truly on the take from us because he wants to take, needs the cash and that's all, wants two pay days, one from the police, one from us. Nothing's clear. Never is. For instance, is he into the boat death that we just get the buzz about from . . .?'

'From Lakeland Percy,' Ivis said.

'Some nobody pilferer, anyway – hopping about the boats, finds Victor and the tale's out.'

'Yes, Lakeland Percy.'

'We ask, don't we, Alf, did Nivette kill Victor, then, because Victor somehow found out about Nivette's

game? Victor used to get around. He might find dangerous stuff by accident.'

Ivis said: 'But the *manner* of the death, Manse – do you
really think Nivette would –?'

'So, then, do we play Nivette along for a while, pre-
tend we believe in him,' Shale replied, '– the way we
played along with people they've tried to put in undercover before? They're always at it. That girl – remember?
We could feed Nivette rubbish information which could
send his bosses the wrong way? That can be a good ploy
in this sort of situation. But perhaps there got to be a
limit. Dicey to let him play for so long he knows the
operation right through, because if we are a bit dozy one
day he can suddenly pull out and finish all of us. There
could be a case if we find he really is doubling on us to
just wipe him out. Obviously. Not just a case for it.
Necessary. Not always easy, especially when he's quite
an officer, isn't he, Alf?'

'Chief Inspector,' Ivis replied.

'You remember that bit in *The Godfather*? "Nobody
ever killed a New York police captain," the Corleone
lawyer says. It would be like that with Nivette. Would
it? But, of course, Mike Corleone does kill the captain.'
They were in the back of the Jaguar. Denzil drove. This
was an urgency thing, too strong for the phone. Shale
wanted a face-to-face with his associate, Ralphy Ember.
It would be a tricky session. There was a body to discuss. There was a body to get rid of, tonight.

'With respect, I've put out an inquiry here and there,
Manse,' Alf Ivis said, 'and as far as I can tell Nivette's
not doing this – the taking I mean – not doing it as an
official undercover tactic. It doesn't look like a proper
HQ operation – Controller, Registrar, back-up, all the
usual apparatus for an organised infiltration. It's my
belief, Manse, that we have him genuinely bought.'

Alfie would sometimes run his own ideas, the big-
headed prick. It was natural. After all, he had a personal
little identity to look after. Everybody did. You ought to

try and treat them with consideration. And you ought to watch them. Alf was the sort who might fancy a top banana role, and he might turn dangerous one day. 'Fuck organised,' Shale replied. 'Fuck apparatus. Boys like Nivette – what they call "fast-track boys" – they act independent. How they get to be fast-track. It's known as flair, Alfred. You heard of flair at all? Harpur did it like that once. Nivette looks at our operation and asks himself how's he going to smash it, win all the gongs. Answer, get within, solo, act purchased, do the job on us, then disclose all and return the bribes from his special account, less a grand or two, but who's counting except God, and forget that until Judgement Day. Mr Untainted. Yes, just how Harpur did it. They want the praise, these boys. It's like their silver buttons. Some of them want the glory more than they want cash, Alfie. This is hard for you to understand, I know. Don't blame yourself. It's hard for all of us. You got to study what's known as their psyches. You heard of them – psyches? Psyches are all the mode, vital.'

This was quite confidential talk, talk it might of been better Denzil could not hear, talk about a police friend – a maybe friend – and about Slow Victor dead. This trip was because of Slow, naturally. Now and then Shale thought about putting a partition in the Jag, so the chauffeur could be blocked out. Always Mansel decided this would be too high and mighty. He hated anything like that. He was only a jumped-up arsehole and for ever tried to remember it. True, Denzil could be a right big-mouth jerk, but you had to give even a jerk like Denzil some tact.

Ivis said: 'I hear what you say, Manse, and yet –'

'Don't say you fucking hear what I say,' Shale shouted. He knew what it meant when Alfie said he heard what he said. This was subtlety, the louse. It meant Alf heard what he said but did not believe it – had his personal views. Well, he was entitled, the louse.

'Mansel, I feel it would be a tremendous risk for Nivette to act bought, *only* act it. I don't mean the risk that we might find out he's doing a con on us, but that Iles, say, or Harpur hear from somewhere he's taking, but not taking as official, undercover policy. Then where's his glory and career? Maybe where's even his life if Iles hears he's taking very freelance. Would the ACC believe him if he said he was only taking as a way to get information on the firm? That's been tried as a defence a million times by people on two pay days. Iles can get very sceptical. Iles can be a wild one, but one thing he won't put up with is a copper who takes.'

'Of course Nivette would have risk,' Shale said. 'That's the trade we're in, Alf. And the trade *he's* in. He's what's called opted for it. Heard of opted? If he wanted a safe clean-as-clean career he would of opened a launderette.'

Denzil spoke over his shoulder: 'Richard Nivette? The buzz says he's a pet of the Chief himself. I don't know if it's a bed and flesh job with them, but the Chief's religious, so it could be. Either way, you fuck about with Nivette, Manse, and so much shit flies it's Pearl Harbor.'

'Just drive, will you?' Shale replied.

'The Chief got a Christian streak to him, yes,' Denzil said, 'with mercy and all that, but he's never going to forgive damage to Nivette. He'd come hunting.'

'Implications are what Manse is unparalleled at spotting.'

Denzil said: 'All the same, I –'

'Drive,' Shale replied. 'And where's your fucking cap?'

'Do I need that? A trip to see Ralphy in a caravan, that's all.'

'Manse is well able to decide the status of the journey. If he feels the cap is right for the occasion it's right.'

Denzil picked up the cap from the passenger seat and put it on.

'You look a total prick with it or without it,' Shale remarked, 'but *with* it you're a prick with a role.'

'Did Ralphy do this lad on the boat?' Denzil replied. 'To me – I say to *me* – this don't seem decent.'

'Mansel has a view on it, naturally. You don't have to concern yourself.'

'Just drive, will you,' Shale answered. 'How come you heard about that, anyway?'

'Same as you,' Denzil said. 'The noise is around.'

'It's not in no papers yet, nor on TV,' Shale said.

'Around – you know, Manse,' Denzil said. 'Buzz.'

'What Manse is telling you, Denze, is to keep quiet on such topics or people like Mr Harpur and Mr Iles will be wanting to ask *how* you know about it. This is not a situation Manse would want you in.'

'Do *they* know about it?' Denzil asked.

'No bugger knows about it,' Shale replied.

'Manse sees it as totally regrettable – what happened to Victor. Apparently what happened.'

'Atrocious, if it's true,' Shale said. 'Corpsed in a wardrobe. Insulting. And primitive. Is that what you heard, Denzil – the wardrobe? We got a lovely peaceful state of things going here – me, Ralphy, headquarters – and then something like this. Where's fucking decorum? One thing I hate, it's disorder.'

'This is an attitude you're rightly famed for, Manse,' Ivis said.

Denzil drove into a nicely kept Mobile Homes field. 'You're looking full of enterprise and style, Ralph,' Shale said when Ember came to the door of a big caravan to greet them, smiling like a brilliant day. 'Denzil, have a drive around for an aeon or two. See if you can discover any little known plant life. I don't want my number plate standing here, winking at the world.' Ember had Beau Derek and his red cabbage complexion with him in the van, but this could not be helped. If you went into a partnership with Ralph, you took his other partners, too.

'So right of you to call this meeting, Manse,' Ember
said. 'Oh, so right.'

He could get a bit lordly. Ember did not *live* in this
van, obviously. Ember had a big place in the country,
paddocks, possible furrows, wheat, called Low Pastures.
And for a couple of years he was a mature student at the
university, not just looking for young fanny but getting
proper learning. It seemed back-burnered now.

'I guessed you'd of heard about Slow, Ralph. He got
to be brought off the boat and lost tonight. Otherwise,
when he's found, Iles or Harpur or the Chief will decide
there's a battle on among the firms and we can't deliver
street peace no longer. They'll come trouble-making,
big-style trouble-making. Is peace someone hanging
shattered on a beam, for God's sake, even someone like
Slow? I don't ask who done him or why but all the
reports I get from reliable voices say he's definitely out
there in that condition. So he got to be moved fast. You
remember that message in *The Godfather* –'

'Manse loves *The Godfather*, Ralph,' Ivis said.

'"Luca Brasi sleeps with the fishes." Old Sicilian cus-
tom. Bring Slow out of the cabin and drop him to the
timeless depths somewhere. Victor put out of sight for
ever, that's one thing. But Victor mid-aired and pot-
shotted head to toe, that's filthy provocation. The Chief
would not let Iles and Harpur ignore that. The Chief's
against the peace arrangement, anyway. Thinks it's surrender to us. Lane would regard Slow torn by bullets as
a terrible dark symbol of our times, especially in a
wardrobe. A wardrobe should be civilisation – suits tidy
on hangers, moth balls fighting wildlife. Instead, a
slaughtered body. And then there'd be the poncy Press
– whining about gang fights. We don't want it, Ralph. It
would put us back years. Plus the chance of getting
framed for it.'

'I don't ask who did it, either, Manse,' Ember replied.
'Where d'you hear of it from?'

'Ralph has never even mentioned your name as

responsible for the death, Manse,' Beau said. 'I'll vouch for that.'

'Thanks, Beau,' Shale replied.

'And I can wholeheartedly say the same about Mansel and *your* name, Ralph,' Ivis remarked.

'Thanks, Alf,' Ember replied. 'Get him off the boat?'

'Like tonight,' Shale said. 'People will be back aboard soon, maybe checking on him, or the divers. How did you know he was out there, Ralph?'

Shale did not mind caravans. They looked just what they was, long boxes for living in, no fucking heavy history to talk about such as old stone chimney breasts going back to Sir Walter Raleigh. Of course, Shale was not against history in total and his own house, which used to be a rectory, had quite a slice of history itself, but you did not want history all round. The drugs game was now. Also, he liked the way caravans were up off the ground – all that damp and mud. Nature was pretty hopeless. It did not seem to know what it was for. If you stuck a caravan there you were doing it a favour by making Nature useful. Ralph Ember was friendly with the lad who ran this site and he could always get the use of a caravan – for a session with a girl or meetings. You could not do better for privacy.

'You mean put him over the side weighted?' Ember asked.

'No good. Not in the dock,' Shale said. 'Big vessels churning about on twin screws. They'd flush him to the top.'

'Nothing's churning now.'

'They will eventually.'

'Eventually there might not be much of him left, Manse. As you said, fish.'

'Enough of him to identify. The lab can do magic with bits and pieces these days.'

The caravan had a three-piece suite in it and was tasteful in a caravan way. Ember must have brought some Kressmann Armagnac with him from the club he owned and sloshed it out for them now, that big showy style of his. 'This would be a tough operation,' he said.

You could see a bit of the old panic he was famous for get to work on Ralphy when he thought about shifting Victor. Ember had a scar along his jaw line that he always fingered when he felt a full fright come. It was like he expected his scared soul to pop out through this old wound where the skin was weakest and make a run for cover. Shale said: 'Plus it saves Slow's parents and his boyfriends from the stress of hearing how he was cruelly messed about. If he just disappears under great fathoms he could be anywhere as far as others know – such as starting a new career as the maturest rent boy in Valparaiso.'

'Who did him, Manse?' Ember asked. 'I wondered about Nivette.'

'Ralph did mention *him*,' Beau said.

'Of course. We all wonder about Nivette. Maybe Slow saw him taking payment one day from Beau or Alfie, and Nivette found out. Maybe Slow even been trying to squeeze Nivette for silence cash. This is another aspect of it – we got to move him out. What we don't want is the body found, then Harpur sniffing around and deciding it was Nivette. There's the end of our briefings from inside HQ. All right, so Nivette might be a doubler. But only might, Ralph. So far. And if he did do Slow it *could* say he's *not* a doubler, or he wouldn't have to shut Slow up like that and torture him to find who he's told.'

'A task bringing him down the side of the vessel,' Ember replied. His voice had a squeak to it now. 'This is a big ship they say.'

'He's a corpse, not a peritonitis case with injurious banging to avoid. We got gravity going for us. Ropes, Ralphy. Heard of them at all? Plus a big clean-up of the cabin. This becomes just a lad who've gone AWOL. It's thoughtless of him, but nothing to shake our world into chaos.'

'If there's one thing Manse can't stand it's chaos,' Ivis said.

'It's a fact then, Manse, that you didn't do Victor, or you'd have disposed of him at the time,' Ember remarked.

'Of course it's a fact,' Ivis replied. 'Would Manse –'

'But is it a fact *you* didn't do him, Ralph?' Shale asked.

'Of course it's a fact,' Beau said. 'Ralph would never –'

'Just the four of us to transfer him,' Shale replied. 'Very private mourning only. He'd understand.'

Chapter Five

Harpur managed another bit of breaking and entering. Well, no breaking this time, only entering. Nivette and his wife and small son were in Paris and Disneyland for ten days. On the first evening of their absence Harpur used his plastic card on the front door. It worked. Police officers were famed for casual security in their own places. He worried over Nivette. Harpur was here to vindicate him. Harpur was here to look for money, big money. It would be bribes Nivette had hidden away for eventual disclosure and surrender, once he chose to end his performance as bought cop and tell everything he'd learned about Mansel Shale and Panicking Ralph Ember. If there was fat loot concealed here, Nivette was all right. Harpur had followed the same sort of hoarding procedure himself now and then when he played the detective who'd sold out.

Of course, no detective was supposed to go fake-corrupt without the knowledge of superiors. It was perilous in ten different ways, indisciplined, mad. Detectives did it, all the same, especially good detectives, in the hard and competitive hunt for victory. Harpur longed to clear Nivette. He would have longed to clear any subordinate accused of taking. He especially wanted to clear Nivette before Iles set up something special for him. After that it might not be possible. And he wanted to clear Nivette because the Chief liked him. Lane's mind would not take many more shocks, and if he discovered somehow that Nivette was on a second salary, the Chief might slide into breakdown again. It could not be, could it, could it, that a fine prospect like Richard Nivette had tumbled into treachery, and might have tumbled so far that he'd torture and kill a nobody like Slow Victor?

This would be different from the visit to Victor's place. Harpur could take it slowly here, *must* take it slowly: he would need to empty drawers carefully and then refill them just as carefully, pull back carpets, perhaps open up the back of pictures and look for hollowed-out books on Nivette's shelves. He could have done with some help, but it was not the kind of help he would ask anyone to risk with him. In fact, Denise was the only one he'd asked for support – moral and philosophical.

Lying legs entwined after love-making in her single bed at the student residences, Jonson Court, this afternoon, he'd said: 'Here's a problem for your trained mind. You do that fancy French philosophising stuff, don't you – Sartre, existentialism and what all?'

'I do French. That doesn't mean I want to be involved in another of your smelly ethical dilemmas.' Now and then, she'd press him to come with her to this room, as a change from Harpur's place in Arthur Street. It was a kind of possessivenesss. That pleased him in a way. The room itself was pretty grubby, and the sheets, usually, but he thought it kindly of her not to mind being seen in the corridor with someone of his age and looks. He always tried to regard the dirt as bohemian. Denise was an intellectual. She was everything else she needed to be besides that, but she definitely was an intellectual. 'I have to prove someone innocent,' he'd told her this afternoon. 'A mission. It will involve committing an offence and invading his privacy to do it. Am I justified?'

'You'll do it anyway.'

'Of course.'

'Col, you just want the comfort of being told your filthy tricks are not filthy tricks.'

'But I don't want to be told by any Tom, Dick or Marjorie that my filthy tricks are not filthy tricks. I want to be told my filthy tricks are not filthy tricks by someone who's in habitual touch with subtle thinkers and who is herself exceptionally bright and insightful.'

'That's true. Who the fuck's this Marjorie? You're going to do a bit of burglaring again, are you?'

'Along those lines. That's what I mean – you're so bright and insightful you can spot what's happening without being told.'

'But I *want* to be told, Col. Who are we talking about? Whose house are you going to pollute?'

'In principle, though, you think I'm right,' he had replied.

In Nivette's semi, he worked systematically from room to room. If he found nothing in the main house he would have to do the garage and loft. He was not looking only for quarantined money, though. Arty ornaments or gold taps or high-class pictures could signify that Nivette really was taking and spending, really was treacherous. Would Harpur recognise high-class pictures? As for art, he knew what he liked and what he liked was generally what Jack Lamb told him was good and valuable. But Jack was not here.

Did a spell in Paris Disneyland speak of fat, improper funds? Had they taken the loot with them, for ice-creams and claret? Please, Nivette, be a doubler. Harpur started to work through some cereal boxes in the store cupboard, shoving the corn flakes and crispies about, sniffing for old currency in biggish bills.

Chapter Six

In his private rooms above the bar at The Monty club Ralph Ember put on old clothes and then changed back out of them into his hand-tailored three-piece Cachape and Drew navy pinstripe suit. He was jumpy. He'd had some drinks but was still jumpy and would not risk drinking any more because things could turn out bad aboard this damn boat tonight, shifting Slow Victor towards the shrouding deep. Perhaps Ember would need his wits and agility.

He went to a wall safe, opened up and brought out the short-barrelled .38 Smith and Wesson Model 49 Bodyguard revolver he was using these days. No, no, *storing* – not *using*. Was he a hit man, for God's sake? He had become a commercial figure with almost genuine local distinction. As Ralph W. Ember, didn't he publish letters in the Press from time to time on environmental issues and charity matters? Quite often these days he could see the happy glow of long-term respectability and prominence not far ahead. He should be beyond guns. But, then, he should also be beyond going out at night to recover the savaged body of a low league pusher and clean up the site.

Ralph put the Bodyguard into his jacket pocket. Along with the gun the safe contained a stamped, padded, sealed envelope addressed to himself, emergency funds of twenty-five thousand in four packs held with rubber bands, and a shoulder holster. He thought about the holster but did not take it. Wearing that would turn him back into what he was once long ago, a piece of professional lawless crudity. Now, he had a daughter at a damned pricey finishing school in France, and the other one rode at gymkhanas with the kids of high civil servants, surgeons, main street hair stylists and even county people. He was hardly someone to wear a leather harness himself. He was someone in a Cachape and Drew town suit, and Cachape and Drew did not cut their jackets to conceal shoulder holsters. They probably did not make pockets to house a .38 revolver, either, but it was a neat little gun and Ember thought no severe damage would be done to his outline. He felt he had a duty to look good. He closed the safe.

Ralph loathed the plan for moving Slow, but understood why he had agreed to it. Manse Shale would come up with these far-fetched ideas sometimes and turn them into a test of guts and manhood. If Ember backed out, or had even queried the scheme, Shale would mark him down as feeble – would mark him down again as what Ember knew some unwarrantably called him, Panicking Ralph, or even Panicking Ralphy. He could not allow this – to be reduced before Shale and Alfie and Beau, especially Beau, that loud little crawler and colleague by accident.

After checking the bar area on a couple of surveillance monitors he prepared to go. The staff could cope with the rest of the night and close up. He left his rooms, then turned and went back, opened the safe again and brought out the padded envelope. It was for an emergency drill. His hand holding the envelope shook a bit. Did he really need it tonight? For a moment he stood in front of the safe wondering whether to replace it. Were the risks at the docks actually so bad? Just a kind of private funeral, surely. He leaned forward to put the envelope back, stopped, then drew away with it still in his hand. Yes, sod it, the risks were bad. He slipped it into his empty left jacket pocket and secured the safe once more. The envelope was a safeguard against errors, and he foresaw errors – not specific or in detail, but a general dread had touched him. Although he knew he must not dodge out of the quest for Slow, there was something that tortured his mind and said transporting the body could slip into foul disaster. Victor's might not be the only corpse. Oh, Jesus, would Ralph himself get on the wrong end of something tonight?

Now and then throughout his career Ember had noticed this ability in himself to detect early, inexplicable warnings of future catastrophe. When he could, he acted on them. Ralph knew above all about running, and in good time. It was why he had stayed alive, while some of his old crooked companions were killed, probably cursing him as they died for letting them down and cornering the loot. It was why his body stayed reasonably all right, while some of his old crooked companions were in wheelchairs, probably cursing him for letting them down and cornering the loot. It was why he had never been to jail, while some of his old crooked companions would be behind the wall for years, probably cursing him for letting them down and cornering the loot. It was how he had become rich, owning The Monty outright and his fine country spread, Low Pastures, plus a very decent mound of capital mostly in deposit box notes. It was how he could give his adored, wonderful family the best, and his girlfriends close to the best. Tonight, though, he knew he must not respond to this bit of vague but terrifying clairvoyance about Slow Victor and complications. Otherwise, his honour was in shreds, and occasionally he did have a thought about his honour, or even slightly more than occasionally.

The arrangement was for Ember to pick up Beau in the Saab and then drive to Alf Ivis's place, a converted lighthouse not far down the coast. They'd transfer to Alfie's car there and make for the *Dion*. On the way to Beau's, Ember stopped and posted the envelope. Inside were keys of the bank deposit boxes in Britain and his code tag for an account in Switzerland. As long as things went all right, he would be home in time to open it himself, transfer the items to a new envelope and seal, readdress and stamp it ready for the next crisis. In case he failed to return, these items should be still in the post if the police or other enemies came to ransack his places immediately after whatever had stopped him getting back. Whatever and/or whoever had stopped him getting back would be some murderous trade enemy, or the police, or someone who had always hated him and had now decided that they *really* hated him.

Of course, Margaret knew what to do with the envelope's contents. She had a sheet of paper locked away which identified the keys and gave the other half of the Zurich code and that bank's address. Naturally he had told her about the funds in the safe and in The Monty loft. They were helpful amounts but not major and even if these reserves were found by invaders, she and the kids would be fine from the bank capital. Perhaps such provisions were hard on girlfriends but, since the terrible death of Christine Tranter, he had no lover he regarded as unarguably important enough for a legacy. If he favoured one it would only set up degrading bitterness among the others. Anyway, he bought them all sorts of tasty things now, when he was alive. Most likely they would not expect to cash in if he were killed. They wanted him for himself rather than gain, possibly – his kindliness and famed Charlton Heston profile, but Heston when young.

After posting the envelope he sat without moving for a while in his car alongside the pillar box. Although sending the keys and papers was a familiar drill, it always gave him at least the start of a panic and occasionally the entire works. He began to sweat a bit, but that seemed all. He had no further trembling or loss of power in his limbs and no impression that his jaw scar was due to fountain mucus. He passed a hand over one thigh, to get the feel of his suit's tip-top material. It reassured him. The sweat was nothing like enough to produce that unpleasant odour from wet, quality wool which he sometimes got.

He was glad he had changed back, although this would most likely be a mucky job at the *Dion*. There would be ship's oil and grime, dock water, dried blood, maybe fresh blood. Ember always kept a set of old clothes at The Monty in case of such emergency tasks. Victor would not be the first body he had made disappear. But he'd decided to remain in his decent gear tonight because if he was noticed leaving the club late and looking scruffy people would guess something special was on, and this might bring trouble eventually. Should things turn evil on this damn vessel there'd almost certainly be dire aftermath, even publicity. Club members might hear of a calamity and recall that Ralph had gone out just before it happened, whatever it was, wearing clothes that showed he was on his way to rough duties again. Many members of The Monty were damn gifted at making connections, especially dark ones. Some members of The Monty talked on the quiet for cash or favours to people like Colin Harpur, or even to people like Desmond Iles, except there was nobody like Desmond Iles. Alternatively, some members of The Monty would offer Ralph silence for similar cash or favours. He longed to turn The Monty into a distinguished, elegant spot for clean folk of solid class like the Athenaeum in London, or at least the Cavalry and Guards club, but how could he do that if regulars guessed the proprietor had been out trying to waterhearse a third-rate villain to extinction?

He drove on and met Beau. When they arrived at the lighthouse Shale was already there. He had cycled from his one-time rectory through back lanes on the 1930s Humber bike he used, with an ancient Sturmey Archer hub three speed, and heavy metal case over the chain to protect his trousers. Ember knew Mansel would do that sometimes, just to make himself look like an ordinary man of the people. At least it meant Shale's pushy chauffeur, Denzil, was not on this trip.

Ivis had a newish Land Rover. Tied to the roof rack was an inflatable rubber boat in two shades of grey, perhaps a beach model belonging to Alf's children. Ivis had been down to look at the moored vessels. He said that the quayside gangplank was kept hoisted but, from the far side of the dock, he spotted a divers' platform and a rope ladder hanging from the *Dion*. 'We'll row out,' Shale said. In the rear of the Land Rover Ember saw a long coil of rope, and alongside it several fishing rods, probably in case the docks police turned up to ask what they were doing. Some tale. By arrangement, Ember had brought from The Monty a couple of buckets and three mops, plus several cleaning cloths, and three flashlights. He and Beau put all these into the Land Rover.

Ivis drove and they unloaded near the vessels. Then Alfred took the car to a less obvious spot and walked back. Because the inflatable was not big enough to take them all, there would be two trips out. Ivis and Beau went first with some of the equipment and fishing tackle. Ivis would return for Ralph and Shale. To Ember it seemed right that those two dogsbodies should freight the clean-up stuff, lights and rope. There might need to be three trips when they brought Slow. Perhaps someone on his own would have to row him to the dockside from the ship because he'd take a lot of space stretched out, and it would be unseemly to fold him, although rigor would have passed by now. It made Ember think for a moment of poetry he'd been forced to read in his foundation year at university, describing how King Arthur's body was sent to Avalon by barge. Probably Slow was not in the Arthur league for aura, although they said he almost never plumped out coke with baby powder beyond the reasonable.

Ember and Shale stood on the quayside and watched Alfie Ivis row the dinghy to the far side of the *Dion*, buckets glinting like silver treasure at the feet of the two men whenever the moon came from behind clouds. Ember thought they looked damned miniature and vulnerable in that tiny boat trekking slowly across the stretch of black water under the three high sterns of the D vessels. He would be in that position soon. Although this was frightening he managed to stop himself massaging his scar and instead paced a bit about the quay, keeping his steps unhurried, relaxed. This bastard Shale would notice everything. 'You were brilliantly quick to see the need to move Victor, Manse,' he said. 'Vital.'

'Well, I know you'd have suggested it if I hadn't. That's the grand thing about a true partnership – the minds work together like, in every respect. There's something binds us, Ralph, and it's that eternal lust for a wholesome fucking peace. That's all this is about. We're lucky Alfred loves the sea – I mean, would he be living in that daft place if not? Anyway, he got a motor launch in the estuary for fishing and we'll need another little voyage with Slow and some for-ever sinkers to lash him to. He'll have to go under a good way from the coast for permanence. Alfie won't want to be up in his lamp room one day enjoying vistas and see Slow coming in full of bullets on breakers. I'd say what we both are when it comes to corpses, you and me, Ralph, is thorough.'

'It's out of respect for the dead as much as anything, Manse.'

'Decorum. So right,' Shale replied. 'Even arseholes like Slow deserve privacy in death. When I say "arseholes" this is not to do with his gayness, not at all. I hope I got nothing much against gays. Tolerance – I love it. "Arseholes" I just meant as a run-of-the-mill term for Victor, exactly the way I personally used to be pre-success. The other thing I got in mind, and I'm sure you got it in mind, too, Ralph – this rapport between us as it's called – you heard of rapport at all? – our other objective, maybe the main one, is pick up something off

Slow tonight if we can, say something out of his pocket, something that would have an identity aspect, and then if this sod Nivette ever turned out to be a doubler – and it's still only *if*, Ralph – he still could be totally clean and truly bought – but if he *did* turn out a doubler and was trying to fuck us up we get this item into his car or his house at some hidden spot and anon calls to head-quarters and the Press ask are they aware this Chief Inspector Nivette got private knowledge about the van-ished traditional old back street trader, Slow Victor or All Passion Bent? My mother always used to say, "A word to the wise." So they go through his house and his car and suddenly that boy Nivette got tangles around him and no credibility, nothing, not even if he been taking on police orders. He stinks so much nobody could ever put him in the witness box.

'As you know, Ralph, this is a profession like Heinz foodstuffs where you always need a business plan that goes a bit ahead of today's problems and even tomor-row's. There got to be vision, you'll agree. Always, always, this search for lovely peace and happy toler-ance.'

Ivis came back and they climbed into the inflatable. Ember took the oars. With something to do he felt more or less all right, although the boat seemed well down. In fact, Ralph almost chuckled, thinking it was most prob-ably the first time a man in a three-piece Cachape and Drew suit had rowed out to the middle of this dock after midnight looking for a corner-boy pusher's body to lose again. The cloud had densened and it was very dark now. He could only just make out Shale's and Alfie's features where they sat facing him in the back of the boat. He did not mind having only a dim sight of them. Shale was snub and wily under a lot of dark hair. Alf was slabby, solemn, a waiter's face, perfect for someone who lived in a lighthouse. Shale said: 'When you realise the way *I* realise that I'm just a flash in the pan of life, Ralph, you got to do everything you can to make sure that flash lasts more than other flashes. What was it someone said, some head of NATO or Nelson Mandela – "Know thy fucking self"? I hope I do. So, we scavenge Victor. This is a lad who when he was alive was less than a write-off but as a dead he got real upsetting potential. He got what's known as overtones.'

'Oh, well, with respect, I suppose we're all, in a sense, flashes in the pan, Manse,' Ivis replied, 'namely in the context of eternity. But I know everyone would say that *your* contribution to the central pattern of things is high and substantial, even historic.'

Ember thought maybe he was supposed to say something confirming, but concentrated on the oars. All this conversation and the compliments did not seem right in a rubber boat in the middle of a dock at night. Shale still had his cycle clips on the bottoms of his trousers. Perhaps he was scared black ship's rats would run up his leg and bite his balls with plague. He did not need cycle clips, anyway, with a case like that over his chain. He wore them as part of his act, the stately twerp. They moored at the platform and Beau went first up the ladder with the coil of rope around his shoulders. He climbed easily. Beau was like this. Looking at him and especially his skin you would think the slob of slobs, but if you gave him a physical task such as this ladder or a safe or cutting through razor wire, he would handle it so sweetly. From the *Dion*'s deck he lowered an end of the rope and they fixed the buckets and mops to it and put the flashlights in the buckets. Beau and Alf had left the fishing gear in the dinghy. Beau hauled the gear up and then Ivis, Shale and Ember climbed the ladder.

Shale had the information, from wherever he got his information, that Slow was in a wardrobe, which seemed to mean one of the bigger cabins, maybe the captain's or owner's. Ivis said these would probably be what he called amidships or in the stern. Alf knew a bit about vessels. He led the way to a group of five cabins beneath the *Dion*'s bridge and at each one Beau put down the buckets and mops and opened the doors with some of his special keys. They found nothing and moved on. 'Or somewhere like this,' Ivis said, and pushed a door open. 'It's unlocked, which means trouble.' Three of them shone their flashlights into the cabin. Ivis went forward and stood for a second in front of the closed wardrobe doors. It was like theatre, Alf in three spotlights, that meaty face glowing. He was enjoying it, anyone could see. Since they boarded the *Dion* it was as if he was in charge on account of his maritime connections. This was all right. He deserved a moment or two out from beneath the shadow of that arrogant thinker, Shale. Alf pulled back the wardrobe doors.

'Ah,' Shale said with depth.

'Oh, it's noble of you to come here and save him from this disgrace, Manse,' Ivis said.

'After all, this was a kind of colleague, with a strong entitlement to our concern, Alfie, ' Shale replied. 'What's the fucker said to whoever done the target practice before killing him? That's what we got to ask. A bit of rubbish like Slow is not going to keep his mouth shut, is he?'

Beau turned one of the buckets upside down and sat on it, clutching the erect mops hard to him for comfort while he gazed at Slow. Beau said: 'If we had a vicar with us he could say a few words, just to bless Victor and sort of tidy up the tragedy a little.'

'Well, looking around I don't think we brought a vicar, Beau,' Shale replied. 'Vicars on ships are bad luck. Every sod knows that.'

'Slow's already got bad luck, without a vicar,' Beau said.

'Ralph can perhaps help. He studied Religious Knowledge at the university, I believe,' Ivis said.

'We didn't do death,' Ember answered, 'it was more theoretical — what the Muslims believe and Shakers and Foursquare Gospel.'

'Something from the Bible,' Shale said. He intoned:

'"Life's too short, saith the preacher." Is that one of them Psalms, or the top prophet, St Francis Ecclesiastes himself?'

'Possibly,' Ember replied. He widened his voice. '"And there shall be no more death." This is Revelation.'

'That one I go for,' Beau said.

'Yes, nice,' Shale replied. 'Did they tell you at coll how to get this message through to someone in Slow's condition? I'm looking forward to them days. We'll need to let down buckets over the side for docks water. Nothing on tap here. Then swab this place. Ralph and I will hold him, Alfie cut him down.'

Beau went to fill the buckets. Ivis brought out a penknife. 'Things are going with exemplary smoothness, Manse,' he said. 'This was remarkable planning.' Shale took Slow's legs and feet, Ember put his arms around his shoulders and chest. It felt intimate and Ralph was comforted. Slow had been a nothing, but amiable enough, and less grasping than several. He was entitled to some contact. Two business leaders crouched in a wardrobe – unbecoming, and yet there was humanity to the occasion, generosity. It was unpleasant the way Slow's head hung back over Ralph's shoulder with no control, his hair trailing. There would not be much staining of the Cachape and Drew suit because most of the blood had hardened. Alfie cut the ankles binding first, then the wrists. There was some weight to him, but not too bad. Ember and Shale lowered him to the floor and Shale began to search his clothes.

'What you'd expect,' he said. 'Some bastard been through already. This was disrespect on top of disrespect. This was someone professional. This was someone who heartlessly dredged this ruined being.' Victor's mouth was open and Shale did a little fingering in there and unhooked a plate with two front teeth on it. He put it in his pocket. 'If we plant that it will tell a tale and give a name as good as any driving licence or DNA. Dentists' records.'

Beau came back with the two buckets full of water and he, Ivis and Shale began to clean up with the mops and cloths. The back of the wardrobe showed bullet chips as well as harsh spatters of blood, and it would be impossible to conceal there had been shooting in here. Without a body, though, nobody would be able to work out why. Ember began to think that perhaps Shale had things right after all. Ralph helped by directing the torchlight for them, then took over the cleaning from Beau. Ember did not mind sharing duties with his own man. That was only hands-on leadership, and no slide in status – the way he would sometimes help the gardener with slug pellets at Low Pastures. He would not have acted as substitute mopper for Shale or Ivis, though. It would have been like housemaiding.

They carried Slow Victor out to the deck, Beau and Ivis a leg each, Shale and Ember at his shoulders. It was done decently, Ember thought. They had nothing to wrap him in and no flag, but otherwise it might have seemed like a proper procession for burial at sea on a warship, except that it was at night and in darkness because nobody had a hand free for a flashlight now. They laid Slow down and Beau went back to the cabin for the mops, cloths, buckets and flashlights. Beau descended the ladder first. They lowered the equipment to him, then pulled the rope back up and Alf Ivis fixed it around Slow's chest and under his arms in a secure loop. Alf knew about knots as well as ships. It would be unspeakable if the body broke free and fell. Ember went down and joined Beau on the platform with the equipment. Shale and Ivis got Slow over the side and lowered him to them below at a sensible pace, though he bounced against the hull and spun slowly now and then. The way Alf had tied him, Slow was upright and did not look too bad, except for the way his head slumped forward. He dislodged flakes of muck and rust each time he hit the ship's side and Ember and Beau were showered but that would all brush off.

It was getting on for 3.30 a.m. and still dark. Ember and Beau received the body and stretched him out on the platform. They unfastened the rope and tidied his clothes. Ivis dropped the other end of the rope to them and then he and Shale came down the ladder. Ivis said two would have to go with Slow to the quayside because a man alone could not get him out of the inflatable and up the steps. Alfie was still admiral of the fleet. It seemed reasonable what he proposed. He thought it should be Ember and Shale who accompanied the body as they were the principals of the two associated firms. This would give proper dignity to the journey. One would stay with Slow at the quayside, a proper, dutiful guard, while the other rowed back for Ivis and Beau and the buckets, mops and flashlights. None of this gear could be abandoned because forensic science traced from all sorts these days. Ivis thought the dinghy would be all right to take three men plus the equipment.

Ember wanted to be the one who stayed with Slow at the quayside. Although hanging about there with a shot body was dangerous if the docks police did patrols, he hated the idea of this little craft being overloaded and going under in the middle of the dock at such an hour, with only those mops as floating items in the gear. This was a kids' boat, that's all. He could swim, but not very far and he had never tried it in shoes and a three-piece suit.

It horrified him to think of Beau, Ivis and himself in the water fighting for the mops to cling on to, although obviously no mop could ever support the weight of a man, anyway. It would be just the frenzy that possessed people when they were drowning, grabbing at anything, pushing others under. Ivis could be ruthless. Hadn't he killed Big Paul Legge? That had been a shooting and years ago, but probably he would drown people, too, if it came to it, and it *would* most likely come to it if that boat sank. Ralph had never had a panic in the water.

Although, clearly, there would be no sweating, and he would be unable to tell whether his scar was weeping, it was sure to be a full-out panic all the same, he knew it. The boat had already carried three men safely enough, yes, but it was low in the water when he took Shale and Alfie out to the *Dion*, and the heavy buckets, the mops, cloths and flashlights might be just a bit too much. These were brand new buckets and Shale would not have them dumped in the dock in case they were recovered somehow and linked to him through the shop where they had been bought. Well, if the small boat sank they would be dumped in the dock all right, and so would whoever was with them.

Beau held the inflatable hard against the platform and Ember, Ivis and Shale gently loaded Victor aboard. It was not easy. Ember stood in the boat and the other two handed Slow to him head first. When he had a grip on Victor's shoulders Ivis came into the boat with Ember and Shale eased the body forward until they had his full weight. Once again Slow was laid out, this time along the length of the boat. He did take a lot of space. Christ, the damn thing could go down on *this* trip, just Ember, Shale, the body and fishing gear. If Ember and Shale had to sit to one side because of that damn corpse it might capsize. It might actually be safer to travel with the gear and two men who were alive.

Things had been decided now, though. He had to do it this way. Shale climbed in with Ember and Slow. Ivis returned to the platform and Beau pushed them off. Shale rowed. 'I wish this fucking peppered poofter knew the bother he was giving us, Ralphy,' he remarked. Ember allowed nobody to call him Ralphy to his face, but he said nothing now because he feared setting off an argument or angry movement in the boat and causing an upset. At the steps they moored, then both carried Victor up to the quayside and put him down. Ember returned to the dinghy and brought the

61

fishing gear which he put near Slow. 'I'll stay with him if you like,' Shale said.

'Oh?'

'Yes. My operation, my responsibility. If anyone comes I'm the one who got to deal with it.'

'Oh? How?' Ember replied.

'Deal with it. I'm made for vigils.'

This was one of those tests. The sod probably realised it was perilous to come back in that boat with two men and the gear. He wanted to push Ember into a fright again.

'Right, Manse,' Ember said. 'This is the kind of courage we all expect from you.'

'Thanks, Ralphy.'

'I'm Ralph, not fucking Ralphy, Mansey.'

Ember rowed out alone. The docks water reeked of petrol and decay. They loaded the gear aboard and then Ivis and Beau joined him. Beau offered to take the oars, but Ember said no. He felt safer if he had control and he managed things very gingerly. More hands-on leadership. The water was about two inches from coming over as they returned.

Suddenly Beau seemed to get tense. He was staring ahead towards the dockside. 'Christ,' he said, and at the same time Ember heard what could be a man shouting in anger or fright and then two silenced shots from the quay. Noise carried well across water. As he rowed, Ember was facing the other way and could not turn to see what had happened for fear of disturbing the boat's balance. 'He's shot him,' Beau said. 'Shale's shot him.'

'If Manse shot him it will be only because it was unavoidable,' Ivis replied.

Beau started to stand, eager to see better. 'Sit still, will you?' Ember remarked. 'Shot who?' But, God, to have to depend on Beau as reporter.

'Just shot him,' Beau replied. 'They were fighting, wrestling. Shale stepped back and shot him.'

'Who?' Ember asked.

'Get us there, will you, Ralph,' Ivis replied.

'Don't come the bosun with me, Alf,' Ember replied.

'Manse might need help,' Ivis said.

'It doesn't look like,' Beau said. 'Don't come the bosun with Ralph.'

Ember kept his same safe pace. When they reached the steps, Alfie was out first, a pistol in his hand, so valiant. Ember followed, but kept the .38 pocketed. Beau came last carrying the coil of rope, the flashlights, buckets, cloths and mops. Ember saw a man's body lying on top of Slow's.

'Get the Land Rover, Alf,' Shale said. 'We load these two fast.'

'Who is it?' Ember asked, as Ivis ran for the car.

'His pockets say someone called Finnane,' Shale said. 'I think one of Slow's paramours. Maybe *the* paramour.'

'Finnane?' Ember said. 'The politico?'

'What politico?' Shale asked. He still had cycle clips on. This was an eminent death, yet he still had fucking cycle clips on.

'It's catastrophic,' Ember said. 'There'll be hellish repercussions.'

'Look at him,' Shale replied, pointing at the bodies. 'He looks like he's at Slow even now. He come at me like a maniac, Ralph, screaming he been looking all over for Victor and what had I done to him? And he's bending down to him weeping, kissing Slow on the eyes and forehead, and yelling where was his teeth, yelling at me I'd knocked his teeth out brutally. This is someone shot to bits along his whole body and all this Finnane could think of was Slow's looks, his teeth. How come he did not know Slow had a plate and it was missing if they been French kissing, which is commonplace today? He could of strangled me. This was true passion. I tell you, I was fucking moved. I've never said gay love was less than man and woman, and this was immense, Ralph, this was an inspiration.'

'How could he have strangled you if he was bending down to Slow?' Beau asked.

'Prick. He bent down to him and then when he saw what he saw he stood up and was going to strangle me, shouting I'd destroyed his life, meaning Finnane's life, because of Slow's death and his teeth. Well, I said, "Not fucking yet I haven't destroyed your life, you fucking raver" and I got the Walther out and self-defenced. It was him or him, Ralph.'

Ivis brought the Land Rover. They put the two bodies aboard and the buckets, mops, cloths, fishing gear, flashlights and rope.

'This is two lots of sinkers now,' Shale remarked.

'There's a famous novel where a brother and sister who were always fighting drown in each other's arms and people put on their gravestone, "In their deaths they were not divided,"' Ember said.

'I got nothing against stories,' Shale answered. 'Gravestones I'm not in favour of, though. There's not going to be one. Or two. This pair disappear, that's all. It's an elopement.'

'If I may say, a lovely concept, Manse,' Ivis replied.

'It's what Ralph had in mind, I think,' Beau said. 'That final togetherness for Slow and partner.'

Chapter Seven

Harpur threw £17,000 in twenties and tens on to Iles's desk. 'Nivette's obviously storing it for ultimate return, sir,' he said. 'Only mock-taking, like anyone playing at being bought would. He's turned his place into a bonded warehouse. He's all right.' Harpur felt wonderfully relieved. The money was in three unsealed Jiffy bags. It was the morning after his nice little break-in at Nivette's house.

Seated on the corner of the desk, Iles looked down unexcitedly at the cash. 'Col, we've no way of telling whether this is *all* he's collected from them. He could have been secretly spending, indulging himself, like a . . . like a bought cop.'

'Of course we've no fucking way of knowing. Of course it's not all he's fucking collected from them. If you're supposed to be on the take you've got to spend some of what you take on things they can see, so they'll believe you're genuinely on the take and enjoying it. Didn't I buy myself an Avantage watch at £2700 and two silk shirts for display when l was playing on the take? Did that make *me* corrupt, for God's sake?'

Iles had quite a long think about this, as though he found it tough to decide whether Harpur was corrupt and if so whether the watch and shirts did it. 'Yes, whatever happened to that Avantage item, Harpur?'

'It was handed in.'

'I'm almost sure I can believe that.'

'Thank you, sir.'

'Hard to think of silk against your kind of skin.'
Iles flicked the money bags with his fingertips. 'Where was this?'

'Usual kind of thing. He'd cut and lifted some floor-boards in his boxroom and bathroom.'

'Floor safes?'

'No, just enveloped. l wouldn't be able to open a safe, would I, sir?'

'I've no bloody idea what you can do, Harpur.'

'Thank you, sir.'

'If he tries looking for it now?' Iles asked.

'He and his family have gone to Paris Disneyland. I'll return it before they get back. But I knew you'd want to see it, actually see it, sir, touch it – wouldn't be able to take my word, or wish to.'

'Paris? Expenditure?'

'Yes, some. As I said, he'd have to.'

'Jesus, I've got chief fucking inspectors who go to Disneyland? As to taking your word, Col, I've always found you remarkably plausible, on small matters.'

'Would this be a small matter, sir? It's an officer's integrity.'

'I've heard of quite a few with some of that and don't necessarily exclude you, Harpur.'

'Thank you sir.'

'We'll need changes.' The ACC jumped down from the desk and paced for a while. At the far side of the room he carried out a series of exercises to strengthen his Achilles tendons. Iles revered his legs. 'Col, if Nivette's building a case against them undercover on his own initiative and only play-taking the money, it's going to shatter everything when Lane puts him in charge of targeting.'

'It will make it tricky, yes.'

'Either Nivette deliberately misdirects the targeting to preserve relations with Panicking and Shale, in which case Lane will quickly want to know what's gone wrong. Or Nivette does the targeting properly and

Panicking and Shale decide he's been doubling on them all along and probably see him off some convenient evening, with full brutal preliminaries.'

'Along those lines, yes.'

Iles returned to his desk and fondled the money. 'He might be saving for a yacht.'

'I believe in him.'

Iles bowed his head in a kind of awe at this declaration, his kind. 'I've known two or three occasions when your judgement was right, Harpur. Two.'

'Thank you, sir.'

'I'll have to make Lane put someone else in charge of targeting,' Iles said. 'That's if we can't get targeting junked altogether. We must protect Nivette. I like a bit of maverick activity.'

'That right, sir?'

'But remember, Harpur, what we do will be solely on your say-so – if this all turns tragic.'

'Mr Lane's determined it should be Nivette.'

'We block him.'

'Really determined. The Chief's soul and future are in this project. I don't think he'll shift. We can't tell him Nivette's working undercover without authority.'

'I love Lane, as you well know, Col. His soul I prize and his future I know will be hallowed and banal. I'll talk to his wife.'

'She loathes you, sir.'

Iles nodded sadly. 'She's a sage old thing whatever anyone says. Col, women can be like that towards me – an intense contempt.'

'Oh, not just women, sir.'

'Mainly.'

'And not *every* woman,' Harpur replied. 'There's Sarah, and the juvenile ethnic whore, or is it whores, at the docks, and Lady Ambin, a sweet, busy fuck, I should think?'

'That's all true. Thank you for your kindness, Col. Only Honorée at the docks. Mrs Lane will be at this

Coastal Waters Television party we're all invited to tonight, won't she? I'll go.'

'She sticks by the Chief's decisions always, sir.'

'A fine wife, in her plain, chest-of-drawers-shaped way, Col, and everything that Lane deserves. Yes, I'll talk to Mrs Lane. You tell Francis Garland he'll run the targeting operation, *if* it happens. This will be a round-the-clock commitment for him, so he puts all his lech appointments on hold. All.' The ACC's voice moved briefly into screech and Harpur checked the office door was properly closed. 'I think I've told you, my wife can't imagine now what she ever saw in him. Nor in you, for that matter, Harpur. She laughs, actually laughs, at the mention of him or you. You're an amusement to us on evenings when Radio 3 is poor.'

'Thank you, sir.'

Iles sank into normal tone again. 'Yes, Col, when I've got Nivette off the targeting it's quite possible Lane will shut down the whole fucking idea. Obviously, this is my basic aim. The Chief's a dear brave wreck but can only take so many hammerings a year.'

'And you dish out more than that, don't you, sir?'

'He'll probably come to see the wisdom of a non-aggressive approach to Panicking and Manse. Containment. Peace. These are my watchwords. At Staff College I was known as "Desmond the Reconciler". Stay near me for at least a while at the CWTV vulgarity, will you, Col?'

Harpur did. Iles, greeting the Chief and his wife there, said with quite a decent tremor: 'Mrs Lane – Sally – I have to tell you, and tell you in the presence of the Chief, if I may, sir, that I think you've helped him brilliantly towards a most wonderful recovery. Would anyone know looking at Mr Lane tonight that he had been ill at all only such a few months ago?' Iles paused, but this was not a question aimed particularly at Harpur and he gazed silently about the crowded boardroom, its walls decorated with framed photographs of smiling local and national television celebrities.

'Back I'd say – entirely back – to exactly what he was,' Iles continued. The ACC wore a single-breasted grey flannel suit, its jacket as with all his jackets sweetly conscious of the ACC's shoulder curve. The suit must have cost somewhere near a thousand. He had on another of his murkishly striped club ties, worn to affront.

Sally Lane said: 'And the beauty of it is that when Chief does return he is brilliantly full of energy and new projects.' There was fervour in the words. Her long, nice face throbbed with approval of her husband. She dropped into a powerful whisper. 'This targeting of major crime, for instance. Utterly his own notion, of course.'

Lane glanced towards Iles, held up one hand and said hurriedly: 'Now Sally, perhaps I shouldn't have mentioned that to –'

She softened her voice and became confiding: 'Oh, please don't imagine, Desmond, Colin, that Chief has spoken to me in any *detail* about this targeting operation – *proposed* operation. Never would he do that. We both know there are boundaries to what l may be told, even as his wife. I simply mention the targeting plan as evidence that, upon recovery, he is able once more to initiate bracing policy, to *create* bracing policy. He still has his glorious impulse to fight and fights for the cause of good.' She spoke in that superbly warm, affectionate, dictatorial way she had. 'Command is natural to Chief.'

Lane also had on one of his typical suits tonight, which was understandable enough all told. They were at a retirement party for the chairman of Coastal Waters Television, Lord Ambin of Istalle and Main, a friend of the Chief. 'Sally and I spoke only of the *concept* of targeting, of course, Desmond,' Lane said. 'Absolutely no names were mentioned, no specifics.'

'It's perfectly . . . it's perfectly, well, *predictable* that you should wish to discuss important police moves with Mrs Lane, sir,' Iles replied. 'She's not one to be pushed into a corner and kept in the dark, I think, like an old chest-of-drawers.' He gave a mixture of smile and chuckle at the preposterousness of that placing. 'I certainly would not be one to regard such talk as sloppy big-mouthing, though I can't speak for Harpur, of course, who is severe sometimes.'

A second unquestion, and Harpur stayed quiet. This CWTV function was the kind of thing Iles would not normally have spent a minute at, not even to disrupt and cause pain. The long boardroom was packed with all sorts of other folk he despised, additional to Mrs Lane: media people, national and local politicians, at least two university principals and their wives, a couple of vicars and a priest wearing their gear and a bishop in mufti, plus Round Table and Chamber of Commerce contingents. Specifically, though, Iles detested Ambin. Harpur thought it might be something sexual to do with Ambin and Iles's wife, Sarah, or something sexual to do with Iles and Ambin's young, twitchy third wife, Harriet, or the way CWTV presented police matters in their factual shows, or because Ambin and Lane were friends or because Iles just detested Ambin for not being someone else. He hated many for being undifferent from themselves. Sarah Iles was here tonight, hidden now in the scrum. Harpur might be able to ask her.

Mrs Lane said: 'I'm entirely with Chief, and with several of his major colleagues, when they resist the fashionable relaxation of attitudes towards drugs and seek instead more effective counter-measures. Targeting of specific large-scale dealers such as that gross, allied pair –'

'This relaxation has come to us from the United States, I fear,' the Chief said swiftly, to put a stopper on his wife before she reached the names he must have spilled. 'I know I am right to resist it. On this patch will begin and flourish the reversal of that frighteningly dangerous process of concession, concession.' Lane did what Harpur had often seen him do before – rearranged his feet carefully on the ground as if for more solidity in case Iles hit him.

'As a matter of fact, I half expected to see that gross, allied pair, Shale and Panicking, at this soup kitchen tonight,' the ACC replied. 'Panicking at least. He's worked his way so far towards respectability he'd fit fine into a grab-all crew like these.'

'Dismaying prospect,' Lane said, 'the blurring of ethical lines, the social acceptance of evil. I'll never countenance it.'

'*Never* countenance. Chief will *never countenance* such a snaking into bogus worth. Target, target, target these two men of disorder,' Mrs Lane replied.

Ambin himself arrived and there was a flurry near the door. One of the local MPs accompanied him – the Home Office Minister. Harpur had a general sense of well-tended but thinning grey hair over there, and of bulbous profiles and top-line aplomb. Iles turned his back. 'I've had a thought about the actual programme of targeting,' he said. 'We discussed it, Harpur and I.'

'Oh?' Lane said.

'Oh, yes,' Iles replied.

'But, of course, it is entirely *Chief's* project,' Mrs Lane said. She stared at Iles, ready to spot and kill any take-over ploy. Always she guarded Lane. Harpur found it lovely to watch, thought it what marriage ought to be about.

'This is why I wanted to talk to you both,' Iles replied. 'The Chief might be vulnerable.'

'Oh?' Lane said.

'Certain hazards,' Iles replied.

'But perhaps, Desmond, these are not quite the circumstances for such a talk, or the place,' the Chief muttered.

'I feel Mrs Lane should be present, sir,' Iles replied. 'And I know Harpur would think the same.'

Lane said: 'Sally present? This I do not understand. Sally is a wonderful partner, but I want to assure you, Desmond, that she has no substantive knowledge of –'

'The woman's – wife's – view in this could be so valuable. Col and I agreed on that. Oh, yes, indeed.'

The Chief moved away suddenly to greet Ambin and officially wish him well in the scrapyard.

Iles said: 'In every way he's a most attractive laddy, as you probably know, Mrs Lane.'

'Who?' she replied.

'When I say attractive, I mean entirely in the all-round, professional sense, of course. It can be such a, well, sexual word, I suppose. Sorry. It's clear why the Chief is intent on pushing him. Oh, yes.'

'Pushing him? Who, Desmond?' she replied. 'Whom does he mean, Colin?'

'Sorry again.' Iles said. He struck himself a mild blow on the side of the head for jumbling his message. 'The officer the Chief has selected to lead the targeting operation. Clearly, I can't disclose a name because of the risk for him entailed, but he is in all senses a winning figure – young, intelligent and passionately devoted to the Chief. Oh, absolutely passionately.'

'You mean Richard Nivette?' she asked.

Iles put a finger to his lips. 'What is between the Chief and him I regard as entirely positive.'

'Between them? Positive?' she said. 'Positive?'

'And I know Harpur regards it as positive, too. And *only* professional. Definitely *only* professional, regardless of a deliberate misreading of the situation by some.'

'Misreading? How misreading? Which some?' she replied.

'Harpur and I will do all we can to quash these off-key rumours, rest assured, Mrs Lane, but we do feel it is as well that you and he know they exist.'

'Do I understand you, Desmond? Colin, have you heard this murky gossip?' Mrs Lane asked.

'Colin is disgusted that because a young and gifted officer's assets are recognised and embraced by his Chief this appreciation is regarded by a few – a very limited few, believe me – disgusted that such appreciation is regarded by this malicious few as dubious.'

'Embraced? Dubious?' she asked. 'Positive? Dubious how? Which few?'

'Any Press interest in their relationship, for instance, will be vigorously resisted by Harpur and me. Ah, here's the Chief now, and the spent Lord, plus our very own MP Minister.' Iles dropped his voice for a moment. 'Such a covey of ramshackle talent!' Then he called in greeting: 'Lord Ambin – George – how sad to hear you are quitting terrestrial television – in fact, perhaps, all things terrestrial soon.'

Harpur could see Sarah Iles in an elegant blue cotton suit beneath photographs of two famed weather women at the other end of the room. He edged away towards her. She was talking to Angie Hyde who presented CWTV's investigative current affairs programme, *Light*. 'Colin, I think I'm being professionally quizzed,' Sarah called. 'Come and save me. Angie seems to believe I know things – as if Des and I actually *talk*.'

'Or you'll do instead, Mr Harpur,' Angie Hyde said. 'Do you know about a pusher gone missing?'

'Sarah, you're looking great,' Harpur replied. She was, though he saw the old sadness in her, the old certainty that she had made a mistake, the old determination to stick with it more or less now she and Iles had a daughter.

'Where's your lady, Colin?' she asked. 'Aren't you allowed to bring her where the Chief and his wife are guests?'

'She's a student,' Harpur said.

'Yes, I heard you'd crossed a few time zones. That's

73

what I meant – why you can't show her at a do like this.'

'She's busy with her studies.'

'Frustrating for you,' Sarah said.

Angie Hyde said: 'The *disparu* – it's a tip I had.' She was tall, thirties, cheerful-looking, unpretty for a TV face – in fact just unpretty, gifted, very dogged. Harpur liked her. God, what did unpretty mean, anyway? More or less everything, as far as Harpur was concerned, he'd found. But he still liked her, admired her for holding the job regardless.

'Oh, pushers are always on the move,' he replied.

'This is *really* gone missing,' she said.

'They drop the trade. They go to other cities, better pickings, easier policing.'

'What, easier than here?' Sarah said. 'Easier than Des's live-and-let-live?'

'It's Slow Victor,' Angie Hyde said. 'You know about this, don't you, Harpur? Don't you?'

'About what?' he replied.

'*Do* you know him, Colin?' Sarah asked. 'Are you brickwalling again? Can you help?'

'Well, I know *of* him, naturally. There's a dossier. He does move around. But is he big enough material for *Light*?'

'Angie says there's a political aspect,' Sarah replied.

Yes, Angie was gifted and very dogged. 'Well, there are plenty of politicians here tonight. Ask the Minister if he's heard anything.'

'I don't know enough to put to him yet,' she replied.

'You're asking Mrs Iles and *me*,' Harpur said. 'What kind of political aspect?'

'A relationship,' Angie said. 'That's what I hear.'

'Sexual?'

'Listen, Harpur, you *do* know about it, don't you?'

'Who with?' Harpur asked.

'Don't know,' she said. 'Not yet.'

'You don't really *know* anything, Angie, do you?' Harpur replied. 'Nobody's reported Slow missing.'

'Who is there to report him missing?' she said.

'This relationship? A partner?'

'A partner wouldn't want to do that – unleash an official, public search,' Angie replied.

'Ah, you mean political reasons?' Harpur said.

Angie Hyde stared at him for a while, maybe trying to decide whether he was playing dumb or was truly dumb. She seemed to see she'd get nothing from him either way and moved off.

Sarah shuffled closer to Harpur, though not exactly touching. Why not exactly? He could see the weave of the lovely suit, and the unevennesses in her lipstick, and the pores in the skin of her delicate nose. He could catch, just, the whiff of a scent he recognised, might even have bought her. 'So, how is it now with the giving student?' she asked.

'So, how is it now with –?'

Iles joined them suddenly. 'Desmond,' she said, 'you look unserene, darling. Not like your true as it were self.'

'So, here you are, you two, hob-sort-of-nobbing,' Iles said. 'Just like old times? Ambin is going to get a presentation and the little Minister will do the honours. I'd like us to leave, Sarah.'

'Well, OK,' she said.

'Not exactly now, obviously. When the presentation's actually under way. We take the longest most awkward route towards the door. Mess it up. I'll stay and talk to you and Col until then. Isn't it nice? If only Francis Garland were here, the four of us could pose for happy pictures to show how adult and forgiving we are. Or how fucking forgiving *I* fucking am. I don't suppose Ambin would get them hung on the wall, though, do you, Harpur?' He was yelling again, his face a hacksaw. The Minister had just begun his speech, standing on a small, temporary stage, and people tried to shush the

ACC. He gazed towards the platform. 'Christ, doesn't long grey hair look poignant, like a dead seal?' He touched his own grey hair, kept full since he abandoned that close cropping affected for a while following revived Jean Gabin films. 'I'll have this lot pudding-basined tomorrow.' In a while the Minister turned to pick up from a table the parting gift for Ambin. 'Now, Sarah,' the ACC said, and began to barge a path for himself and her through the crowd, occasionally braying 'Excuse us, do.'

'Colin, are you coming, as well?' Sarah said.

'No, he's not,' Iles replied from deep among the assembly. 'I don't share any more, not gestures or wives.'

The presentation resumed when Sarah and Iles had left. Gerald Vesthal, the Minister, spoke of Ambin's great support through CWTV of 'wholesome popular culture, and one does stress *wholesome*.' He finished and went to join the Lanes. After a few minutes the Chief beckoned Harpur. The Lanes did not seem so much at ease with each other as earlier. Iles had instilled the poison? The Chief said: 'Detective Chief Superintendent Harpur's the one to ask about this, Minister. Colin, Mr Vesthal and the Home Office and Government generally are worried at the way the middle classes are being sucked into the kind of criminality that until now they would have shunned. There have always been middle-class crimes, of course – embezzlement, fraud and so on. But now, probably because of the increasing social acceptance of drugs and of sexual liberalising, such people can find themselves drawn into cruder and, yes, violent areas. Do you see this happening, Colin?'

Vesthal said: 'None of it is statistically proven to date. An impression. There are well-established, unhelpful icons for the educated – you know the novelists Self, Amis, Hawes, and the film-maker Tarantino? Their works imply approval of what one might call the under-side of life. They inculcate moral confusion.'

The Minister turned aside to talk to Ambin's young nervy-looking wife, Harriet. Mrs Lane said: 'Colin, of course the targeting project is only at this stage an *idea*. Chief and I are not wholly committed to it. Not at this stage. He will certainly fight what he sees as dangerous evil, a dangerous evil to which Mr Vesthal added another frightening dimension in his recent words. To carry out that fight, though, targeting is one option among several. Other methods may yet gain Chief's favour.'

'One option among several, Colin,' Lane said.

Yes, Iles had put the poison down. Iles usually could when he wished, and he often wished. Mrs Lane feared she might lose the Chief to a love affair with Nivette. She would fight to hold her husband even if it meant ditching a valued bit of police strategy. There were priorities and, of course, Iles had counted on them.

Chapter Eight

At home in Arthur Street, Harpur heard someone give a gentle, almost apologetic, knock on the front door and when he opened it saw Angela Hyde in the porch. She spoke quietly, hurriedly: 'A very hefty rumour says Slow Victor is somewhere in the docks. You know this? Please, Mr Harpur, take me down there, would you? Help me look for him.'

Harpur's daughters had heard the knock on the door, too, and came out into the hall behind him, though he did not think they could pick up what was said. He took Angie into the sitting room and the children followed. The two girls recognised her from the screen, of course, and Jill said: '*Light,* your programme, is very anti-police. But is it anti-police *enough*? You should be watchful on behalf of the people, and especially of youth,' she said.

'Oh, God, listen to Madam Misunderstood,' Hazel said.

'The media have a vital role,' Jill replied.

'That the lesson for today, babe?' Hazel asked. 'You want us to leave, dad? Like make some tea?'

'Would you mind?'

They minded but did go to the kitchen. Angie Hyde said: 'We picked up this sort of half tip Slow Victor might have a watchman job down there. I asked around. No luck, naturally, but someone said a man had been doing the same thing – inquiring about Slow, night and day, a bit careworn, even desperate. I get a description, but it doesn't mean anything. Late forties – early fifties, decently dressed, middle height, round face, probably white collar.'

'Someone looking for a fix. Bad habits are rife among the middle class. I hear about it all the time. Apparently it's their reading.'

'Why at the docks? That's not Victor's beat.'

'I told you, Angie, they change – no reason. Or no reason anyone else can see. Not like a Civil Service career.'

'And then I'm informed this man who's been asking the questions and whom nobody recognises has been seen in a car with someone who *is* recognised.'

'Oh, yes?' Harpur tried to go opaque.

'You, Mr Harpur. Everyone seems to know *you*.'

'It's an area that has some crime. I catch a share of cases.'

'One man I spoke to couldn't remember your name but said, "You know, the heavy cop who can terrorise. Looks like Rocky Marciano, though fair and taller." I don't remember Rocky Marciano but I thought it might be you.'

'I don't remember Marciano, either. Very refined features, I believe, however.'

'The bloke at the docks said, "His face all pushed about and spread, like a few hammerings."'

'And you said, "Now I *know* you mean Harpur." As a matter of fact, Marciano retired unbeaten in any professional fight, unmarked.' It was all jokey, but why was he having an argument with this unpretty woman about appearances? Pathetic.

'So, who's in the car with the unbeaten, unmarked, refined-looking tall heavy?' she asked. 'What were you doing, patrolling so late? I think you know a hell of a lot more than you show, Mr Harpur.'

'There'd be no point in even a police officer being wilfully secretive.'

She gazed about the living room. 'Nice. Airy. I came to

your house, not the nick, because I thought it might be something you were doing confidentially at this stage – that way you're famed for.'

'It's nice of you, but no.'

'No. Right.'

Hazel and Jill returned then with tea and some cake on a tray. Jill poured and passed the cups and plates around. She said: 'This has to be something big if TV's chasing it. We get all sorts here, but not TV. I mean, not even *local* TV, like you.'

Hazel carved the cake and said: 'So, it has to be drugs. What else is big? Probably you're after barons, are you, Angie? Where *we're* at, I mean street level, caff level, school gates level, drugs is just some little nobody pushing what's often crap stuff for kids, but obviously there must be a flash organisation behind it and empires and emperors, which would interest *Light*, due to sensationalism. It's a giggle really, because I suppose the programme would go all worthy and say how evil drugs are – you sounding off to viewers about needing to clear it all up, and all the time the people making the programme are snorting and smoking, even doing H. This is well known in media to help their creative flair and they've got the money for it what with expenses. Do you do some, Angie? Which?'

'Hazel,' Harpur said.

'Many are hypocrites these days,' Jill said, 'like the Pharisees in the Bible.'

'Is that so, Your Reverence?' Hazel replied. 'Angie, what we always tell people who come here is dad might help you, probably *will* help you, but you've heard of grey areas, have you? He's into grey areas. I think he and Des Iles invented grey areas like a painter named Monet invented dodgy light. We believe dad *wants* to do things right but –'

'He *does* do things right, but sometimes it's hard to actually see he's doing things right, that's all,' Jill said.

'What kind of drugs situation, Angie?' Hazel asked. 'Is this gangs fighting to protect their turf, and so leading to violence? Have there been deaths lately, dad?'

'My mother was killed, murdered, you know,' Jill said.

'Yes, I remember,' Angie replied.

'That was a gang thing,' Jill said. She spoke in a flat, informative voice, as if to show everyone, including herself, that she could talk about it now without breaking.

'Yes,' Angie replied.

'We're all right,' Jill said in that same Now-hear-this tone. 'We don't forget her but it's all right. Nearly all, right. Dad's been pretty good, single-parenting et cetera, when he's got the time, what with Denise. And then his work, also. But mainly Denise. This room used to be all dull with mum's books, real cardboard-cover padded out stuff from far back like *Crime and Punishment*, but he got rid of them after like a decent time because of mum's memory, though, of course, they were both at it on the side. He's thoughtful, in his own way – well, like anybody's father. I'm not exactly against reading, but this was shelves and shelves. This was definitely *literature*.'

'I want your dad to help me find someone,' Angie replied.

'Like a police trawl, or on the quiet?' Jill asked.

'On the quiet.'

'He's not bad at that,' Jill said.

'If it suits,' Hazel added. 'That's if it suits him *and* Des Iles, so things can be tricky.'

The children left again then to do something to plants. Angie said: 'A lockgates man told me a good spot to lie low was one of the moored vessels laid up at Invet Basin. I'd like to look.'

'It's mad.'

'I'd like to look.'

'You've got permission?'

'I don't want it public, and it would have to be if I approached the owners.'

'Why do you need me there?'

'My producer says I can't go trespassing on a ship without some kind of official presence.'

'This won't be official.'

'It'll do. Probably. You've got credibility.'

'I have?'

'Not with juries, maybe, but with general folk, like docks officials and my producer.'

Harpur said: 'We don't even know Vic's missing. Of course he isn't. He's off somewhere – or *in* somewhere, behind bars. We certainly don't know he's working at the docks.'

'*I* know he's missing. I think you do. You've been scouring the docks. You want to come?'

And so he met her on the quayside later. Boarding was by the same rope ladder, and once more it was a night trip with flashlights. Angie wanted the visit kept as secret as it could be, so that if there were revelations on any of these vessels they would be exclusive to her and her programme. Harpur wanted it secret, too. There was the promise to Jack Lamb. Possibly that did not make sense any longer. Angie had decided on her own and from her own information that the D ships were important, no help from Harpur. All the same, he still felt bound. Contracts with Lamb were holy.

Angie had arranged for a docks boatman to row them out and told him the fee included a special element for silence. She went up the ladder even faster than Jack. She was in dark jeans and a dark sweater, dark plimsolls, a burglar's outfit. The cameraman she'd brought took longer, but he was carrying his equipment. Angie wanted to start the search systematically from the dockside vessel and then outwards to the third. They could cross between ships by wooden walkways. The examination of the first two was very swift, because everything was locked up – swift and useless, of course. They simply walked around the deck trying doors, Angie striding eagerly on her long thin legs, expecting success but gradually sinking into disappointment.

Then, on the *Dion*, she found the unlocked cabin and revived, sure she was about to discover something at last. And so was Harpur. Angie pulled open the wardrobe doors. Harpur, standing just behind her with a flashlight, felt himself sway slightly with shock and worked on keeping his face empty, at least as empty as the wardrobe. He wasn't sure how well he managed it. Angie seemed to notice nothing, or nothing in Harpur. She was looking away from him, staring into the wardrobe. 'What are these marks on the back wall?' she said.

'Marks?' Harpur replied.

'Look.' She pointed to the small indentations that made a rough line across the steel bulkhead below the clothes bar.

Harpur went forward and examined them with her. Hadn't there been a string of blood splashes, too? 'Mystifying,' he said.

'As if –'

'Maybe the captain's uniform brass buttons banging about in heavy weather.'

Angie had things right twice, but didn't know it. Yes, Slow Victor *was* missing, was missing.

Angie closed the doors. 'Where next?' she asked miserably. 'The bridge?' They moved out of the cabin and towards a ladder leading to the upper deck. 'All right, I admit it,' she said, 'I'm starting to feel I've brought both of you out here for nothing. It looks like Slow's not on any of the ships.'

'It was worth a try,' Harpur replied. 'At least we know they're clear.'

'Don't be so fucking long-suffering.' They could not get into the *Dion*'s wheelhouse or chartroom, but peered through the windows. 'I'm sorry,' Angie said.

'Oh, he'll turn up, unless he's in the cells somewhere. I'll ask the computer,' Harpur said.

'Why was that cabin door unsecured? It has to mean something.'

'A slip-up.'

The three of them walked back towards the rope ladder, ready to leave. 'And you're not going to tell me who was in the car with you?' she asked.

'Not relevant, believe me,' Harpur replied.

'No,' she said. 'I won't do that – believe you. I still think you know so much more than you show, Mr Harpur. But that's policing, I suppose.' She screwed up her face a bit in irritation, like someone familiar with brick walls, especially police brick walls.

'There's no point in even a police officer being wilfully secretive,' Harpur replied. He would have to explain to Jack.

Now, they descended from the bridge and looked for more open doors and then for a way into the hold of the *Dion*. Nothing. 'Listen, Mr Harpur, could those dents be bullet scars?' she asked.

'Bullets? In a wardrobe?' Harpur replied.

'Could they?'

'What – the captain, drunk or high, shooting at his own clothes for fun?'

She stopped the questions for a while, then said, 'OK, I give up. But don't you worry if someone just drops out of the scene, Mr Harpur?'

He wondered for a second or two – no, only *one* second – wondered whether if she were not unpretty he would still obstruct her like this. God, he was disgusting. 'Slow's adult,' he said. 'He's entitled to go where he likes, without informing me or anyone else.'

'But of course you worry. Why else would you be ferreting down here by car at night, with companion?'

'I'll do a quiet little check around and locate him. But would that kill your programme?' Harpur replied.

'Exposure TV's no good if there's nothing to expose.'

84

Chapter Nine

In his drawing room Mansel Shale had a sharp memory for a moment of Alfie Ivis with his pistol almost against Finnane's ear in the bottom of the motor boat, but not quite touching. And then the two shots. Shale said: 'That was a true crisis, Alf, the only word. And you handled it beautiful. With all the humanity I'd expect.'

'Thank you, Manse.'

'I've seen unpleasantnesses like that before, but never so bonnily handled. Someone who everybody thought was . . . well, dead sure was dead suddenly starts the noises and the fluttering, this fucking inconvenient return to life out of the fucking blue. Disturbing, Alf. That Finnane must of been a real tough one – nearly indestructible, except for you. I don't want to talk crude money about what's obviously a tragedy, but there's a bonus in that for you.'

'No need, Manse. Just a duty.'

'I'm talking of half a grand at least here, Alfred.'

'Generous, Manse – well, as ever.'

'But there's implications.'

'Certainly, Manse.'

Shale took a drink. *Generous, Manse – well, as ever.* Now and then Shale wondered whether Alfred was sending him up. Ivis did not know anything in proper detail about the firm's real accounts, but he might be able to make a bit of a guess at how much money went through the firm, and how much reached Shale and Ember in profits. Half a grand could look measly to Ivis. Was he

85

getting dangerous, the way anyone close to you in this business could get dangerous? Shale said: 'Yes, implications, Alfred. So I'll break into that fucker Richard Nivette's house tonight. Got to be tonight. He's due back from Paris after his stay with Minnie Mouse, right?'

Ivis had a think. 'With respect, Manse, maybe I'm thick, but I really don't see the connection between the sad business of completing on Finnane and a search of Nivette's property.'

No, Alfie wouldn't, not yet, not without a direction arrow or two. Yes, Alfie *was* thick in some aspects. Shale asked: 'This *is* our last chance to get in there, isn't it? Nivette's coming home.'

'Tomorrow, Manse, but –'

'Myself. Not something I'd ask you or anyone else to handle. You handsomely did *your* job at sea in the *Cormorant* when them come-back groans got under way from Finnane.'

'If you personally were caught in Nivette's place searching at night, Manse, it would –'

'No, you've handled your share of responsibility, Alfred. And would I ever ask Denzil to try a break-in? Christ, could Denz do someone's place with subtlety? Subtlety? He never heard of it. A quick look around for funds, that's all. We know how they work, these doublers, if Nivette's a doubler and, oh, yes, he could be. They stack the money so they can give it back intact more or less. Sometimes the cash is at home, sometimes in a bank deposit. I'll take a glance. If it's there it will be behind a picture or under floorboards and it will tell the lot. They got no invention. If it's in the bank there'll be a certificate for the box and a key. We got to know him in full, Alf. Tell Denzil, would you – about the driving? We take the Ford, not the Jaguar, it's a screaming advert. Just after midnight. Denzil stays in the car and does a circuit or two while I'm in there to check no officers, mobile or other. You hang about in the garden, give me cover.' Shale sat back, as if the talk had finished. 'So slip upstairs and brief Denz now in his flat, would you, please, Alf? It's like urgent.'

Ivis did not move, though. He said: 'I'm sorry, Manse, but I still can't help thinking that –'

Shale held up a hand but friendly. You had to listen to arguments from staff, listen to them like they mattered, especially when the staff member had done so well giving that Finnane a decent timely end. 'All right, Alf, you ask me what's the link. You want to know, how come Finnane given final rest on your boat means I got to get into Nivette's place for a search tonight? I'll tell you. The link? Panicking Ralphy's the link, that's who. Why? How? That bugger's upset, upset, upset by what happened on the boat and could talk to Nivette, if Nivette's a doubler. Panicking *might* know he's a doubler. I got to know, too. Why I'm going into his nest.'

'Manse, I just don't follow how you –'

'Did you get a look at Ralphy on your boat during that trip? Would you say his heart was truly in it? He was bad enough on the dinghy and the *Dion* in the dock. But then when we drive to the estuary and go to sea in your fine little motor boat, *Cormorant*, Alf – well, suddenly he's a complete dangerous ruin.'

'Jumpy, I agree,' Ivis replied. 'But –'

'I looked at Panicking and saw someone who had no real commitment to the enterprise, Alfred. Well, Panicking always been like that, yes, or why is he Panicking?'

'He *was* badly affected by –'

'He was turned, Alf. Ralphy won't recover. What he heard, what he saw, it tore him, Alf. I can almost understand it. Always, always, there's them terrible sounds when someone comes back to the living like that Finnane, like they seen something foul while they been away and want to tell about it, like the one called Lazarus resurrected in the Bible– one Sunday School tale we all remember most probably. This with Finnane reveals the remarkable strength of the human body, so important for the survival of our species, obviously, but now and then . . . well, very trying, Alf. Finnane was smacked point blank with two 9mm H and K Parabellum rounds in the target area on the dockside by me and he can still make a noise like that more than a couple of hours later. It was strange because, in a way, our journey in the *Cormorant* could of been regarded as pleasant and bracing up till then – smooth sea, sky black but silvering sweetly at the edges, a lovely grey-dark loneliness, no other boats, not even early day fishermen. And then suddenly from nowhere these very personal sounds, like a communication.'

'Panicking went into a genuine –'

'Panic. Of course he did. The trembling and that stinking all-over sweat and pawing at his face, his own face, like checking up it's still there. He's saying to himself, "Get clear of them, Ralph. Now."'

'Of whom, Manse?'

'Me. Us.'

'No – I'm really unable to believe that.'

'He decides to spill to Nivette – getting out from accessory,' Shale said. 'And he's still clutching at that fucking jaw.'

'I think at those times Ember fears his scar is going to open up through stress, like the stigmata weeping blood,' Ivis replied.

Shale nodded. 'Well, I've heard of that, when I had Carmel living in here for a week or two.' They were talking in the long drawing room of his home, the former St James's rectory, a big, gaunt, grey-stone comfortable house in grounds and a good top floor for Denz. 'Or it could of been Patricia or Lowri. One of them's a Catholic and mentioned stigmata. Probably Patricia. Or it *could* be Lowri, a Welsh girl. There are Welsh Catholics. Catholic girls will cohabit these days, it's known as liberalisation.'

'Ralph was able to recover, Manse. Entirely. With respect, I don't think anything drastic is needed at this stage. Certainly not housebreaking.'

'Something like that's going to stay for ever with Panicking, Alf. Do you know what I saw? I really looked at him while you bent over so uncomplaining to complete things for Finnane, the wheel on automatic pilot.'

'It was unavoidable, Manse.'

Shale leaned across and gripped Ivis's arm, fingering hard in reassurance. 'Do you have to tell me that, Alfred? I don't think so. It was basically a wholesome act. For God's sake, am I going to put somebody still breathing over the side weighted? Disgusting. You dropped the pistol into the sea, didn't you, the one you used on him? Not at the same spot, obviously, but got rid?'

'On the way back.'

'And mine's down there, too, naturally. Basics. Did Panicking see you do it?'

'Do what, Manse?'

'I don't mean saw you finishing Finnane in that considerate way – of course he *did* see that.' And Shale saw it again for a half-second then, too. He trembled slightly. He was sure that in a moment there would be other grim pictures. 'Ralphy was staring when you went down to Finnane's ear, Alf. But I meant did Panicking see you ditch the gun?'

'I don't think so.'

'I wish you knew for sure,' Shale said. 'You never know what they can recover from the depths these days. Think of that fucking *Titanic* on the bottom with divers in and out the portholes. I didn't let him see me sink my pistol, just a hand over the side with the 9mm in it, and then it's gone, no splash just swallowed up in the fathoms. Next time he sees my hand, no gun, but it could be anywhere, holstered, my pocket.'

'But, with respect, what are you saying, Manse? That Ralph Ember would mouth to . . .'

'Oh, yes, mouth. I've got to get ahead of him.'

Ivis went quiet. He had an armchair under two Edward Prentis paintings in the Pre-Raphaelite style. Shale was entirely in favour of the Pre-Raphaelites and had a work by another artist of that time who did their kind of stuff, Arthur Hughes. Girls' tresses Shale regarded the Pre-Raphaelites brilliant at, often auburn, and he wondered why so few modern artists did good tresses. Ivis and he were drinking gin and peps from earthenware nursery mugs, Ivis's decorated with 'Tom, Tom, the Piper's Son' pictures, Shale's 'Hey-diddle-diddle the Cat and the Fiddle'.

Shale said: 'That's what I saw when I looked at him during the death – someone who could mouth, spill. Just after the blood and so on got to his shoes this was someone suddenly wondering who he was partnered with. It was still dark, yes, and the *Cormorant* was doing a little bit although so calm, but I could see his face and what his mind was telling him. All of it was done as respectful as it could be, but for Ralphy Ember this was a new and horrible development. Following this Finnane event he thinks I'm some animal, and even you, Alf – me for what happened on the quay and you for helping Finnane into peace.'

'Oh, Manse, if I may say, you really mustn't speak in –'

'Yes, some animal, his view. He wants distance between us, a lot of distance. And he's thinking to himself, *How do I put myself right if someone such as Harpur or even Iles finds out about this Finnane, someone important in the political scene and with important mates, probably, who can stir?* I mean, washed up, or someone spotting things at the docks or jetty who we never saw. So, how *does* he put himself right? He puts himself right by going to this Nivette if this Nivette is a doubler and telling him the whole lot he knows – Slow Victor, Finnane shot then given a finale in your boat, and the both of them capably wire-bound to them concrete pillars down below. They're deep and at sea, yes, not just in a dock, but like I said the sea bottom is not what it used to be. So, I got to know first if Nivette's a doubler. After that, other decisions, clearly, which could be grave. I don't want you fretting, Alfred. OK, you're the one who killed Finnane in full view. But we can make sure we get this information nicely sealed in one way or the other. Why I'll do Nivette's place tonight.'

'It's good of you and typical, Manse, but –'

'Yes, I hope it's typical.' Shale was getting tired of Alfie's conversation. 'This is leadership. This is looking after one of my people who could be in difficulty because of . . . Well, because of possible behaviour by someone supposed to be an associate, but really a panicking liability to us instead.'

Ivis wagged the weighty face. 'Yet I do have to ask, Manse, whether you might be exaggerating Ralph Ember's reaction. I think I can say we were all very troubled, yourself included. You've always had a sensitivity about things in cold blood, even when so vital.'

'Oh, yes, *troubled*. Certainly. Finnane shouldn't even of been a part of any of this, the poor gay shot bastard. I don't know, it could be they got a more vivid, lively sort of life, gays – some say that, I've heard it – so even two rounds from a H and K Parabellum don't do it straight off because of all that inner friskiness. But for Panicking this was not just *troubled*.'

'I –'

'Go and tell Denzil we'll need him tonight then, will you, Alfred? He needn't wear the chauffeur's cap.'

Shale did quite enjoy discussions with Ivis, but all discussions had to end sometime, and sometimes Shale liked ending them. His voice now said he was ending this one and Alfie recognised it and stood up. Alf was a great lad probably, with an education, so he said, and perfect when you got someone so defiant and unexpected frightening folk in a small boat at sea before dawn like Finnane. But Alfie was not good on the wider picture. Not ramifications. Perhaps it was best like that. If he *had* started thinking about the wider picture it might make him a bit ambitious, a bit dissatisfied, a bit dangerous.

When Alf had gone upstairs to find Denzil, Shale thickened up both drinks with more gin. He had acted pretty settled with Alf because a leader must look after morale. All the same, the events in Alf's boat at sea and even events before that still gave Shale very rough memories, memories he waited for the gin to wipe out for a time or at least soften. It was not good to recall chucking Finnane into Alfie's Land Rover at the Invet Basin the way they had with Slow, when Finnane was still alive. To Ivis, Shale had said the treatment of the bodies was respectful, but with a live body you ought to be *more* respectful if you knew it was alive. Well, they didn't and it should definitely not of been, but Shale disliked going over that part in his mind. The same when they took the bodies from the Land Rover down the little jetty and on to the *Cormorant* for their trip out of the estuary to open sea. They were like cargo, that was all, Slow and Finnane, but all the time this Finnane's body was getting ready to perk up. The treatment had not been right, when you looked back on it.

Shale had a brief but very clear mind-glimpse of them dragging those two bodies, and to get rid of it he gazed around this grand drawing room with its good furniture and pictures and thought it wrong that someone sitting here should have to recall grubby moments like all that with Finnane and Slow. He hated to think this comfort and style depended on such roughness. The gin was taking a long time to get a blanket over those recollections. They still kept on at him. They still hurt.

Alfie had been at the wheel of the motor boat heading far out when the noises from Finnane started and probably he did not hear them at once above the engine. At the time, Shale and Beau were devotedly wiring Slow to the concrete, which meant they were very close to

Finnane because they had been laid out together along-side their individual pillars for convenience. They had a reel of wire and cutters and Panicking was slicing off lengths and handing them down to do the binding. Things were moving along really nice. These pillars were about six feet high and say 8" by 8", hefty – they could not be better. Ivis had stopped the Land Rover on their way to the estuary from the docks and with spades they dug out these pillars and their concrete bases from a road fence, then cut them free from the fence. They had brought the spades, the roll of wire and the cutters to the *Dion* in the Basin, knowing they would have to sea-sink Slow Victor. The cutters and spades had come from Shale's garage, but they had had to buy the wire. That could be a problem one day through sales records if the bodies were found, though they had paid cash, no cheque or credit card, naturally.

Anyway, the thing to do was to make sure they were deep and did *not* get found, and Shale and Beau were doing a really thorough operation on Slow when Finnane began the sounds and twitching. Shale did not blame Finnane. Life was such a powerful item that if there *was* any it would always push to the front no matter how things looked. This was true of many folk, not just gays.

Beau had turned out great at the work, tightening up wire on Slow, knotting it good, no skimping. Obviously the best place on a body for fixing the wire was around the neck because it could not slip up or down from there – either the chin and head would stop it or the shoulders. Beau did a really skilled unmovable binding of Slow's neck to the pillar, four strands and then a triple twisted knot. This knot had to last a wet century. It was so good it would of strangled Slow if he had not been dead from bullets, cutting right into the flesh. But he did not bleed owing to the time he had been gone. This knot and the tightness was what Shale meant when he said they had offered the bodies respect. Beau gave Victor true craftsmanship.

But Beau said the neck on its own was not enough, and Shale did not mind taking orders from the bastard about this – it was only a low-rank job and not the sort that would come up often. Slow had to be wired around his ankles and waist as well so no amount of waves and tide could work him free, regardless of if his size went down because of time and fish, making the wire slacker regardless of how tight it started. It was a good job they had bought a full roll of the wire, even though when they bought it they thought it was only for Slow because Finnane was not in the scene at that point. By the time they had Slow nearly complete it was getting close to day, but Beau still would not rush. Luckily there were holes in the pillar for strands of the fence to go through and Beau said to use these in the binding of him, so the wire could not shift up or down on the concrete during sea movement at great depths which there always was. The big jagged foundation blob of concrete on the end of each pillar gave grand extra weight. That blob would be beneath their feet which meant they would be pulled down like standing, like Slow had been coming down the side of the *Dion*, giving dignity.

They had Slow fastened with real neatness and permanence when Finnane who was lying by his own pillar started this groaning, wheezing noise from far down in him. A shock, yes, but at first Shale thought it was just air escaping from the body as could sometimes happen with a deceased. The noises went on, and then Shale thought he saw the eyelids start that fucking flickering. It had been hard to be sure with so little light, but in a minute Finnane's eyes opened altogether for a while and he was staring up at the dark sky, or that's how it seemed. Perhaps he could not see, but the eyes were wide. And there was the groaning getting louder. Now and then it seemed to Shale to become almost musical, like the start of some miserable old hymn – some hymn that had stuck from Sunday School, like Lazarus raised from the dead. It might be 'Abide With Me'.

It was obvious Beau Derek did not like this. He stood up in a hurry to get away from Finnane and stared down at him. A minute before, Beau had been a real careful operator, tending for Slow with such method, yet now he was like frozen, just stiff and staring alongside Panicking in the stern. Christ, some couple. Well, by then Alfred must of heard the sounds and he saw the movement – Beau jumping up like that, jerky with nerves before going frozen. Ivis put the wheel on automatic and came over to Shale, then bent to examine Finnane. Panicking did not say anything but he looked like he wanted to get that wheel off automatic taking them outwards and turn the boat around and head back to the jetty. Probably even in full daylight they would not be in sight from land by now, to be sure of depth. Did he think what it would be like, arriving back there, one body unmistakably wired to concrete and the other not a body at all, a life? Or perhaps he thought, put Slow Victor over, but take Finnane back for hospital. Just as crazy. Suicide. Probably he did not even *have* thoughts, only these rushes of fear. On the whole this *Cormorant* was quite a sight then. There had been a definite atmosphere.

'Regrettable, Manse,' Ivis had said, still crouched by Finnane.

'I'll finish him.' Shale whispered it, worried he might get some sloppy intervention from Panicking or even Beau.

'With respect, Manse, not your kind of work at all,' Ivis answered. 'You've given your wholly justified heat-of-the-moment contribution. This is a different kind of duty.' He stood and turned away so that Finnane could not see him, if Finnane could see anything. Shale, who had remained down with Slow and the concrete, stood, also, and saw Alfie had produced a Smith and Wesson Model 52 automatic. Panicking must of seen it, too, and grabbed at his fucking jaw line again like somebody with the communication cord in a train. He looked as if he wanted to shout something, something like 'No' or 'Stop' or 'Give him mouth-to-mouth', but probably he did not have any voice. It might of all seeped out through the scar.

Alfred seemed to wait until Finnane's eyes closed again, maybe for good, maybe from weariness. The singsong groaning had kept going, though. It was more 'Rock of Ages' now. Well, we were all looking for one of those to hide under or inside if it had a cleft. Alfie stepped across to him and bent down very swiftly. He put the gun half an inch from Finnane's ear so he would not know it was happening, and fired twice. Alf did not want to shoot him like a horse or a dog with the metal right on him. This was consideration and tact. Alfie had to get really low so that if the bullets went right through they would go up through the top of Finnane's head and then away, not hole the boat. It was messy, of course it was messy, and some of it caught Beau's trousers from the knees down, plus Panicking's shoes. Shale reckoned this was what really finished him. He was staring down, still comforting his jaw. Shale thought it was then – the shoes moment – then that Panicking decided he had to get out of this partnership. He was troubled already, yes, about Slow and especially Finnane, but seeing it on his shoes was what really hit him. The shoes were only ordinary black lace-ups, about £50 or £60, but quite often it could be little things like this that would turn into a crucial bother for some. Following these incidents, the time together on the *Cormorant* grew quite tense, even after Slow and Finnane were gone with their pillars, and Shale had been glad to return to the jetty and then home.

Now, Alfred came back into the rectory drawing room after giving Denzil instructions and sat down again, his big face weary-looking and lost. Shale handed him the stiffened gin and pep. Probably he needed a drink after getting orders into Denzil. 'I'm still remembering the *Cormorant*, Alfred,' Shale said. 'It was when he saw the blood and so on on his shoes. I know what he thought. He thought this is some well-known figure in politics and when the trouble starts because he's missing it will reach everyone.'

'It was unfortunate, Manse.'

'Unavoidable. Panicking and Beau were not the only ones to get stained.'

'Hardly, Manse.'

'I mean, taking Finnane's clothes off for non-identification, and then the wire-binding when he was in that state.'

'Quite.'

'We ended up with a lot of garments to be destroyed, yours, mine, Finnane's. Panicking and Beau burned their own, I hope, as well as the shoes. Notice Beau wouldn't do any of the wiring when it was Finnane? Not because it was Finnane, but because Finnane was bleeding. What did Beau expect? If you put two bullets in someone's ear from close there's bound to be blood. So, anyway, for fixing Finnane to the sinker it was back to the old firm – you and me, Alf – which is something for additional thanks. You did get rid of that suit? Yours, I mean, as well as Finnane's.'

'Absolutely. And a good hosing for the *Cormorant*.'

'So sad to see them naked like that, bullet-holed, close together and wired up to concrete when they must of often been naked in a more relaxed, loving situation with each other previously when alive,' Shale replied. 'And I almost hope Finnane was not seeing anything when he opened his eyes because it would be an agony if his final memory of Slow was him in that happily familiar naked state, but without some teeth and metal-lashed to a great lump of . . . why, here come those two rapscallions Matilda and Laurent, back from school.'

Shale's children skipped into the room wearing their blue and black uniform, laughing and yelling greetings to Alfie. They loved it when Ivis was here, especially Laurent, because one of Alf's genuine slabs of knowledge was history of the Royal Navy, right back to 'Splice the topsails me hearties' and stalking the *Scharnhorst*. Laurent loved to hear his grand tales of bravery and honour on boats. In former times boats usually did bring the best out of the British. Generally Shale let Alf dribble on with it because the children deserved plenty of friendship after their mother went off. But this afternoon Shale felt a bit pressured. He wanted to think about how to do Nivette's place. They called Ivis Uncle Alfred. Shale did not mind this. He did not mind Alfie getting bodily quite close to them now and then, even an embrace. The world was a tricky place to be in and they would have to get used to looking after themselves among all sorts. 'You promised you'd tell me about the battle of Cape Matapan, Uncle Alfred,' Laurent said.

'A wonderful victory,' Ivis replied. 'Three enemy cruisers sunk off the island of Crete.'

'Daddy, do you sometimes get letters from mummy?' Matilda asked. 'In English today we were doing letters and the teacher asked us who we would like to write a letter to. And I thought mummy, but I didn't say it, I said Mel Gibson. But I wondered if mummy sent letters to us, so I could send one back to her.'

'Of course she does,' Shale replied. He tried to remember when Sybil had written last. Less than a year ago? Was she still living in Wales with that stockbroker or one-armed-bandit manufacturer or equivalent, the other end of Wales from where Lowri came from? 'Mummy always wants to know about you, both of you,' he said.

'Does she?' Matilda said. 'Will you show us the next letter, please?'

'Now you go and get your homework out of the way, you ruffians,' Shale replied. 'Uncle Alfred and I are talking about ships and boats, too, as a matter of fact, Laurent, but not the Royal Navy, really. This is only a bit of boring old business, I'm afraid – hardly the rough glories of wondrous battles.'

When they had gone, Shale said: 'I wish I could have put them together on the bottom, Alf, like in that tale Ralphy mentioned about the brother and sister. The fucker's *so* into heavy books, you know, because he went to the coll, as you'll hear and hear from him. That would of not been wise, two bodies close, if ever there was a search. But in a way, a sort of *spiritual* way, they're still joined, Alfred, by being dropped over the side on the same morning and identical sinkers.'

'Once they'd gone under and especially Finnane I think Ralph returned more or less to normal. And Beau wasn't too bad either.'

This was a thing about Alfred, he would stick at it, his opinion, regardless of how fucking mad. 'Panicking's going to remember it all,' Shale said. 'It's going to reshape the bastard, like jelly in a new mould.'

Around 1 a.m. Shale used a bit of plastic on Nivette's front door and went in with a flashlight. Cops had no idea of security. It took him about twenty minutes to find where the floorboards had been cut. He brought out the packets of money hidden there and counted the notes on the kitchen table. They came to £17,000. He did not know how much Nivette had had from him and Panicking but that would not be far off. Alfred might know the figure. He was good at chickenfeed accounts.

So, Nivette *was* a doubler. Shale replaced the money and the carpets and left. Alfie was sentrying in the garden and they walked down to the corner of the street to wait for Denzil patrolling somewhere in the car. When he was driving them back to the rectory Denzil said: 'Well?'

Shale was alongside him in the front, it being only the Ford. 'What?'

'Is he ours or only pretending so he can fuck us up?' Denzil replied.

From the back Ivis said: 'This is not something that can be decided just like that on the basis of a necessarily hurried visit.'

'He's going to fuck us up,' Denzil replied.

'Just drive,' Shale said.

'This means his house is bulging with loot, does it?' Denzil replied. 'You left it, Manse?'

'Stay away from there,' Shale said.

'Some obvious place to hide it – behind the toilet tank, floorboards, in the back of some pictures,' Denzil replied.

'Stay away from there,' Shale said.

'It would be doing us a favour if someone took that loot,' Denzil replied. 'When it's gone he can't fuck us up because he wouldn't have it to hand back and make himself look clean in court.'

'Mansel doesn't need your advice on this kind of matter.'

'Stay away from there, Denzil,' Shale said.

'Well, it doesn't look like the police know he's taking or they'd have been through the house already and lifted the lot for themselves,' Denzil replied. 'What sort of amount, Manse?'

'There's been no mention of a find of money,' Ivis said.

'So what will you do about him, Manse?' Denzil replied.

They dropped off Alfred at his lighthouse and then went back to the rectory. When Denzil had gone up to his flat, Shale took the Ford again and drove down to Nivette's place once more. That was a smart notion from Denzil. If Nivette could not produce his stored back-handers, no jury would ever believe he had only been privately *playing* at corruption. They would think he had been taking because he liked taking, a second career. His

word would be next to useless. But, of course, he'd
never risk having to give his word to a court, anyway, if
he did not have the money. It would not matter if
Panicking went along to him with some tales about the
Dion and the *Cormorant*. Nivette would never be able to
pass on those stories because he'd know he stood a
grand chance of going to jail for fifteen years as a bought
copper and accessory. And that was without them nail-
ing him for Slow Victor. Did Nivette do Slow? God what
a picture it all was – chaos, disintegration, no values.

He worked the plastic again, lifted the carpets and
boards, filled his pockets with the money then replaced
everything nicely. As he drove back to the rectory, he
wondered whether he should tell Denzil and Alfie what
he had done. Usually he liked to praise staff really well
if they had come up with something bright, such as
Denzil's idea – just as he had praised Alfred for settling
Finnane down. But Denzil was such a prick basically,
and it would probably not be good for him to think he
had been cleverer than Alfred and Shale himself.
Although Denzil had some good elements to him, obviously, it would most likely be a mistake to let him get
the idea he was suddenly creative. In any case, that
would offend Alfie, make him feel a fucking chauffeur
was being treated as brighter than he was, which Denzil
might be, but Shale had to look after Alfie's pride,
especially since the *Cormorant*. This was elementary man
management.

Of course, there was one danger if Shale did not tell
Denzil he had taken the money. This was that Denzil
would break into the house himself, hunting the loot for
his own selfish gain, and he could easily get caught, he
was so clumsy. Then there would be inquiries, ramifications, maybe involving all of them. Or when Denzil
looked for it and it was gone he might think Shale had
taken the money first time and pretended he hadn't so
he could keep it for himself. This could make Shale look

to Denzil like a lying sneak thief, and there would be a full loss of respect.

It was tricky, but Shale decided on the whole it would be best to retain the money and not speak of it. Did that ugly lout Denzil run this firm, for God's sake?

Chapter Ten

Harpur had a call at home late in the evening from Iles on his mobile asking if Harpur could 'pop down post haste' to the docks where the Assistant Chief was waiting in his car with Honorée, one of the very young black girl tarts who worked the area, and whom Iles was especially given to and often. He loved ethnicity and youthfulness because as he had once told Harpur such girls were more sensitive to his 'diffident almost retracted glamour' than other people. Harpur thought this might be true. At least they could not be *less* sensitive to it. There was a case some while ago now when he bumped into the two of them at night in the Valencia Esplanade district near the docks, and it had been clear then that this was not their first meeting. Probably few Assistant Chief Constables had such a relationship going. Iles used to say there could be what he called 'a kind of fidelity' between a client and a girl and girl and client.

'Which kind of fidelity is that, sir?' Harpur had asked him.

'Oh, a workaday kind. An intelligent unbothersome kind – reciprocally unbothersome, obviously.'

'Ah.'

Tonight on the phone Iles said: 'Honorée has something powerful to report, Col. It's the kind of thing you ought to hear direct and face-to-face, I feel, you being at what Lane always with his flair calls the nitty-gritty. Honorée says she would not object to speaking to you,

103

although you've never given her the least business. She's a kindly person, a credit to the rising generation, which is so often maligned. She's even nice enough to say she thinks she remembers you, though I said unlikely given your towering subfuscness. But she asked, "Wasn't he the one with the circus clown suit?" so perhaps you *did* impress. Oh, she's shaking her head, denying she ever said that now, but you'll know better, Col, in your circus clown suit.'

'What kind of powerful thing to report, sir?' Harpur replied.

'Yes, get down here, would you?'

Hazel had answered the phone first. At the time, Harpur was in a corner of the living room with a cup of tea, trying to list on a writing pad all possible removers of Slow Victor's body and all possible destinations: not a lying in state. On the other side of the room, Jill had been performing a coffin scene from Joe Orton's *Loot*, doing all parts and using a cardboard box as prop. Could Finnane have recruited people to help take Slow, supposing he had found him eventually? Why would he want to shift him, anyway? Sentiment? Decency? Hazel chatted away on the hall phone and when she came back in for Harpur Jill said: 'Haze, it just has to be Des Iles calling. There's flirt sweat on your top lip.'

'Belt up, sheep tick.'

'Did he praise your deportment and unique vitality again?'

'I think he had someone with him, dad,' Hazel replied, 'overhearing.'

'His wife?' Jill asked. 'Chatting you while *she's* about – the nerve.'

'He might be in a car,' Hazel said. 'That kind of echo.'

'Oh,' Jill replied. 'The nerve – but even more so.'

Harpur had gone to take the call, then returned to the living room. 'Does he want to show off someone new?' Jill said. 'Some other child?'

'I have to go out,' Harpur replied.

'Will you be able to find them?' Jill asked. 'Did he give good directions – some bit of waste ground, or a nice dark spot on the docks?'

A nice dark spot on the docks. 'It's a small emergency at headquarters,' Harpur replied. 'To do with overtime payments for plain-clothes officers on football duties.'

'That was a mobile,' Hazel said.

Harpur drove down to the Invet dock. The ACC's new Rover was parked in shadow between two tall disintegrating Victorian warehouses, like a soft-sell car ad. He and Honorée were standing by the Rover talking. Occasionally she pointed towards the dock and the three moored vessels, as though describing something she'd seen. The ACC was right – there did seem to be a harmony to the two of them, a rich fittingness. 'Ah, Col,' Iles called, 'I was just telling Honorée about the deportment and unique vitality of your daughter, Hazel.'

'He's so let's call it appreciative, Mr Harpur,' Honorée said in a kindly sing-song voice.

Iles said: 'Apparently among the girls, Col, I'm known as "Insightful Iles".'

'Is this place significant?' Harpur replied, waving a hand around to take in the dock and buildings.

'The general area is certainly significant to Honorée and me,' the ACC said.

'Oh, yes,' Honorée said. 'Frequently, yet not frequently enough, Des.'

'And, of course, to Honorée with some others,' Iles said.

'She brings all her car toms here?' Harpur asked. 'She saw something?'

'She was here with a friend the other night, yes,' Iles replied. 'Not in a car. A car would have been spotted and what happened would not then have happened, probably.'

'What *did* happen?' Harpur asked.

'They were in the warehouse here.' He pointed to the

huge ruin on the left. 'Oh, yes, very basic, but there are comfortable patches. Honorée was with a marriage guidance counsellor or primary school head – someone along those lines. People like that admire her nice way with grammar, and so on. They heard what they both took to be shooting. At least two shots. They did their best to see what took place.'

The girl sort of spun to face Harpur direct and gripped his arm for a second: 'Listen, I don't grass, ever.' It was ferocious, like a defiant statement of faith to persecutors. Then she softened and let go of Harpur. 'But Des . . . well Des is Des. I talk to him as to a grand chum. We all do.'

Iles chuckled for a while. It turned out to be about life's ironies: 'When I tell Honorée and the other girls that there are people – colleagues, I mean – associates – yes, when I say there are colleagues and associates who fear and even loathe me these girls are mystified, Col.'

This was not a question and there was no need for Harpur to reply but he felt he should contribute: 'Oh, yes, Honorée, the ACC is genuinely detested by many very close to him.'

'Thanks, Col, for confirmation.'

'Never,' she cried. 'Des? So generous, so conversational, so loving.' Her words echoed confusingly from the shell structures on both sides. Honorée could be eighteen just about, wearing a denim trouser suit now, her hair cut *en brosse*, as Iles's was again, too, after his revulsion at long grey hair at the Coastal Waters Television party. Harpur thought her accent was South London, considerably improved, not local. Iles plainly regarded her as a winner, and who wouldn't agree?

'Apparently among the girls, Col, I'm also known as "Integrity Iles" – meaning I don't blab. I assure you, it took me a while to persuade Honorée that you could be told, despite everything.'

'Thank you, sir.'

Iles's tone grew considerate: 'It disturbed them in

their love activity, this shooting, Col. Well, when you're a marriage guidance counsellor or headmaster lying out accompanied on rubble by someone not much above sixth form age more or less naked in the middle of the night, you don't want to get drawn into things, do you? You above all, Harpur, will understand that.'

'This *can't* be grassing, can it, Des,' Honorée said, 'because I don't know any names, and it was too dark even for descriptions?'

Iles walked over to what had been a double doorway to the warehouse on the right, wide enough to take a pair of dray horses and a wagon in its original bustling era. The actual doors had gone and anyone could enter. Iles went in, then beckoned Honorée and Harpur. They joined him. Iles produced a pencil beam torch and shone it on to the warehouse floor. 'Honorée says she and her friend were lying here,' he said. 'That's about right, isn't it, love?' The ACC indicated a space on the ground where the debris was not too deep or perilous: no broken glass and only small denomination brick bits, cushy more or less. With a sudden elegant swoop, Iles lay down there and got comfortable. The ACC was in a fine navy herringbone double-breasted suit, almost certainly another London job. He signalled to Honorée and Harpur to join him. Honorée stretched out close to Iles and Harpur folded down next to her, nearest to the door space. She smelled of what Harpur thought might be Red scent and, now, rotten wood and powdered masonry. Her face and head were level with Harpur's and he could feel one of her shoes against his ankle. He had not noticed when they were all upright, but she must be tall, possibly as tall as Iles. She was a slim brilliantly made girl of a teenage style the ACC prized. There would be a grail element to Honorée for Iles.

The ACC climbed on top of her. 'I don't think there's any need to take our clothes off for verisimilitude at this stage,' he said. Honorée kept her legs together. 'This roughly would be how they were when they heard the shots,' Iles remarked. 'Both were extremely puzzled, as you'd imagine, Col. There's already stress for her partner, coming to a dump like this with his status and Marks and Spencer clothes – and then what seemed to be firing, for God's sake. They look out towards the dock through the doorway there, maintaining this position. They were scared to move in case they caused a noise. Honorée's work locations are not secret, Col, and she feared the least sound could remind folk outside she might be here.'

Harpur turned his head on the floor to look towards the dock. He could see the stern of the *Dion*, a patch of water near the vessel and a stretch of the quay in front of the warehouse doorway.

'Your perspective, lying there uninvolved, Col, will be slightly different from that of Honorée, but more or less right, since you are at ground level. Whereas her friend was positioned, as I am myself now, on top of her, nothing experimental. It's possible that he from this slightly raised point could see a little more than Honorée herself. But, of course, they did not discuss what they observed, because silence was key. And when it was all over she and her friend left very quickly, no swapping of impressions.'

'When what was all over?' Harpur replied.

'They understandably wanted to be away from here immediately things seemed clear. Impossible to consider completing the interrupted act and then chatting over events in a relaxed state later. Luckily he had paid up front as it were so there was no reason to linger.'

Harpur knew Iles would enjoy speaking down at him from his elevated crouch on Honorée while Harpur was flat, one cheek and one ear in the timeless muck of the floor as he took in the outside view.

'Clearly, it might be necessary to attempt a trace of Honorée's friend, because his account of what occurred will possibly be fuller than hers,' the ACC said. 'Get a search under way, would you. This could be difficult,

Col. Honorée does not recall ever having done business with him before and was guessing when she said he might be a marriage guidance counsellor or headmaster – just that kind of mild, responsible jitteriness about him, you know, and the general caring professional level of frantic sexual craving. But, good Lord, is it for me to talk? Hardly. Was I here? Not then. You'll be interested in a first-hand version of what happened, I know. That's your training, Col – prime sources. And Honorée is prime, as ever.'

Harpur turned his head towards her now to listen and his other cheek and ear were to the ground. To talk to him, Honorée also turned again to Harpur and he was aware of her breath, warm and odourless on his face, her tone confiding. It seemed not altogether right to have an intimate conversation with Honorée while another man was mounted on her. 'I could see a body on the dockside – male,' she said. 'But perhaps it was two bodies, one almost on top of the other. I couldn't be sure. It was very dark. Another man stood near, walked out of sight, came back again, then went out of sight once more. Like pacing. Let's call it anxiety. That was my speculation at the time, and still is.'

'With a gun?' Harpur asked.

'Yes, with a pistol in his hand. He did not look at the body or bodies much but was staring out at the ships. He seemed sort of . . . boss-like? Commanding? Then I saw a small boat approaching the quay, one man rowing. This was what he was waiting for. It looked like a rubber boat, as might be used at the beach by children. I think three men in it. It seemed crowded. I mean, nearly awash – the load too heavy. Some gear in it, too. There was an occasional gleam of metal.'

'But she could only see it for a couple of minutes, Col, because from where she was lying under her friend she had just a limited stretch of docks water visible. As the boat neared the quayside it would naturally pass out of her sight – well, as you'll appreciate from where you're lying now. Honorée could move her head all right, but not her whole body for a better perspective, because of the weight of her friend and his actual situation, preventing any swing from the hips by Honorée to change angle. I don't know whether you'd want me to get on top of you, Col, to show you how limited your movement would be if as a woman you'd been getting fucked in the routine position and had to keep to it for security reasons.' Iles began to ease himself thoughtfully off Honorée and towards Harpur.

Harpur said: 'I believe I can imagine the burden and restriction, sir, thank you.'

The ACC settled back on to Honorée and said: 'At any rate, the boat was undoubtedly making for the quay. There are stone steps not far from where my car is.'

'Just the body or bodies – that's all I could see for a while,' Honorée said. 'After a time, I heard someone running, running away from where I was – the footsteps receding – and then the noise of a car – well, a vehicle. Another minute and it drew up closer but I couldn't see it. Sounded like quite a big engine.'

'We have to assume the three men had brought the boat to the quay and come up the steps, I think,' Iles said, 'and then one fetches the car, which must have been parked somewhere hidden. The other two probably carried the boat and equipment up.'

Honorée said: 'I think four altogether. One of them – a dumpy, scruffy man, I believe, maybe bald – this man was carrying mops and buckets and fishing rods – that's how it looked, don't ask me why, and a coil of rope around his shoulders. They began to move the bodies. I think they loaded them on to the vehicle. Its engine had been left running and very soon afterwards I heard doors slam and it drove away.'

Iles said: 'She and her friend remained like Honorée and I are now for, say, five or six minutes, Col, though, as I indicated, without sexual progress, only concerned about safety. Not sure everyone had left, they listened for further footsteps. Then they disengaged and stood. At once, the man ran off, up towards Valencia Esplanade, despite the fiasco making no claim for refund. Honorée found her own way back.'

Iles removed himself from Honorée and got to his feet. He helped her and Harpur to stand. They brushed one another down and Honorée gently removed some filth from Harpur's hair and ears with a small handkerchief. This was an all-round sympathetic girl. 'I expect you know who these deads on the dockside were, Col, do you?' Iles asked.

'Are we sure it's deads in the plural and that they were deads?' Harpur replied.

'I expect you know who this body or these bodies on the dockside were, Col, do you?' Iles asked with a plod rhythm.

'How, how *could* he know?' Honorée asked.

'Harpur tends to know,' Iles replied. 'Fishing tackle? A blind? Buckets and mops? They've been sprucing up some scene on one of the ships, do you think, Col? But why on a ship? Anyone suddenly missing? More than one?'

'That's a thought, sir,' Harpur replied. 'The men you saw, Honorée – age, clothes?'

'Thirties? Dark clothes. Or they seemed dark in . . . in the dark,' she replied.

'Great,' Harpur said.

'Who's missing, Col?' Iles asked.

'These are adults. Who knows who's missing?' Harpur replied.

'You?' Iles asked.

Honorée's voice grew squeaky for a second in bafflement: 'But he'd tell you, wouldn't he, Des? He's police, like you, isn't he?'

'He's Harpur,' Iles replied.

She dwelt on that, then said: 'There was a woman around two or three times a few days ago – that TV woman, you know? The *Light* show? – she was asking if anyone had seen a pusher called Slow Victor. All Passion Bent? And then a man asking about him, too. Both of them *really* asking, trawling the streets.'

'Slow?' Iles said. 'Has he dropped out of view, Col?'

'I'll have to check.'

'He has, has he?' Iles replied. 'What sort of man asking around?'

'Good suit, good shoes, decent accent,' Honorée said.

'Who can this be, Col? A lover?'

'He sounded truly anxious for Slow,' Honorée said, 'sad.'

'Did he make an offer to you?' Iles asked.

'He wasn't interested. Just in Slow.'

'Fool. A lover?' Iles asked.

'I'll have to check,' Harpur replied.

'Get hold of the TV woman, Angie Something, isn't it?' Iles said.

'That's an idea,' Harpur replied.

'If there were two bodies on the quay, we don't assume they were both killed at the same time,' Iles said.

'There were definitely two shots,' Honorée replied.

'All the same,' Iles said.

'Can we get out of here now, Des?' Honorée asked. She walked to Iles's Rover. It was the swift, energetic, elegant stroll of a tall, lithe girl. She climbed in and lay out on the back seat, covering herself with the ACC's Bonnie Prince Charlie grey overcoat in case the docks police were about. Perhaps in summer the coat was kept there only for this kind of duty.

Iles drew Harpur a little away from the car and spoke softly: 'Clearly, it would be best the Chief did not hear of these events, Col.'

'Oh?'

'He'd become very intense again, possibly restart the foolishly hazardous targeting mission, which I gather he'd decided to drop – I don't know why.'

'No?'

'Possibly even with Nivette – really fucking up things. Harpur, what we have to consider is that . . . Col, if Lane begins agitating again, with a focus on this place and incidents, it's going to look as if Honorée might have seen and talked to someone. As I said, many know she comes here. If suddenly there's information about they'd assume it came from her, and they'd fear she can identify.'

'Honorée *did* see and talk to someone, sir.'

'Yes, we're privileged. Keep it like that.'

'But, sir, we can't exclude the Chief. This is –'

'Yes, you're so right, Harpur,' Iles replied, 'keep it like that. Quiet. We don't want a murder gang hunting Honorée to silence her. This would be an appalling loss.'

'Des,' she called 'please, can we go?' A rear window of the Rover must be open and her voice came strong and agitated, though muffled by the overcoat's good wool.

Iles said: 'Have you thought, Col, that one of the bodies on the quay could even *be* Nivette? They've rumbled him already? Do we know as fact that he's in Disneyland?'

'I expect you'll be taking your daughter there yourself soon, sir, when she's a little older,' Harpur replied. 'It's your kind of place.'

'You *do* know who those deads are, don't you, you deep sod?'

'Des, I could be missing tricks,' Honorée yelled.

Chapter Eleven

Harpur went up to a conference with the Chief and Iles in Lane's suite. The Chief seemed to have struck a disturbing mood of resolve, even poise. Usually he drifted informally into Harpur's or Iles's office when he felt like a discussion. Today, though, he sat very square and open-chested at his desk, as if at last he knew he belonged there. Harpur wanted to believe he was right, but couldn't get even close to the notion. 'We proceed with targeting and put Richard Nivette to run it now he's back from Paris,' Lane said. 'It's a matter only of deciding *whom* we target – whom we crush – first, Ralph Ember or Shale. That's my basic reason for bringing you here this morning, Desmond, Colin. Plus, of course, I wished to announce that targeting in principle is definitely on, in case there were doubts still. The sequence 'is probably not important. As soon as one of them is destroyed we can apply all our energies to the other. We pick them off.' His voice sang like an arrow.

Iles said: 'Sir, Colin and I both –'

'You have valid objections in principle, Desmond, and I do take account of them – have given them thought, be assured. Plus, of course, your rather more marginal reservations.' He giggled. 'It was a wickedly comic idea that my interest in Richard Nivette's career, his advancement, might appear dubious in a way to some – in a sexual way, specifically. One of your famous, extravagant but quite disconcerting jokes. Yet no resentment, Desmond, none.'

Harpur was unnerved by the Chief's friendliness to the ACC. Something terrible would happen.

Iles said: 'Well, sir, I'm happy to hear that you and Mrs Lane can be so confident about –'

'Oh, at the serious level, your philosophy is to "leave well alone", Desmond – meaning as ever that the drugs business carved up between Ember and Shale is a comfortable, peaceful arrangement and should be tolerated for fear of something worse. And I admit that has its apparent attractions. Apparent. When things come to basics, I find I still simply cannot accept this. It is a betrayal of our role. Yes, Desmond, betrayal. We are not here to make pacts, spoken or unspoken, with evil.' He turned almost impish, the lame imp. 'And if my alternative plan means that some folk think I have suddenly fallen in love with Nivette and gone gay, let it be so.' He moved beyond a giggle now and guffawed for quite a while.

Harpur found it hellish – loud, empty, miserably uncertain, scared. Lane's laughter skidded off the panelling and polished furniture of the conference space like a kid's paper plane then nose-dived to the floor. The Chief must know Iles would retaliate. Harpur knew it, too. There was the ACC's tender, ratty subordinate's pride to protect, there was his best-of-a-bad-job belief in tolerated local villainy to protect, but probably above all and again and for ever, or at least a month or two, there was Honorée to protect from all the ripples and rippings that might follow an onslaught on Shale or Ember or the pair. Harpur watched the ACC, trying to read his supremely blank face. Rage should have been on show, perhaps contempt, possibly ruthlessness. Yes, all these, but especially the last. Iles smiled with bright affection at Lane and said cheerily: 'There's a bit of a snag, as you might see it, sir. Dick Nivette's on the fucking take.'

For a moment the Chief did not budge or speak. He looked like a head-and-shoulders photograph, dignified and lifeless. Then he pulled a foolscap pad of paper towards him and took a pencil from a tray. He seemed about to make a note, perhaps in case the idea that one of his senior officers was bought by villains might slip from his mind. But he did not write, simply stared past Iles, eyes suddenly void, his doughy skin going doughier than ever as Harpur looked.

Iles said: 'Or is playing at on the take. Probably that, though we're not wholly certain. He's receiving lumpy funds from Panicking or Shale or both jointly. As a result, sir, we can't let him target either. Sorry, but out of the question. If he did it properly they'd think he'd been stringing them along – which, of course, perhaps he has been – and he'd be dead in days. I don't know what you and Mrs Lane would feel about that, someone you've taken to your kindly hearts. And if he didn't do it properly . . . well, sir, the policy would be a disgusting and dangerous failure. And one thing we've all learned is that you're not a leader to countenance failure. In fact, targeting by *anyone* has become impossible. It could hopelessly disturb whatever Nivette might have already built inside one or both firms.'

Lane stuck his head and neck forward, a shift rich in assertion and dreadful frailty: 'This cannot be. Nivette? Desmond, you speak ill of a man's reputation for your own ends. It is a disgrace.' His voice sought volume but wavered.

'Ask Harpur,' Iles replied. 'He might give you a decent answer. He never gives me one.'

'Colin?' the Chief said.

Harpur yearned to spare him but said: 'Yes, he's taking, sir. Pretending to.'

'Without authority?' Lane asked. 'No organisation behind him?'

'Detectives do sometimes, sir,' Iles replied. 'Egomaniac, undisciplined detectives. Harpur did it. They believe themselves too big and talented for the system's safeguards. Oh, yes, very much Harpur. And probably Nivette.' Iles briefly falsetto crooned: '*They do it their way.*

116

Nelson: *I really do not see the signal.* Nivette's been given such gorgeous encouragement here he might have fallen into that sort of arrogance.'

'No, this cannot be,' Lane muttered again.

'The money's been seen,' Iles replied.

'Seen how?' the Chief asked.

'Seen,' Iles said. 'Seen and counted. Harpur's seen it, I've seen it.'

'Seen how?' the Chief asked. It was repeated, like an interrogation, but not like an interrogation: weary, doomed, vanquished. His desk looked too big for him now, a kid piloting Concorde.

'Oh, seen, sir,' Iles replied.

'Is this true, Colin?' Lane asked. 'Not that I don't believe Desmond, obviously, but –'

'How could I resent that fierce distrust of me, sir,' Iles asked, 'me being me? It comes with your job, like the salutes.'

'Yes, I've seen the money,' Harpur said.

'Handled it,' Iles said.

'How?' Lane asked.

'Harpur's magnificently thorough about these things,' the ACC replied.

'And how are we certain Nivette's only *pretending* to take?' Lane asked. 'Because the money is intact?'

'Exactly, sir,' Iles replied. 'Ah, you've met this kind of situation before, have you? Possibly even did something of the same yourself when you were a young, pushy, successfully corner-cutting detective?'

'You've penetrated his bank, Colin? Or, my God, his home?' the Chief asked. 'That would be unforgivable.'

'Yes, Harpur's *very* thorough,' Iles said. 'Not inspired or clever or incisive but thorough. It's in his dossier. At training school he was known as "No-Stone-Unturned-Col".'

'Where is the money now?' the Chief replied.

'Nivette has it, naturally,' Iles said. 'He's lost without.'

'You actually took it then replaced it, Colin?' Lane

asked. 'Brought it away and went back with it? But why
– as long as you'd seen it?'

'You'll want to know why you weren't kept informed,
sir,' Iles replied.

The Chief sat back in his chair and gave a small,
dismissive right-handed wave in front of his face. Then
he repeated it with his left hand. In these gestures
Harpur read vast and sickening humility. God, where
were the resolve and poise now? With the first wave
Lane seemed to say he did not expect to hear con-
fidences, because he knew he had failed to win his
inferiors. And, in case this was seen as a sudden, hyster-
ical response, he then confirmed it with the left hand.
'We hoped Nivette would justify his breach of rules
by producing evidence otherwise unobtainable, sir,'
Harpur said.

'Justify?' the Chief replied.

'Ah, you have in mind the end justifying the means,
sir,' Iles said. 'Shaky morality we'd all admit.'

'No morality at all,' Lane muttered.

'That is certainly the belief of the Catholic Church, sir,
your church. But I believe Harpur considered Nivette
was too far committed to his activities to interfere without causing –'

The Chief made the same gesture once more, this time
only with the right hand, though. He was beyond fine
points. Lane stood up. He wore uniform today, decently
fastened and the buttons clean. He had intended a
strong presentation at this meeting. 'Targeting cannot
proceed. That is plain,' he stated.

'We knew you would recognise this at once, sir,' Iles
said.

'For now,' Lane said.

'Oh, certainly, only for now, sir,' Iles replied. 'Very
likely reappraisal will be possible in due course. Nivette
might even make targeting unnecessary, if he is
genuinely only *mock*-taking, as it were, and if he can
deliver Ember or Shale or both by his own means.'

'It is essential he retain the bribe money,' Lane said. 'This alone shows he is still our man.' The Chief gave a snap and a ring to these last two words. He had to show some contact with command, despite everything. Harpur loved him for that sad effort in retreat.

Iles said; 'Both Harpur and I would plead with you, sir, not to condemn yourself for having especially favoured an officer who might prove a filthy dud – and, of course, when I say favoured I mean exclusively in a career sense, not that sexual sense you found droll. It is by no means proved as yet that Nivette is bent, in either sense, is it, Col?'

'We'll do all possible to ensure he remains safe, Mr Lane,' Harpur replied.

The Chief walked across the room and stood by a chain-of-command wall chart which showed him at the top as a thick-lined scarlet rectangle with the letters C.C. in purple at the centre. Harpur had seen him fall back to this situation for support two or three times before when things with Iles were exceptionally harsh. 'I still believe well of Chief Inspector Nivette,' the Chief declared. 'He thinks he is doing what is necessary, perhaps even regards it as inevitable when people like Shale and Ember are apparently allowed to operate as they wish.'

'Harpur and I admire the typical fine loyalty you show him, even though he may turn out comprehensively rotten and chargeable, sir.'

In the lift on the way down with Iles, Harpur said: 'If you had to tell him at all you could have told him more strongly that Nivette's almost certainly only play-acting.'

'I told him.'

'Stronger,' Harper said.

Iles moved his eyes up and around the lift to signify it might be bugged – a persecution fiction he liked to keep going. They went to the ACC's room. 'We're all right here. I've had a damn good look around, as you can imagine, Col,' he said. Iles sat down in an armchair and draped his legs over the side, a pose he adored for the way it displayed his fine shoes and the murderously slim cut of his trousers. 'How else would I have stopped him going for targeting?'

'One of these days he'll crumple finally.'

'Finnane,' the ACC replied.

'Sir?'

'You've got this name, Col?'

'What is it, sir?'

'Ah, you *have* got it. This comes to me roundabout – like so much of the best stuff often does, rather than from you. Finnane is the Minister's constituency agent here.'

'Ah, yes,' Harpur replied.

'Ah, yes,' Iles said. 'He's missing, though not yet reported so, for reasons of delicacy. This reaches me from a pal in the Metropolitan Force.'

'Useful pals, those,' Harpur replied. 'London's such a –'

'Such a vortex. I love your *mots justes*.'

'I'm glad, sir.'

'The tale is that this Finnane, although a staunch political figure and family man, lately developed new tastes – rather as the Chief says he hasn't – and took up with a gay pusher. Finnane has possibly eloped with him. That is the supposition. The name they have is Victor Goussard. Slow Victor. Honorée tells us the TV lady thinks he's missing, too. The Minister knew about the awakening relationship, pretended to Finnane that he didn't and hoped it would pass. But he consulted party headquarters in, as you say, the vortex.'

'And so your pal in the Met heard.'

'And so I heard,' Iles replied. 'They're afraid, naturally, that Finnane and Slow may turn up somewhere as a couple. It would not be fatal for the party nor for a Home Office Minister whose portfolio includes drugs policy, but it would not really be a plus.' He sighed. 'You know all this, naturally. Tell me, Col, did Honorée see these two dead on the dockside, Slow and Finnane?'

'It might be an idea if she moved away for a while, sir,' Harpur replied. 'London? A vortex, but she could conquer it with legs and grammar like hers.'

'But where does that leave me?' Iles said.

'Oh, as assistant to a great man, sir,' Harpur replied. He knew Iles hated that word, assistant – the creepy feel of subordination and servileness in the rush of s sounds. Sometimes it would shut him up.

Chapter Twelve

At night Ralph Ember drove down for a look at Invet dock, another look. He worried that Beau might have left something traceable there, or that any of them might have. He thought above all of Beau Derek, though, who had been in charge of equipment. Beau was a talent but a talent with safes and wire cutters and break-ins. Handling other kinds of jobs he could be casual.

Naturally, Ember had counted the buckets and mops back, and they were correct, no question. But were all the cleaning cloths returned? Ember was not sure how many there should be. Such carelessness in accounting he regarded now as idiotic, as sloppy as anything Beau could be guilty of. The cloths, like the buckets and mops, came from The Monty and might have been improvised originally from any old bits of material – say a discarded shirt of his or a slice from a replaced curtain. Since he first began to make good money Ralph had had all the formal dress shirts he wore for main functions at the club tailored to his personal measurements, and fragments would tell a tale via the maker. Some shirts even had name tabs. And curtains which had hung in The Monty might be remembered. After all, Harpur and Iles looked in quite often to terrorise and check up on members. Ralph's dread was that someone might have secretly observed the incident at the dock the other night and spoken about it afterwards. Tarts used wrecked buildings at Invet Basin with clients. If one of them started talking, the word would spread, and next thing is a police trawl and a lump of waste cloth on the quay picked up and sent for examination. They could do all sorts with modern forensic, some of it accurate. Several of the tougher bloodstains in the *Dion* cabin had been rubbed off with those cloths, Slow Victor's blood. Jesus, Ember was accessory to a murder, maybe to two murders. He would go to jail for ever.

For a while he wondered about taking Beau, to make the search more thorough. But he did not want Beau to observe him in a full Ember panic. He felt he was not far off collapse, and might slip further at the docks. Ralph had a leadership image to guard, especially since Beau saw that mad sod Shale so decisive with a gun and concrete pillars.

At a little after midnight Ralph told the barman he was going out for an hour and prepared to leave. His self-addressed envelope with the keys and bank papers in it had been delivered to him through the mail, of course, and was restamped and ready for another journey. He wondered about posting it again on his way to the Invet, but decided this was not needed. He would simply walk about there, eyes open. There should be no immediate peril, only the peril of recognition. Just the same, he put the .38 Bodyguard into his pocket. He resented having this kind of life imposed on him by colleagues, reimposed. For the present, Ralph saw he was just a street heavy again. Yet this last year or two he had liked to think of himself as one of what Scotland Yard called 'the 400', a select group of criminals grown so successful they did not bother with bread and butter villainy. They relaxed and watched the profits come in, like so much of the British ancestral peerage. But now he was back to dumping shot corpses and grubbing about on the dockside for bits of aftermath. His environmental and other civic concerns had been brutally shoved into nowhere by Shale and Alfie Ivis. Did he need them any longer?

Naturally, he would need to check first that no girl

was operating in one of the warehouse ruins this evening. Perhaps he had not been identified last time, but he might be now, scouring the quay. All sorts knew Ralph Ember through The Monty, and occasionally a head and shoulders picture accompanied one of his letters on environmental topics in the Press. People told him he was memorable – the Charlton Heston profile and his fascinating jaw scar. Although these features could obviously be advantageous with women, they also brought an awkward distinction now and then. Now. After all, they would not suspect the real Chuck Heston of crossing the Atlantic to cart bodies off the quay.

He parked where Alf Ivis had left the Land Rover, away from the dock, and walked. First, he went to the warehouse shells, to make sure he was not observed. He had brought a torch with him and worked through the ground floors of both buildings. There seemed to be no girls here tonight. Perhaps there had been none here the other night, either. He could hope. Near the wide doorway of one of the warehouses he saw a patch of ground which looked as if it might have been cleared of the worst debris, perhaps allowing a girl and her client to lie in basic comfort. Wanting to check what might be visible from that kind of position, Ember lay down on the floor, at first on his back, as a girl might, and then crouched on his knees, simulating a client. From both situations he found there was a limited vision of the dock and the dockside. Possibly in the darkness the distance would be too great to identify people or even describe them in detail.

He stood and brushed himself down, feeling comforted a little and not really threatened by disgusting panic, after all. A kind of shame, though, he did feel. Lying down in the muck like that had been totally necessary, but it simply was not the type of role he saw for Ralph W. Ember these days. Thoughts like this kept troubling him, and made Ralph wonder hard about his present business association with Shale. Manse had sucked him into the present situation. It was bad. These days Ember did seek dignity in life, and play-acting a docks tart in the middle of the night did not fit. As he saw it, a more suitable evening activity for him at this stage of his career was to host a big celebration in the club *wearing* a custom-made shirt, not looking for bits of one here – say at a Monty confirmation party for someone's child, or acquittal of a member in a big trial.

He went out on to the quay and had a thorough look around but saw no dropped hunks of cloth. Walking to the edge, he descended the steps to where the boat had pulled in. He searched the steps themselves and stared out across the dark water for darker patches where a rag might be floating. He found nothing. His anxieties had been foolish. Thank God he had told nobody. How unjust to accuse Beau of slackness.

He began to remount the steps and was almost at the top when suddenly he heard a couple of footsteps above him on the quay. He stopped. His hand moved towards the jaw scar to gauge its dryness, but he forced his fingers away from there and on to the Bodyguard pistol in his jacket pocket. Ember did not draw the gun yet. He crouched hard into the wall, making himself the least possible target and ready to retaliate.

A woman appeared, feet in court shoes and legs in trousers, then body. She stared out towards the vessels and only after a minute or so noticed Ember. She grunted in surprise. 'Hi. Something wrong?' She peered harder at him. 'It's Ralph Ember, isn't it? The Monty? Are you looking for the same people as I am – Slow Victor Goussard and Bernard Finnane?'

Ember did not speak, could not speak.

'We've met. I interviewed you once in your club, on traffic pollution. Angie Hyde, Coastal Waters Television. The *Light* show.'

'Of course,' he muttered and pulled his hand away from the gun. Legs weak but basically all right he resumed climbing the steps. Did he remember her? 'Is this research for another environmental programme?' he asked. 'So late? The neglect of valuable acres in redundant docks? Quite a topic. I've thought about it myself.' He joined her on the quayside.

'But not why you're here tonight,' she said. 'What's down the steps? And you were going to pull a gun?'

'I like to get out briefly from the club for some fresh air in the night and a look at the water,' he replied.

'Pretty, isn't it?' She flicked some muck off the shoulder and back of his coat. 'You're in a mess. You had the tip, too, did you, that Slow Victor and Finnane might be around here? But what's their connection with you?'

'I've certainly heard of Victor Goussard,' Ember said. 'He appears now and then at the club, though not a full member. He's here? Why?'

'They're both missing.'

'I don't know the other name,' Ember replied.

She brought a photograph from her shoulder bag and held it out to him. Ember could not see clearly in the darkness, though clearly enough. Finnane was smiling in the picture, not at all as Ralph remembered him, yet recognisable. 'He's a political agent in the Hewlett constituency,' she said. 'The Minister's. Suddenly he's dropped out of sight. Our Parliamentary man in London had a tip. All sorts grow agitated, though nothing said publicly yet. Finnane might be with Victor somewhere. There's a *tendresse*.' She put the picture away.

'But Victor's not in politics, is he?'

'These things cross professional bounds, Mr Ember – *amour* and drugs.'

'Well, I –'

'I've been looking for Victor for weeks. Someone said the docks. And then suddenly I hear of Finnane, too. But how did *you* find out about them? Are there angles to this I don't know?' She lowered her head dramatically as if for the axe. 'Oh, hark at me, the great omniscient! Arrogant. *Of course* there are angles to it I don't know. What I mean is – you have business involvements out-

side the club and so on, don't you? These two – they're
concerned somehow? Well, I know Victor pushes. Very
low level by your – But –'

'You've lost me,' Ember replied with a decent sigh.
'I can't help you with either of them, I'm afraid.' He
switched on some aggression, had to for this know-
ledgeable insolent cow. 'I don't understand when you
say I have business *involvements* outside the club. What
would they be? And when you tell me Victor pushes
drugs *but very low level by my* . . . by my what?'

'Standards.'

'I push? Is that what you're saying?' He was aware of
his voice crackling angrily across the water. It pleased
him.

'I admit it's a meagre word, given the scale you and
Manse operate at. You *supply*. Wholesale. Others push
for you – Slow Victor, for instance. It's hardly a secret, is
it? Some police blind-eye – anything for blood-free
streets.'

'You should be careful what you say,' Ember replied.
'Especially someone in television.'

'Oh, I'm not going to put it on the screen, am I? Not
without unbreakable proof, and how do I get that?'

You fucking don't.

She gazed out at the dock and the ships again. 'The
rumour is they've eloped, Slow and Finnane. Can't
believe it. That wouldn't be much of a story for me,
anyway. Gay couples are allowed to push off together,
even when one's a Home Office Minister's agent – nothing more than a tiny embarrassment to the party and
Finnane's family. But look, Ember, Slow Victor went a
while ago. Very dark tales began, none I could stand up,
though. I came to the docks because there were pointers
this way. Then I hear someone else has been asking
about him, really working at it. I didn't know who – just
male, middle-aged, middle-classish – a big field. Afterwards comes the whisper from my London colleague
that Finnane's missing. I find an election night victory

picture of him in our library and show it down here on spec. And people say right away this is the man who was asking about Slow. In other words, Slow disappeared ages before Finnane. OK, so Finnane might have located him and *then* they flit. I don't think I buy that.'

'Very shadowy.'

'Shall I tell you my reading of it?' she replied.

'I ought to be getting back to lock up the club.' He found it strange to be talking to a youngish woman with not a bad body in a waterside setting that had its flavour of bleak historic and industrial beauty, even romance, yet their words remained entirely sexless. Women generally responded to Ember. Some would remark on that resemblance to the younger Heston, even finger the jaw scar, as though it gave a shortcut to his essence and glamorous past. Always it confused Ralph when a woman seemed indifferent to his aura, and especially when it was plain that this one knew about his commercial power and wealth. What the fuck was the matter with her? Flicking a few chunks of warehouse muck off his jacket did not rate as a come-on. But then it was true a lot of media women fancied women.

She said: 'Isn't it possible something very rough had happened to Slow, then something very rough happened to Finnane as well, because he grew intrusive?'

Yes, it was very possible, Angie, dead possible. Ember said: '"Something very rough"?'

'Killed,' she replied. 'A dispute in the drugs trade, and then Finnane's swept into it.'

'My God,' he said.

'The police are no help. I brought Harpur down here to look, you know. He says nothing. We searched the ships.'

'Harpur? Really?'

'No luck.'

'Really?'

She laughed. 'And you're not much help either, Mr Ember.'

'How could I be?'

'I wouldn't disclose where information came from,' she replied.

'I haven't any. I'm not the mighty figure you imagine.'

'Really – as you'd say? Mighty enough. There'd be no question of your having to appear in any programme.'

'You're trying to get a programme going on all this?'

'What else?' she said. 'My job.'

'Isn't it dangerous?' he asked.

'I hear a threat?'

'Well, hardly. I meant, if this man Finnane was, as you say, "swept into it" –'

'Might I be?'

'I think of that terrible case of the woman reporter killed a while ago in Dublin,' Ember replied.

'I hear a threat?'

Hear what you fucking like. 'I do admire that kind of journalistic persistence, naturally, but –'

'Mr Ember, tell me, did I miss something on one of the ships?'

'Miss? I don't know what kind of thing you mean.'

'Some hint of Slow. Or even Slow himself.'

'Didn't you say Chief Superintendent Harpur came, too? I'd have thought that between the both you'd have spotted anything important.'

Abruptly, she turned away from him: 'OK, you're going to stay blank, are you?'

'Born so.'

Driving back to The Monty, Ember felt battered. He had almost broken down when talking to her, but somehow kept going and stayed careful about what he said. *Blank* as she termed it, intelligently blank. That eternal hazardous jerk, Shale, had killed someone important who was linked to people even more important. Christ, a Government Minister! This disappearance could not be ignored by the authorities or treated as minor. Eventually, when Finnane failed to show, there was certain to be an all-out search. Not just the police would be in on it but all the media. That damn woman had seen him there tonight. Everyone knew that reporters' promises of confidentiality were a ploy and breakable. In any case, she might only be offering confidentiality if he helped her with information. Had it been an error to try to block her? He could tell her such a lot – not everything – not what had originally happened to Slow – but plenty.

The club was still busy when he returned. Beau sat alone at the bar, drinking rum. Ember topped up his glass and poured himself an Armagnac. 'I need to know about Nivette, Beau,' he said.

'To check if he's doubling?' Beau asked.

'I expect he's back from Paris, which makes it tricky. Could you get into the house when they're all out one day – have a look around?'

'Of course. I'll see whether he's sitting on the funds for eventual return? Easy.'

It did not sound glib coming from Beau. This kind of routine practical work he was made for.

'What's your thinking, Ralph?'

'Just safety.' In fact, he hoped Beau would come back from the house and tell him Nivette *was* squirrelling the money and that therefore they knew he meant to betray Ralph and Shale and Beau and Alf, eventually. This was not something to say now to Beau, though. Ralph had to start separating himself from Shale and Ivis before the official Slow and Finnane search began and it became too late. He had heard a whisper that Mark Lane, the Chief, wanted a targeting campaign run, possibly against him, Ember, personally. But the trawl for Slow and Finnane would be so intense it would make targeting superfluous. There would be a hellish focus on Ember, anyway. He must try to nail that in advance. If

Nivette did turn out to be taking only as a means of getting undercover in the firms, Ember would feed him as much as he knew about Slow and Finnane, and above all convince him that Ralph had no responsibility for either death. Of course, it was conceivable Nivette knew more about what had happened to Slow than Ember did himself. That risk Ralph would swallow. He did not regard it as large.

Perhaps he might have spilled everything direct to Harpur and Iles, or even to the TV girl. Ralph believed he would be more in charge, though, if he worked through Nivette. That way a bargain would exist, with Ralph entitled to good informant's treatment. Nivette could disclose the information when suitable, as if he had found it for himself. If Ember approached Harpur and Iles it would look like outright grassing, and he could not contemplate that. Police despised some grasses, even while they took the information. An amoral sod like Iles might lap up whatever Ralph offered and still persecute, prosecute, him. And if Ember went to Angie Hyde . . . oh, God, nobody knew what the media would make of material once they were in the chase for what they called 'a story'. As soon as he spoke to her it would go from his control.

'No,' Beau said to Ember next night in the club. 'Nivette's all right. He's spending it. No cash wads in the house, no bank receipts for a deposit box. I always thought he was a good boy, though that's not to say you were wrong to check, Ralph. An under-the-floorboards hiding place, but empty.'

Oh, Jesus. 'You really went through it?' Ember asked.

Beau swallowed some rum and did not bother to answer this.

'Why would he want a hiding place?' Ember asked.

'Nothing there, that's the point,' Beau replied.

'There's a couple of hundred in this for you,' Ember said, retopping Beau's glass. At the head of a business you learned you had to pay for bad news as well as good. *Was* there any good, though?

Chapter Thirteen

Every six months or so, the two firms had a combined board meeting. There was one tonight. Always these sessions were accompanied by a decent dinner and they could be good occasions, really friendly and constructive. Mansel Shale valued them. He thought Ember did, too, though you could never be sure what that smug jerk Ralphy felt, he was so fucking high horse and deadpan. From Shale's outfit he and Alfie attended, and these days Ralphy brought Beau – Ember's previous partners, Foster and Gerry Reid, being probably deceased through office politics. Severely out of sight, anyway.

Beau was all right. He did not always seem too sharp, but neither did Alfred. You could not expect it from also-rans or they would not be also-rans. With that red cabbage face-skin and his garments, Beau also looked short of civilisation, which you definitely could not say about Alfie. In fact, Ivis sometimes showed too much of that, his poncy accent and the wordy wordage. And, of course, there might be something else going on in Alf behind all that polish and noise, something greedy and very personal. He would have to get some observation, the bastard, from now on.

Beau probably had a few useful aspects such as safe cracking, and you could not dictate to an associate about his fellow directors, not even to a flabby fucking associate like Panicking. In business there were all sorts, and you had to put up with it unless they gravely messed you about. Of course, Ralphy might try just that now.

Shale had to admit that Ralph dead would leave quite an emptiness for a short while.

Denzil drove Shale over to pick up Ivis at the lighthouse. Shale thought he noticed a bit of bulk at Denzil's chest, but did not mention it. Denzil liked to holster something biggish when he was chauffering Shale. It made Denzil feel significant. That was all right. One day or night the gun might even be useful, if Denzil knew how to use it.

They were early. Shale wanted a confidential discussion with Alf before they left for the conference and dinner at the usual medieval banqueting hall, imitation halberds on the wall and plastic longbows. Alfie's strange wife and very strange kids were about the lighthouse this evening as they were certainly entitled to be, and to get some privacy he and Shale climbed right up to the lamp room where the big beam once shone to guide and guard shipping from rocks. It gave Shale a warm throb to think of this kindly role, though obviously it was a come-down to have Alf and his sort living here now. Another lighthouse along the coast had taken over the duties, a more modern one, full of electronics, probably. There was plain glass in the circular windows of the lamp room now instead of lighthouse magnification type, and Shale and Alfie stood and gazed with respect for a while far, far out towards where they had finally let Slow Victor and Finnane go. This pause seemed only right.

It was early evening on a superbly clear and warm summer day. The sea looked unbelievably still and a brilliant turquoise. This fine tranquillity was bound to remind Shale of the happy drug-trading conditions won locally, and which could have been splintered by discovery of Slow's body and later Finnane's. The police would have been forced into gross activity, and surely few wanted such disturbance. However, disturbance might not be avoidable now, he knew this, Finnane

being a bit eminent so it seemed and with a family, gay
or not.

In the lamp room, gazing reverently towards the horizon, Shale could understand why some who loved the
ocean opted to be buried in it when they passed on,
getting incorporated in all that splendid changeable col-
our, depending on weather. He sincerely liked to think
Slow and Finnane would have picked this remarkable
world-wide element to finish up in if they had been
asked. Shale considered the evening sunlight still so
clear that if one or both of the bodies had been already
eased out from its lashings it or they would certainly be
visible on the surface now, admittedly introducing an
unhelpful note. But this would not occur. They had been
fixed to their pillars with fond care. That was one aspect
of Beau where you *could* see true civilised polish, the
way he clamped Slow's neck and so on, even though
Beau went jumpy later.

Shale said: 'I want the cleaning cloth kept very careful, Alf. That sod Beau Derek could be in here and take
it back, so easy. He probably never done a lighthouse
before and he'd love the experience. Ralphy's the fussy
sort who'd have an inventory of cloths and might miss
one and start deducing. Oh, you done brilliant to pick
that up, Alf.'

'It was just a thought, Manse, seeing the name tag.'

'But where you keeping it?'

'Secure, Manse, don't fret.'

'Just like the stupid big-headed sod to get shirts
monogrammed. R.W. fucking Ember. Great luck for us,
though. What's the W for, Alf? Worthy? Wobbly?
Wanker? Winsome?'

Alf had a giggle. Often he could recognise a joke as
long as it went on for a fortnight. 'Why I thought that
piece of it was so useful, Manse. Potentially.'

'Inspiration.'

'I dried it out and pressed it, of course.'

'This is a shirt relic as valuable as that Turin Shroud,' Shale replied.

'Two items of value I'm holding – the shirt, plus the seventeen thou from Nivette's store cupboard you entrusted to me. Also, of course, you've got Slow's teeth, which could be planted.'

As usual they had on dinner jackets and black ties for the occasion later this evening. A while ago Alfie had discovered a good spot for their meetings, on the other side of town. It was one of those mock old-tyme feasting halls where punters came to party at fifty quid a head before booze, pretending to be barons and their ladies, and served duck called swan by girls in wench costume, all leg and tit. Mondays the banqueting hall was usually closed, and Alfie had fixed a regular deal so it could be made available especially. They ran the joint boards and dinner there when due. Shale and Ember took turns to pay, just *noblesse oblige*. They said no waitresses in garb, only one girl wearing ordinary clothes, and no minstrels or any of that plucked lyre shit from the special little gallery. There were big comic mirrors on the walls that gave misshaped reflections, and these made Beau look human. Tonight, Shale wore an azure cummerbund. He loved touches of style now and then.

It was nearly time to go. Shale did one more slow half tour of the lamp room, giving the sea another thorough, affectionate survey, although the sun was almost down now and vision more difficult. He would admit there were times when he hated the sea, knowing it would sneak back over every fucking thing in a couple of million years or so, wiping out all Mankind had ever done – cities, art, the lottery, business set-ups, TV. Not even the aerials would show above the top of the bastard then, nor Alf's lamp room. But tonight that bolshy water looked decent, tame, and he could view it without rage. After all, the sea had done him a good turn. In a way, that was its chief job – covering things. He said:

'It's a deep fucking pest this Finnane turns out to be political, Alfred, if the rumours are right.'

'I think they are, Manse. I did a check or two.'

'Who'd expect some dignitary like that to be around the Invet in the night searching, and shouting rage and hate at me like I'd corpsed his dear lover. I believe I'm entitled to be shocked, Alf.'

'Certainly it was an unfortunate coincidence, Manse.'

'This is really going to upset Ralphy, if he's heard of the political aspect.'

'He hears everything – through the club.'

'So he'll expect a super-trawl for Finnane. And he's right, Alf. This is a different kettle from Slow Victor. Finnane will be in a hierarchy, as it's called. People will wonder about him. What's known as ramifications.'

'I'd say so.'

'Ralph will want to put himself OK even more now – in advance. He could leak a word about us and the bodies to – well, maybe to Harpur or Iles direct, or to Nivette, if he thinks Nivette is not a true taker but undercovering. Which the sod is. Of course, Ralphy might of sent Beau into Nivette's place to check, and if he has he'll think Nivette is *not* undercover because there's no money pile there.'

'It's certainly a complex one, Manse. I'm wondering how you'll play it at the meeting tonight.' Ivis had a cummerbund on too, but royal blue, flashier. If you were a fucking nobody you had to be flashy because no fucker would notice a fucking nobody otherwise.

'I got to feel my way, Alf. It's why the shirt morsel is so vital. If Ralphy starts anything unpleasant against us, describing Invet Basin matters and making out he heard of it but was not there – oh, *naturally* not there, not Ralph W. Ember, Mr Intense of the Green Party – if he tries that, this elegant rag is going to turn up again somewhere at the Invet and the police get a useful anon tip about location. Plus maybe Slow's teeth in Ralphy's car. Ember could find out he's not the only one who can grass. And so his credibility's deader than Slow Victor.'

'Justifiable, if I may say, Manse.'

They began to descend the steep stairs from the lamp room. Shale went first and spoke back over his shoulder, his voice echoing a bit against the curved, blank, white stone wall. 'But, clearly, Manse Shale don't want to disturb a beautiful smooth-flow business arrangement with Ralphy, cherished by Desmond Iles, unless it absolutely got to be. What I meant just now – feel my way. One of the last things Mansel Shale would ever seek, Alfred, is for Ember to be stuck in jail, even if that left us his bag of dealers et cetera and gave monopoly. Although this idea looks ducky, Iles wouldn't put up with it. I'd be too mighty, too solo. It would scare him. You ever heard of balance of power in international affairs? This is what's known as a policy, Germany-Russia in the thirties. Famous. It's what Iles believes in – everybody making sure things stay governable because no one bugger's too big. And for just the same reason, I'd really hate it if we ever had to kill Ralphy. And Beau. It got to be on the cards, yes, obviously, but *only* on the cards so far, nothing certain.'

'This is contingency thinking, Manse,' Ivis replied.

Shale stopped near the bottom of the stairs and turned to face Ivis. 'These are subtle matters, as I say, policy matters, Alfred. When I tell you I don't want to kill Ralphy and Beau I got to also think *they* might want to kill *us*. If Ember thinks I'm dragging him into dark areas where he don't want to go . . . well, we better think what probably happened to Harry Foster and Gerry Reid, Alf. Who says Slow and Finnane are the first bodies he was in on disposing of, even though he plays holy now? Ralphy can look like a prick and sound like one, but there's true savage refinement to him as well.'

'I don't know anybody I would trust to handle strategy decisions more deftly than you, Mansel,' Ivis replied.

'Then Nivette,' Shale replied. 'He could be something different. Maybe he got to be done soonest. Even immediate.'

'If I may say, Manse, I do appreciate your argument, but the death of Nivette might also antagonise Iles and lead to nuisance activity. Plus the Chief. Nivette's his protégé.'

'Christ, they at it, too? We'll get another mad grieving lover?'

'Not necessarily sexual, Manse. Career-wise.'

'All the same, I'll have to think about Nivette.'

The Jaguar was waiting in the yard. It had been unnecessary to meet any of Ivis's family, and Shale felt tip-top gratitude. There was something magic about a car with genuine wood trim after not having to see Alfie's children. He went into the back with Ivis.

The car moved off and Denzil half turned and said: 'So, all that bribe loot – still maybe stacked somewhere in Dick Nivette's house?'

'Watch the road, will you?' Alfred said. 'This is not your kind of topic. And kindly don't discuss it with Ralph Ember's driver later, either.'

Chapter Fourteen

'But how, Colin? How?' the Chief muttered. Harpur could have told him how – one biggish bullet in the chest from very close, close enough to scorch. He knew that was not really what Lane wanted to ask, though. The Chief meant 'Why?' and Harpur had no answer, or a lot of answers. They would not reduce Lane's suffering. Harpur longed to do that. He hated to see the Chief veering towards breakdown again, as he would have hated to see anyone veering towards breakdown. This concern was different from Iles's occasional moments of generosity to Lane. As Harpur had diagnosed before, those moments came because by instinct the ACC needed a command structure, with someone settled at the top, even someone like the Chief, and even someone Iles spent so much effort trying to smash, almost smash. Harpur just wanted Lane happy.

The Chief would turn up personally to the sites of some crimes. These were always offences he regarded as not just isolated bits of law breaking but symbols of general returning chaos. And, of course, this was such a death. At Lane's rank you looked for overtones, themes, patterns, most of them sombre. He had arrived here tonight only a little after Harpur. In these cases it was as if the Chief thought he must use his actual body to stop the spread of threat further, like a frontier castle.

'Is this connected with what you and Desmond told me about him?' Lane asked, and then did not give Harpur time to answer. He had to show he could face the worst: 'Certainly it is, certainly. There is a network of evil. We culpably permit it to thrive.' Iles used to say Lane read and reread the prophecies in Revelation, searching for coded references to a Chief Constable so feeble that God let rip with the Day of Judgement. 'This network will ultimately make all of us its victims.' Lane must have left home at a rush as soon as the call came around 11.15 and had put on the jacket of a grey suit with a pair of old navy chinos. He wore very faded blue and white trainers. Often there was a refugee look to him. It was hard to deny Lane pity, though Iles could manage it for most of the time.

Harpur said: 'His wife and child are with the people next door, sir. Perhaps you'd have a word with her in a little while.'

The street door was open to allow the rest of the Scenes of Crime people in, and Harpur thought he saw Iles's Rover arrive and park, then the flash of fine black footwear as the ACC deboarded. The Chief continued to stare down at the body for a couple of seconds. Without speaking, Iles joined them in front of the fireplace. Lane said: 'And what do I tell this lady, Colin, Desmond that her husband was a great, brave officer? Or that her husband was bought?'

Harpur said: 'Well, sir –'

'Oh, but what does any of that matter to a grieving wife?' the Chief said. 'Treachery is but a term of our profession. Her husband is dead. For her, that is all.'

The ACC crouched to look at Nivette on the carpet. Like Harpur and Lane, Iles wore hygiene gloves and plastic covers over his shoes. He touched the side of Nivette's face with his sheathed palm, and then muttered something short and full of consonants, maybe a curse, maybe an expression of shame. He pulled off the glove and touched him again, now skin to skin. His hand lingered. It was nothing to do with guessing at death time from temperature. This was Iles communing. He wanted true flesh contact. There had been other moments when Harpur watched him offer similar acts of affection to someone savagely killed. Harpur thought it would be cruel and not totally true to say Iles always found things easier with the dead, but he was unequalled at mourning and theatre. 'I'll speak to the wife for you, if you wish, sir, although I'm sure she would suspect nothing between you and him but the requirements of our work,' he told Lane, looking up. The ACC was in a navy blazer and another of his club ties, mostly silver, plus some purple and orange. It would be a club full of big voices and money with a ten-year waiting list at the right end of London, not The Monty.

The Chief said: 'Well, Desmond, I –'

'As a matter of fact, I myself have spoken of getting Nivette killed, sir,' Iles replied. 'I suppose that was exaggeration. Yes, I suppose so. But, although you're probably right when you say treachery is merely a professional matter, I *am* a professional, a professional police officer, and I always have this urge to eliminate police treachery, in Nivette or anyone else. Yes. I don't know how you feel about that. No. But then Col in his generous style came to me and built something of a case for Nivette. And I'd heard you were fond of the boy. One held back. These testimonials impressed me. I reasoned that you couldn't *both* be in love with him. Now some other bastard jumps in at his own home and large-calibres him. My latest information on Nivette is Col's assurance that he was still our man and only *acting* bought. And because this information comes from Harpur I'd say it has a 60–40 chance of truth or only marginally less. Plus, sir, there is your own instinctive affection for Nivette, and your instincts are not instincts to be won over lightly. They bear on my judgement. I believe Nivette might after all have been honourable, and one must speak of him as such. At this stage.' He touched Nivette's cheek again.

Pay Days

'Perhaps it is my duty, Desmond,' Lane replied. 'Mrs Nivette will expect this.'

'Haven't you enough stress, sir?' Iles cried. 'Harpur and I fear you might overload.'

'I take it they found he was doubling and have executed him?' the Chief asked. 'They would be unforgiving, as unforgiving as you, Desmond. In their perverted way they would regard *that* as treachery. They want honest corruption!' His voice clanged with sarcasm at the monstrousness of this, at the upending of true order. 'His was a tragic but noble death, tragic in that he should, of course, have sought our official sanction and back-up for what he was doing, which might have saved him, yet noble in that he had the courage to act alone.'

'Oh, no, not an execution,' Iles said. 'A panic shot more likely. An intruder? I should think we'll find forced entry somewhere. Execution is generally the head, two bullets for certainty. Usually they're bound. Ask Elmore Leonard or the IRA.'

'Colin?' the Chief said.

'I thought he might have confronted someone,' Harpur replied. 'Mrs Nivette is not very coherent but she thinks her husband must have heard a noise and come down to investigate. They'd gone to bed quite early and she was awoken by the shot, but by the time she got downstairs whoever it was had disappeared.'

'Perhaps just as well,' Iles said.

Harpur said: 'In any case, this is the night for the firms' joint board meeting at the Agincourt Hotel. It's still going on. We get a tip from the management and keep a gentle eye. Shale, Ember, Ivis and Beau Derek are all there now. None of them could have come here and executed him, sir.'

Lane looked sickened. 'What, we know of their meeting and do nothing but keep a . . . what do you call it, Colin – "a gentle eye"?' he asked.

'We check them in and out, sir, for the Collator,'

143

Harpur replied. 'We'd get spotted if we did more, the meetings there would cease and our management contact might get trouble.'

'We connive, we connive,' Lane said.

Yes, there could be something in that, Harpur thought. Shale and Ralph Ember were given the gentle touch in exchange for peace on the streets, Iles's cherished policy. He called it *realpolitik*, though not to the Chief – meaning it was the best that could be got in any big British city now, as it had been in any US big city for a decade.

'The meetings are only formal, anyway, sir,' the ACC replied. 'Not worth bugging. Shale and Ember are hardly going to disclose real figures to sidekicks like Beau and Alfie Ivis. Panicking and Manse have their own private sessions. *Those* would be the ones to eavesdrop.' The ACC's plastic overshoes rustled as he crossed the room to examine the windows for signs of entry.

Harpur said: 'Francis Garland tells me the kitchen door was forced. Someone crude. Someone in a hurry. Someone on edge.'

Lane seemed confused. 'Someone who'd heard of the stored bribe money you told me about and came to thieve?' he asked. 'It's here?' He glanced about Nivette's living room.

'Upstairs,' Harpur replied.

'It will be gone,' Iles said.

Harpur went to the boxroom and bathroom and lifted the boards. 'It's not there?' the Chief asked, when Harpur returned. 'My God, so we've got no evidence that he was playing them along.'

'You have Col's word for it, sir, and to some degree my own. We've seen the money.'

'Yes, of course, of course,' Lane replied.

'And above all your own instant, steady, blood-felt belief in his worth, sir,' Iles said.

Lane said: 'Oh, but the actual retained cash – to show

the Home Office, the Inspectorate, the Press, sceptics of that sort.'

'You have Col's word for it, sir, and to some degree my own. We've seen the money.'

'Yes, of course, of course. One does crave certainties.'

'Not our kind of game, sir,' Iles replied. 'Truth's a variable. One day it's what the jury believes, then tomorrow the Appeal Court decides the opposite. Nivette was a grey area, as are we all.'

'No, there *are* absolutes,' Lane cried. 'We guard them, or what are we for?' He put his head back as though about to bay in agonised despair at the ceiling.

'I'm always asking Col that, but, of course, sir, you get no intelligent answer out of *him*. Probably no answer at all.'

'They are in filthy session at the Agincourt at this moment, you say?' Lane asked. He brought his gaze down and stared at Harpur. 'I want to go there, go now before they have heard of this. Or before they have heard of it from us.'

Iles said: 'Sir, this is not the –'

'I want them pressured. I want their smugness shattered,' the Chief replied. Occasionally the Chief would do this – somehow fling himself into these fits of resolve. They were wild spasms full of pride and anguish as he struggled for brief fading spells to live up to his title. Harpur found it inspiring to watch, ghastly to watch.

Iles said: 'Sir, we have no cause to enter a private meeting and –'

'Did Colin have a right to enter this house to look for the money?' Lane replied. 'We show we are aware of them, that's all.'

'I think they know this, sir,' Iles replied.

Lane's lips went back hard in that doughy face and he began to snarl: 'Oh, they know we are aware of them and their foul empire, but have come to believe we accept it. This will make them doubt that. If we lean heavily enough one of them might break. You say we cannot target. We try something else, then. Ember – Ember might break. Doesn't he crave respectability? Isn't he torn by panics? We needn't disclose any of this, yet. Just observe them.'

Iles said: 'Well, they might know, sir. Gunfire in this kind of nice street would be noticed. Some neighbour may have rung the media.'

'I want to go there. I want us all to go there. Perhaps I should have broken in upon more such scenes. If so, they might not now be taking place.'

Chapter Fifteen

Looking at the other three, so relaxed, so bloody *amiable* and conversational, you would think things were beautifully normal or better and it terrified Ember. *Oh, Christ, why had he come? Thank God he had the Bodyguard .38.*

Well, mad happiness was what you could often expect from Beau. Give him enough pre-dinner rum and he saw the world and the future as sure to be for ever nice to him personally, and to all he would accept as friends. And, at these joint board meetings in this absurd 'medieval' banqueting hall, there was always enough pre-dinner rum, and anything else he wanted. But Shale and Alfie did not drink like that, and yet they seemed damn blissful, too. Ember could detect no feel of crisis or peril, except what he brought himself. This was plenty but not enough for four.

The meeting and dinner went on late, after midnight, as though those three could not bear to break up such a cheery gathering. Ember tried to put on the same appearance of contentment. He knew Shale would watch for evidence of stress – anything that hinted Ember was near panic and might be thinking of safety and desertion and betrayal. Ember *was* thinking of safety and desertion and betrayal, but hid it, hoped he hid it and hoped he hid the Bodyguard, as well. There was joy at this party, or so it seemed, and, as ever, there was peril. To come with a gun meant you distrusted your associates and was not something to proclaim. That could invite a shoot first response from Shale and

147

Ivis, and especially Ivis, who was famed on the trigger, and not just finishing jobs, as with Finnane. Naturally, they would be tooled up. These two went everywhere prepared, and especially Ivis – part of his job. They might not wait to reciprocate, especially not Ivis. *Especially Ivis, especially Ivis, especially not Ivis.* God, he *was* a problem. Possibly they were here to finish Ralph and therefore Beau, before Ember could do any talking . . . And this was why Ember had brought the Bodyguard. And the Bodyguard might produce retaliation. It was a grim hazardous circle, and quite standard.

At the very opening Shale had told them in his back-street bloody grammar that business during the year had been 'extraordinary bright, never mind them odd and unavoidable blips'. Of course, Ember knew this already and knew it in much more depth and detail than Beau and Alfie could be informed of here tonight. It would be mad to let them discover that Ralph and Manse Shale took something between six and seven hundred thousand a year *every* year out of trading. They would have trouble getting their other-rank heads around such figures, and they were never going to get their hands around them, nor anything like. Too much knowledge would hurt Beau and Alf, make them envious and unreliable. Although there was *this* board meeting and *these* formal accounts, there were the other, private meetings, too, between Manse and him, when the real work was done, and the true allocation of major dividends. He and Shale did not need a minstrel gallery and halberds on the wall for that one, just faith in each other, a more difficult item. Tonight, it was only necessary to assure Beau and Alfie in outline and with a few selected details that the firms continued to move ahead and could finance these fine get-togethers – *and* provide around forty grand, sometimes even fifty, for Beau and Ivis each in pay and bonuses. The labourer was worthy of his hire as the Bible said, and his hire was forty or fifty. Where else could Beau make that much, or even Alfie?

In the meeting and during dinner the four of them discussed how to increase the number and quality of street pushers, and Shale mentioned his determination as a wholesaler to win better discounts from importers for constantly expanding bulk purchases. Ember would admit Manse had a real way with business strategy and bullshit. Probably Alf and Beau knew they were only getting baby talk. So? They ate the dinner, drank the wine and occasionally said something bland – or tactless, if it was Beau. They had to be given their little go. They were directors of the firms in their way-down underdog style.

Although Shale did mention Slow Victor, this was only to call for a brief, heads-bowed silence at his death, and then to wonder about an immediate replacement on Slow's pushing beat. Ivis suggested Luke Malthouse could handle it as well as his own. Apparently Luke had been pressing for ways to make more. Luke was a lout and always scheming for something. Oh, admittedly he was thuggish, Alf said, but most of Slow's customers had been pretty rough, so Luke suited. Watching Shale, Ralph Ember saw a bit of a frown or a wince in his face when Alf mentioned Malthouse. It hung there for twenty seconds, maybe longer. Christ, did Mansel see a dirty alliance, a conspiracy between those two, Alf and Luke? Ember had never thought much of Ivis, except as a baggage man for Shale. Had Alfie at last caught the whiff of big money, though, and decided to get some? Hard, hard to believe: as Alf spoke now, his heavy face and loud blue cummerbund put Ember in mind of the winner's rosette on a silverside haunch in a meat competition. There was no mention of Finnane, either from Ivis or Shale. He'd be one of them odd unavoidable blips, probably. Tell that to his Minister MP and Finnane's family.

Beau started to raise a question, perhaps about

Finnane, but his words were slow and blurred and Shale talked over him. 'Our one problem of the year remains Nivette, of course,' he said. 'The un-fucking-certainty with him. This is risk we got to accept, though, because he could be so great for us at that rank, and maybe going higher, being what's known as a whiz kid. Well, definitely going higher, prized by the Chief, as long as the Chief don't know what's what, which could be for ever. My own feeling now is Nivette's all right and truly ours, no doubler. I think Alfred agrees.'

'Absolutely, Manse.'

'This is a wonderful strength for the firms,' Shale said. 'He haven't fed us much lately, true, because he got to be careful with the Chief watching his career, but he will grow and grow under our influence. Well, he better.'

Did Manse believe this, or the opposite? Obviously, Ember never took anything Shale said as entirely straight. After all, he and Ralph were business colleagues, not friends, and colleagues could be much more evil and dangerous than friends even. Perhaps Shale wanted to stop Ember talking to Nivette. Mansel would be sharp enough to see Ralph might be considering this. Thank God, Beau probably knew even when drunk that he should not speak about Nivette and certainly not about breaking in and finding no stacked funds, meaning Nivette was truly crooked, as Shale believed – said he believed. Beau glanced towards Ember and Ember remained blank, willing that rambling loud-mouth to stay quiet. It might work, but the night and the booze were going to run a bit yet.

When the formal meeting was over, and they had sat down to duck à l'orange, pommes de terre and petits pois accompanied by champagne, Shale had more to say about Nivette: 'This means we got two kinds of police commitment to us. There's Nivette and, of course, that superb, long-time unspoken understanding with his seniors, in the rosy interests of safe streets for the populace, which again this year we been able to deliver for them exemplary.'

Ember stood. He wanted a look around the outside of the building, and maybe the inside, too. Almost always at these meetings he felt trap dangers, but tonight they seemed more powerful than ever. The complacency unnerved him. He smelled set-up. 'I've left the *Eton* accounts in the boot of the Saab,' he said.

'I don't think you should interrupt your din-dins just for that, Ralph,' Shale said. 'We done the accounts now, quite satisfactory in the meeting. The *Eton*'s only an aspect.'

Ember laughed a little. 'But a very heartening aspect, Manse.'

Of course, Shale would know Ember did not need to go out there, at least not for accounts. He would see Ralph wanted a security tour. Well, OK, he saw it. Let him. This was not panic, not even jumpiness, just vigilance. If Shale really tried to stop Ember it would be plain there was something wrong. But Shale only waved a hand, conceding.

On his way out, Ember did a hearty bit of mock oratory followed by a steady chuckle: 'The *Eton*'s one of our best achievements, Manse. I demand the immediate right to trumpet our success there.' The *Eton Boating Song* floating restaurant had become difficult as an outlet for a while after some trouble and deaths there one bad night, and this had meant a very prosperous, high-living clientele was lost to the trade. Now, though, Ralph's and Shale's firms were working their way into the *Eton* under its new ownership.

Ember went to the hotel car park. It was nearly half-past twelve. He had the *Eton* figures in his pocket, of course, but would make a show of going to the car in case he was under watch. The yard looked safe enough. He saw none of Shale's people hanging about, not even Denzil and the Jaguar. The two drivers had orders to disappear with the vehicles until near leaving time. It could be noticeable to have them parked together in an otherwise empty car park, though Ember thought Harpur probably knew about these meetings, anyhow. Ralph was using a small-time pusher, Bright Eddy, as chauffeur tonight and had told him to return at midnight. He was there now. Ember walked over. 'Seen anything worrying?' he asked through the driver's window.

'Quiet.'

'So where's Denzil?'

'Manse must have said he could come back later. Is it going to go on in there?'

Ember went to the rear of the car, opened up and took the *Eton* papers from his breast pocket so he would have them in his hand when he closed the boot. While the lid partly hid him he checked his shoulder holster was unbuttoned and the pistol easy to grip. At home earlier this evening he had wondered for a long while whether he should bring it, and then during a brief saunter in his grounds stopped wondering and only wondered how he could have wondered.

Consoled a little by the feel of the gun, Ralph closed the Saab boot and began to walk back towards the Agincourt, still holding the *Eton* returns in his left hand. Just as he neared the door he heard a car enter the yard and the driver flashed its headlights at Ember. Turning, he saw it was Denzil, alone in the Jaguar. There was no plot, then, no gang of Shale extras being shipped in, no trap, not tonight. Denzil stopped near. He looked as insolent as ever, but strained, too, even alarmed. He came out of the car and stood alongside it. 'You nearly through?' he asked.

'What's wrong?' Ember replied. 'What's happened?'

'Happened? What should have happened?' Denzil said. 'You been patting one another on the back in there, Ralphy? Any doggy bag grub for a minion? Have you got a spare bottle of bubbly about your person?'

'The name's Ralph,' he said, 'or Ember.' Now and

then, when he wanted to be offensive, Shale would call him Ralphy, of course, trying to reduce Ember, make him sound like a kid. This jerk chauffeur thought he could get away with it, too. God, but Ember hated contact with Shale and all his outfit. As Ralph re-entered the hotel he had an urge to turn around, get into his car and tell Eddy to drive home to Low Pastures. Beau could find his own way back.

From the start Ember had not wanted to be here, and from *before* the start – from the moment at home when he had just got into his gear, ready to come. In his dressing room he had put on his evening suit early for tonight's session, but then, when he went downstairs, took off his Edgar and Point black lace-up shoes and replaced them with a pair of rubber boots, folding the legs of his trousers in carefully. He had needed a stroll before he set out, if he did set out. Why should he? He knew the answer to that, but still asked. Although it was a fine evening, there had been rain over the past couple of days and the paddock in his grounds was muddy. Ember had had a chunk to think about before leaving to pick up Beau, if he did leave to pick up Beau, and a walk around the property could often settle his mind and bring clarity. Never had he suffered a panic, not even a mild one, in his own house or spread. Low Pastures and its acres plumped up his soul, and with these lovely possessions around him he had decided that if he did go his enlarged soul needed a gun to protect it tonight.

Back in the Agincourt banqueting hall he read out some of the *Eton* figures. To begin with, there was the triumph of getting into the restaurant at all, and then a real sales climb during the last four months. Old patrons of the *Eton* had confidence back and were reappearing for their gourmet grub and snort provisions. These were TV executives, solicitors, charity organisers, hair stylists, high-level civil servants, snooker professionals, professors – worthwhile folk of the AB social class, with real cash as well as habits, and they spent beautifully on top-class material. Some of these people had actually been to the *real* Eton and loved the idea of getting their trip supplies at the *Eton Boating Song*. Ember read out a score of names of steady customers, and there was applause from the three when he mentioned one or two with their decorations and medals – a Companion of Honour, two Commanders of the British Empire and several Members, plus two ex-Guards officers with the Military Cross. Ember remained sitting while he spoke. He had the feeling that if he stood the bulge of the holstered Bodyguard under his jacket would be clear.

He had known the .38 might be tricky. Although a small gun, it would certainly have been spottable in the pocket of a close-fitting, custom-made double-breasted dinner jacket. Just the same, Ralph had decided it would be insane to come without it, especially as Beau refused to carry anything. There was a duty to look after the oaf. And so when Ember called into The Monty en route to Beau's he had strapped on the shoulder holster this time. He would have preferred not to turn up at the Agincourt at all. Once or twice before when there was big stress between Ralph and Shale, Ember had wanted to dodge out of this farcical event altogether. It was made for ambush. But it also demanded attendance. Failure to turn up would signal fear and even defeat, and Ember had been able to get there and get home again, so far. At Low Pastures before he left for the meeting, Margaret had possibly sensed the tension in Ralph and put on wellingtons as well to accompany him on his walk. Actually, he would have preferred to be alone then in the paddock with his plans and anxieties, but did not say so. That would have been hurtful. As they walked, their younger daughter, Fay, had been exercising a new bay pony called Sparky on a leading rein, and he and Margaret watched with pride. Four horses were stabled at Low Pastures now. Margaret liked to ride and so did their older girl, Venetia, when she came home at vacations from school in France.

Looking at Fay while Margaret held his arm, Ember had wondered how long it would be before most of his life could be passed like this, happy among his family in a distinguished, calm and gentlemanly setting, with only occasional absences to oversee The Monty and his other interests, and to satisfy one or two fine women friends where he admittedly had obligations. Instead of that dignified prospect, though, tonight he had been torn by a horde of doubts in the paddock. How dangerous was this meeting? How long would the two bodies stay under? Should he protect himself in advance by leaking that tale? Who to? Might Nivette be doubling, after all, and so turn out to be safe? How much did the television woman know and how much could the bright bitch guess after finding him at the Invet? Jesus, some catastrophe, that. What happened when all the world started looking for Finnane?

'Daddy,' Fay had called, 'why the gear? Have you won an award for protecting the environment?'

'That kind of thing,' he replied. 'I'm off to work now.'

'Work?' she replied. 'A brill banquet I heard.'

'That as well.'

And at the brill banquet, his report on the *Eton* turned out to be a star episode. Beau gave him a bucketful of 'Bravos', but Ember would have expected that, Beau being such a bonny crawler. Even Shale and Alfred were smiling, though, and clapped and rapped the table in congratulation now and then. Ember began to feel really at ease for the first time tonight. Despite everything – despite those sea-bottom unavoidable blips, Slow and Finnane, plus the lousy television woman – despite all that, perhaps things could go on as Shale seemed to expect, at least as well as they were doing already and possibly better, perhaps up to three-quarters of a big one next year, and even . . .

Shale called out, waving a champagne flute, 'We're there, Ralph. We're built into the fucking fabric. We'll last and last, like the Westminster Abbey.' He looked really solemn, as if conscious of the responsibilities their stout achievements brought.

'Hear, hear,' Alfred said.

'Bravo,' Beau yelled.

'I think so,' Ember said.

The door beneath the minstrel gallery was pushed hard open and Denzil came at a stumbling run into the banqueting hall, his prole features frantic. Ember still had the *Eton* accounts in his right hand, but dropped them on to the table and fondled his jaw scar for a second before reaching under his jacket for the Bodyguard. Urgently, he looked behind him, in case more of Shale's people were coming in from the other door. Always a crazy mistake to think Shale was content when he looked content and talked praise. Beau just sat there, like the drunken corporal he was, his soup-kitchen face still alight with a grin at the triumphant *Eton* tale. Ember saw nobody at the other door. Shale had stayed seated, both hands on the table in front of him. He stared at Denzil. What had the sods done to Bright Eddy?

'The police,' Denzil said.

'What police?' Shale said.

'Well, this looks comradely,' Iles boomed. 'You lads know the Chief, Mr Mark Lane, do you? And then there's Harpur. Mr Lane was convinced we'd be welcome here. I was unsure, but as ever the Chief has things right and I can see warmth and good fellowship extended to us from every eye.' He came grinning into the hall, glancing about with hate and familiarity, the way he did whenever he and Harpur visited The Monty, threatening, staring. The Chief Constable was behind him, then Harpur. Quickly, Ember picked up the *Eton* papers and put them back in his pocket.

'What do they want, Manse?' Denzil said. 'What do the fuckers want?' His voice had gone thin. Ember knew that sort of voice. He was stricken with it himself sometimes in a top of the range panic. Denzil stood close to Shale's chair, like a terrified child looking for protection.

Shale got to his feet and Alfred immediately did the same. There was a kind of big-time graciousness in Shale's movements. He patted Denzil comfortingly on his shoulder. 'They are our visitors, Denzil. Like Mr Iles says and like the Chief expects, we must make them welcome. They come to see us. I believe they come in peace and, yes, friendship. This is a gesture. It's a real privilege to have them with us around our what you could call camp fire, and especially Mr Lane. This is something I really looked forward to for so long, well, all of us, but especially yours truly. This is how it should of been always, Mr Lane, I don't know why not. This is a gesture I appreciate.' His tone was smooth, generous, triumphant.

'What fucking camp fire?' Denzil said. 'This is not Roy Rogers. They're here for trouble, Manse. This is *Iles*. You half cut, Manse? Can't you see?'

'Let's make a place for them at our board,' Shale replied. He walked across the banqueting hall, took a couple of straight-backed chairs from underneath shiny imitation boars' tusks on the wall, and placed them at the table with quite a flourish. Alfie found another one. 'Please,' Shale said, waving a hand in invitation to the three police. Christ, he was brilliant, Ember would admit it. Manse could have been the UN Secretary General hosting world statesmen. Shale kept command. He seemed convinced these officers were here to bring official thanks for the pretty way business had been done lately – the end to bloody syndicate warring on the streets, and on the *Eton*. To Shale, the Chief's presence must mean recognition at last from the summit, formal endorsement of a magnificent alliance between head-quarters and the firms. Did he have it right? Were all Ember's dreads foolish, contemptible? 'I think you could go back to the car now, Denze,' Shale said.

'What do they want?' Denzil yelled.

'Just get back to the fucking car, there's a good lad,' Shale replied. He struck him a short arm blow with his fist under the right ear, part playful, part affectionate, part disabling. 'There might be business talk here and that would only bore you, wouldn't it?' Denzil did some hard breathing for a minute, then shook his head to clear his vision and mind and went out.

Harpur sat down at the table. Iles took a step back and indicated a free chair to the Chief. But Lane remained standing, detached. Iles folded down on to the chair himself and taking one of the champagne magnums from the table, put the mouth between his lips and drank noisily for a while. 'Piss,' he said. He turned to Lane: 'I wouldn't touch it if I were you, sir.' Iles lifted the bottle again and finished what was left. 'We're not stopping,' he said. 'Mr Lane simply wanted to see you all *in* as it were *situ*.'

'What is the purpose of this gathering?' the Chief asked.

Shale said: 'Well, Mr Lane, it's –'

'They carve up the realm here, sir,' Iles replied. 'That's to say, here and at more intimate meetings, more select meetings. Here is creativity, here is gorgeous *esprit de corps*.'

Ember began to sense Shale had things wrong. This was not a peace visit or a recognition visit by Lane, it was for something else. Ralph's fears came back. Was that jaw scar seeping? But he kept himself from probing it.

Beau, one elbow in the remains of his dinner, said: 'Harpur, how d'you know about all this, anyway? But I suppose you think you know every damn thing.'

'It's secret?' Harpur replied. 'I thought I'd read about these reunions in the *Tatler*.'

'You've got someone whispering to you?' Beau said.

This was the point about Beau. Always he might reach the moment when he could not stay silent. Drink gave him this stupid chattiness and courage. He had to speak what it was best just to think. His slob face had gone jagged with fight, all cheek bones and hooter. 'This Nivette been talking to you, yes?' he replied.

'I'll get the girl to bring some whisky, shall I?' Shale said. 'Plus port and lemon, isn't it, for the Assistant Chief and gin and cider for you, Mr Harpur?'

Beau said: 'Don't think Nivette ever fooled – Well, yes, he *did* fool me, I must admit. This Nivette's smart, of course he's smart.'

'They got a fine single malt here,' Shale said, 'brought down special from one of them Scotch islands up Norway way, but not as cold as Norway, more misty, mist being vital for malt.'

Beau said: 'This Nivette could find out about these meetings through his dirty snooping. And then a word to Harpur, who gives a word to the others. I see it as intrusiveness and persecution.'

Alfie Ivis moved around the table to a spare chair alongside Beau and sat down. He took a grip on Beau's arm above the elbow, still in the duck à l'orange remains. To Ember it looked just a gentle grip, the grip of a real friend who wanted to help someone gone feeble-brained and articulate from rum et cetera. Beau was Ember's man, but Ralph would never blame Alfie for trying to shut the stupid sod up. And it worked. Alfie could be quite a frightener even when his grip was only light. Beau made half an effort to shake him off but then gave up and his head slumped slowly forward towards his chest. *Oh, let the twat find twelve-hour coma or even something deeper.*

Lane said: 'I suppose you can all alibi each other tonight, for what that's worth.'

'Alibi?' Shale replied.

'Probably why it happened tonight,' the Chief said.

'What?' Shale asked.

'What?' Ember said. He was beginning to sweat across the back of his shoulders.

Iles said: 'Those papers you made disappear, Ralph – what are they about, then? Been lecturing on red squirrel conservation? Or was it sale returns from the *Eton*? I hear you're in there.'

'You *hear* it, Desmond?' Lane said. He was still standing. 'If you hear it, why have we done nothing? I cannot regard these things with the kind of . . . the kind of lightness and tolerance which you seem to bring.'

Beau lifted his head suddenly and stood up, breaking from Ivis's hold. Beau leaned on the back of his chair, supporting himself. 'Nivette?' he said. 'You ask me about Nivette? Yea, I can tell you about Nivette.' It was as though he had taken in nothing since he last spoke – as though he really had been in coma. 'I personally in person have investigated this Nivette. Ralph will confirm this. And the result of this personal investigation was it looked like this Nivette was all right – no money in the house, no deposit box key, so just an honest-to-God taker. But this is Nivette being smart. He knows how to hide things good. Been trained, most likely. So, he fooled Beau, and because he fooled Beau he fooled Ralph, too. For this, Ralph, I'm sorry. Please try to forgive. Please.' He squeaked this last word, looked as if he might weep. 'Isn't it obvious, Nivette talks to Harpur, Harpur talks to the two above, and they all decide to pay a call and do some more spying, but official?'

Ember said: 'This is all news to me, I have to say, and I think, Beau, it would be best if –'

The door beneath the minstrel gallery was shoved open again and Denzil came in. He was walking this time and seemed a bit bent over with worry. 'I know why these three are here,' he said.

'Certainly,' Shale replied. 'This is a liaison visit, and could not be more valued by us, could it, Denzil?'

'Nivette's shot,' Denzil replied. 'They're looking for likelies.'

'What?' Shale cried.

'So, how do you know?' Lane asked Denzil.

'Is he *dead*?' Shale said.

'On the car radio news,' Denzil replied. 'Neighbours interviewed.'

'This Nivette just lived with peril,' Beau said. 'You have to sympathise, regardless.'

Chapter Sixteen

Jill said: 'Many people with bad troubles call on dad, Mrs Nivette, and sometimes he is able to help. I know this because I've talked to them afterwards. Although he does not look very kind because of that nose he *can* be kind. You are in great grief because of the terrible death of your husband which we saw on TV, and we are very, very sorry, but even in your great grief he might be able to help at least a little bit.'

'Anything to do with an officer being hurt or even killed really upsets him,' Hazel said. 'It's like he feels it's *his* fault. Mr Iles is the same. Some say Iles is the devil, but he's got this good side to him, too, same as dad. It doesn't matter what kind of officer – even useless – if he or she gets hurt or killed dad is really sorrowful and angry, and Mr Iles.'

'She doesn't mean your husband was useless,' Jill said.

'Of course I don't. Mrs Nivette knows that, gruel brain.'

'This worrying about one another, 1 expect you've heard of it – it's called *canteen culture*,' Jill told Kay Nivette. 'Like all-for-one-and-one-for-all through having cups of tea together? This can be bad sometimes, leading to dirty work when they get together and tell lies. But canteen culture can also be good. If you get brought up in a police house you find out there's not just good and bad but different sides to things.'

Harpur said: 'I think Mrs Nivette wants to speak to

162

me privately. Could you and Denise go in the other room and watch the boxing on telly?'

'Dad hardly ever introduces Denise,' Jill said. 'If I was Denise I'd be cross. Do you get cross, Denise? This is Denise, Mrs Nivette. Denise is much younger than dad, well, as you can see, but she's dad's girlfriend since mum died. Well, and a bit before that, I think. They were both like that, mum and dad. This with Denise now, though, is really steady and lovely, but he still acts sort of ashamed sometimes. She's often here, a student, even for breakfast. She gets jealous sometimes of women dad has to meet in his work, but she will not be jealous now, I know it, when you are so affected by sorrow. They'll definitely go to your husband's funeral, probably some in uniform, dad, Iles and Mr Lane. Not dad in uniform because he's CID. But Iles and the Chief. Although Mr Lane looks a shambles in uniform, he'll put it on for special things.'

They were in Harpur's kitchen, where Harpur and Denise had been washing up after a good fish supper he'd cooked, when Kay Nivette arrived at the front door. Now, Denise took the two girls into the sitting room. Harpur realised Jill might be right and he did sometimes hesitate to introduce Denise. It was disgraceful, hurtful, as if he felt shame. What was the matter with him? Didn't he see his luck? He'd put that right in future.

Kay Nivette was sitting now at the Formica-topped table with a mug of tea which Hazel had made for her. She did not touch it. 'Richard asked me to get in touch with you, with you direct, if oh, if anything ever – if anything went wrong. There's a letter.'

Harpur sat down opposite her and waited.

'He said you'd probably be all right, because you'd done something like he was doing yourself. I don't know how he heard that, or if it's true.'

'What *was* he doing?' Harpur asked.

'I expect you know. Yes, you do. He was taking – pretending to take.'

'Did he discuss this with you, then?' Harpur asked.
'The outline, nothing more. It was in case – in case
anything went wrong. Oh, damn, same old dim words.
All right, in case he was killed.' She rushed at 'killed' as
if not sure she could get it out. 'He wanted what he
knew passed on, to you. To you in person. And so I'm
here.'

'He gave you the letter to hold?' Harpur asked.

'As I say, in case.'

'I did the same,' Harpur replied. 'To Denise. For Mr
Iles – in case. She wasn't, isn't, my wife, but there's
nobody closer, not adult. Nobody except the children
anything like as close to me or as important.' There, he
had put things right.

'Richard said definitely not to Iles. He didn't trust
him.'

'The ACC can get misunderstood.'

'As your daughter said.'

'Iles believes there will always be drugs, so make sure
they're traded peacefully,' Harpur replied. 'He calls it
pragmatism – like New Labour. The Chief thinks that's
surrender and can't accept it.'

'How about you?'

'I'm not policy-making rank.'

'Are you dodging an answer?'

'I should think so.'

'But you pretended to be on the take so you could get
information on a trading firm, presumably to prosecute
and destroy it?' she asked. 'You back the Chief?'

'That kind of work *is* more or less right for my
rank.'

'And for Richard's? Did you think he might be just on
the take, not taking as a cover?'

'People acting solo can get misunderstood, too.'

She nodded, weighed that for a while. 'So, *will* you
come to the funeral, all three of you? Even the Chief?'

'Certainly.'

'It would mean all of you accept he hadn't really gone on to salary with Ember and Shale.'

'Right.'

That pleased her and she tried to smile, though the shock and sadness in her face gave this only small chance. At no time tonight had she looked liable to weep. Kay Nivette had done her weeping. But a smile was almost beyond her. Harpur felt glad she did not know about the debate in Lane's suite yesterday on whether they should attend, and on whether Nivette's name could eventually be included on the Halo Wall, as it was flippantly known: that section of brickwork in central hall at headquarters where the names of officers killed on duty were honoured with individual marble panels. 'Can we know, truly know, he wasn't selling us?' the Chief had asked.

And Harpur had immediately answered, 'Yes.' He was nothing like as sure as he pretended. He said it like that – straight, bald – from a sort of kindness to Lane. The Chief would wish to hear this, because he had believed in Nivette.

'Yes,' Iles said. He snapped it out, too. It sounded much better than the 60–40 case for believing Harpur that the ACC had mentioned earlier – 60–40 or marginally less. This must be another of those days when Iles wanted to protect the Chief.

'But what if Shale and Ember were to be laughing at us,' Lane had asked, 'for tainting the Halo Wall with a traitor? I want you to remember, Desmond, Colin, that at least one of the Ministers of State at the Home Office will turn up at this funeral – he is, after all, MP for Nivette's constituency – and quite possibly the Home Secretary herself. This is the death of a high-ranking officer, and the Home Secretary might wish to show personal regret. Will I be allowing them and others to degrade themselves by offering public grief to a damn crook?'

'Nivette was a good man acting outside the due procedures,' Harpur had replied.

'Richard was a good man acting outside the due procedures,' he told Kay Nivette. She was tall with a strong-looking frame and face, handsome and at some angles beautiful, her hair and eyes very dark and lustrous. Perhaps she had Spanish ancestors. She would be the kind of woman who recognised a whiz kid when she met one, and would decide to marry him and make sure he whizzed. He *had* whizzed and been extinguished and fallen to the ground. She would have known this was a risk to be faced. And so, no more weeping.

'You're not saying these kind things, and promising to come to the funeral, just because you want to see the letter he left?' she asked.

As Jill had told them, if you lived with a police officer you got used to deviousness.

'I believe his object was to help law and order', Harpur replied. 'The Chief and Mr Iles believe his object was to help law and order.'

She nodded at the plodding repetition of this formula, then shrugged. 'Anyway, my instructions are to give you the letter, and I will, whatever. He had intended handing back all the monies.' Plural. It was a word from legal contracts and seemed to make the imitation acceptance of bribes sound officially OK. 'I was to do that, hand it back if anything went . . . if he was killed. But the cash was taken. I don't mean by the intruder who shot him. It had gone before that. Richard was horrified. Not because of the loss to us. He did not regard the monies as his. But he was afraid he'd be unable to prove he had been only playing at corruption if he could not hand the bribes over eventually.'

Oh, but the actual retained cash – to show the Home Office, the Inspectorate, the Press, sceptics of that sort. In his head, Harpur reheard the Chief's words spoken – wailed – over Nivette's body. He loved Lane but Lane could be feeble. Yes, the top job had brought him down.

'It makes his death seem almost absurd, doesn't it?'
she said. 'Someone in our house for the monies thinks
Richard is guarding it and kills him, but really it has
already been taken. Perhaps he even thought Richard
had a bank deposit key on him and went through his
clothes. The search of the house must have already
taken place or I'd have seen the intruder. Obviously,
I came downstairs as soon as I was woken by the shot.
He'd gone. Perhaps I heard someone running. I'm not
sure. I told Francis Garland.'

'No, not absurd. No. No. How about a vehicle? Did
you hear a car start?'

'Francis asked me that. No.'

'There probably *was* a car, but he would have parked
some way off,' Harpur replied.

'When I say absurd – well, he accepted the risk that he
might be discovered as a doubler and executed for what
they'd see as treachery. But in fact he seems to have got
killed by a run-of-the-mill burglar, a burglar who arrives
too late, because the loot's already gone. God, farce.'

'Not many run-of-the-mill burglars carry guns, even
today.'

She took a while with that, too. 'You think he might
be a –'

'Francis is dealing with things. We'll get this man. But
unfortunately we've no sightings of him or a car yet.
Have you read the letter? Denise read mine.'

'No, of course not. She must be –'

'Wilful,' he replied.

'You like that?'

'She tore it up.'

Kay Nivette put her hand on the mug of tea but did
not lift it. 'Yes, I can understand why she would. She'd
think that if the letter was ever read by Iles it would be
because you were dead or in trouble. She reasoned that
if she destroyed it it could never be read by Iles, and so
you'd be all right. Reasoned? Well, a sort of superstition.
Superstitions are important. Plus, a letter might be dan-

gerous – as long as you were still alive. By destroying it she was looking after you. I can't do that for Richard.' She produced a sealed envelope from her handbag. 'It's a bit messy, maybe smelly,' she said. 'I taped it to the underside of the sewer inspection cover in the garden. People don't look there.'

'Harry Lime might have. So if it had come unstuck it –'

'Would have had a disgusting trip to the outfall. The stains are metallic, that's all, I think.'

'Yes, of course.' He took the envelope from her. It was addressed in Nivette's handwriting: *To Detective Chief Superintendent Colin Harpur, as and when. To be opened by addressee only.* 'Do you mind if I read it now?'

'Why would I?'

'Oh, possibly I won't be able to tell you what's in it. And it might upset you if he's talking to me and you're excluded.'

'So I'd be excluded wherever you read it.'

He broke the seal and pulled out two folded sheets of white A4 unlined paper. They were covered on both sides, also in Nivette's handwriting.

Dear Mr Harpur,

I've never before composed a letter which I hope will not be read. It's odd to realise that if your eye is on these words it's because I can no longer speak or write any further words. I try to visualise the reading. I've asked Kay to deliver the envelope to you one-to-one and only you, and at your house, not in headquarters. I see the two of you sitting together, Kay sad but controlled, you possibly sad, too, though you would feel I brought whatever it is upon myself by going solo. And you'll feel this even though you did the same sort of thing, I gather, because when you did it you managed it successfully, otherwise you would not be around to receive this letter now.

I will admit that my penetration of the Shale-Ember alliance has not so far produced material which would justify charges. I write 'so far', but the fact that you are reading this means I've gone as far as I'm going. Although I'm not one who would normally admit failure, I have to say this operation has failed.

Naturally I realise that even if it had succeeded it would have been seen by some as only an embarrassment, a nuisance. I know it is Mr Iles's view that to destroy or even target one or both of these firms would be an error because between them they keep the streets tranquil. I find his point of view irresponsible and offensive. I chose the only method I could find of opposing him at my rank. I decided to attempt to infiltrate the firms without official support because I did not believe such a mission would be sanctioned by Mr Iles. And what is not sanctioned by Mr Iles cannot take place officially in this Force, regardless of what the Chief might wish.

As you would expect, Mansel Shale and Ralph Ember treated me with intense suspicion, afraid that I might be 'doubling'. In these early stages I was able to provide them only with very minor items of information and so their suspicion remained. This may have led to my death. Perhaps you have already determined that. The watchfulness of Shale and Ember meant that I was unable to penetrate either firm at the highest level, and it is in this sense that I say my work has been a failure.

What I have discovered, however, is that the position of Shale, and possibly of Ember, may be under internal threat. There is resentment among some subordinates in Shale's company at the amount which he and Ember take from the allied businesses, as against what is paid to those in high but subordinate positions. The rumoured figures are more than £500,000 (five hundred thousand) yearly to Shale and Ember as principals, and salaries of about £40,000 to £50,000 (forty to fifty thousand) to co-directors. This resentment is especially strong in Shale's second-in-command, Alfred Ivis. I have been unable to find whether it also affects 'Beau' Derek, in Ember's firm. Ivis has serious money problems arising from his conversion of an abandoned lighthouse into a home for him and his family. He also intends to send his children to fee-paying schools. But his dissatisfaction is more fundamental than this.

Ivis had some further education, apparently, speaks polished English and is angry at being bossed and outearned by someone crude like Shale. 'Beau' has fewer commitments, appears to be more docile, and does not seem so motivated by gain, valuing his position as Ember's lieutenant for itself. He seems genuinely to admire Ember.

I believe Ivis may attempt to displace Shale (and possibly Ember). Manoeuvring for power has probably already begun within Shale's firm, though unknown to him, of course. By the time you read this you may have heard of the disappearance of Victor Goussard (Slow Victor), a low-rung pusher. My information – inconclusive at this stage – is that Goussard was tortured and killed because he somehow discovered that Ivis was contemplating a revolt against Shale (and possibly Ember). Such action would not be beyond Ivis. As you will know, he was suspected of killing 'Big Paul' Legge in the early 1980s, though this was never proved. He would probably be capable of murdering Goussard if he were thought to menace the coup. At the time of writing, no trace of Goussard has been found, alive or dead.

I understand from observation and rumour that it is likely Ivis has formed a secret partnership with another street pusher, Luke Malthouse, in preparation for the move against Shale. Again as you will know, Malthouse specialises in violent enforcing, and between them he and Ivis should be able to dispose of Shale, especially if they have surprise. Ivis will seek to advance Malthouse in Shale's firm, perhaps by adding Victor Goussard's pushing beat to Malthouse's own. I understand he wants Malthouse at a point where he would have easy access to Shale, and which would secure Malthouse and Ivis in spots from which they could assume control of the firm if Shale were displaced/eliminated.

I realise that much of this material is speculative, and is certainly not yet evidence. I pass it to you in this form because I believe you would wish to investigate it as fully as you can, regardless of the passive policy on drugs policing which prevails in this Force.

If any of my work is instrumental in taking the fight

against Shale and Ember forward, I hope that my wife may be informed of this. I do not wish her to think I wasted my life, nor that I spoiled hers and our child's by behaving stupidly.

Richard Nivette, Chief Inspector.

Watching him as he finished reading, Kay Nivette said: 'So you were right. It *is* material you can't tell me about.'

'No, I'm sorry, I can't,' Harpur replied.

'I'm glad. It must be good. It must be important. Richard wasn't a failure.'

'He was a good man –'

'Acting outside the due procedures. Yes.'

'He was a brilliant police officer.' Harpur refolded the sheets, put them back into the envelope and placed it in his breast pocket. 'If all that he suggests here is true, we –'

'Will you be able to do anything with it?' she replied. 'Will Iles let you? Is Richard still an arrogant pest, even when dead?' She nodded towards the envelope and when she spoke again her voice was tired and hard: 'Is that the archive in there – stuff that never again sees the light?'

'It will need some –'

'Richard thought you were a wonderful detective – the best he'd ever met. And he had faith in you.'

'It will need some more work,' Harpur replied, 'but it's remarkable even as it stands.'

'You think it might not be true?'

'Some of it's true. We know that now,' Harpur said.

'He was very methodical, very careful. He wouldn't write things unless he had reason.'

Yes, Harpur could see he was methodical, careful. The amounts in words after the figures reminded him of Mrs Nivette's use of the term 'monies'. There was the same bank clerk flavour.

'What will you do if Iles says drop it?' she asked. 'Or

perhaps you won't even tell him about the letter, just look into it on your own. That's like you, isn't it?' Now she sounded full of joy. 'It's what Richard would have hoped, I think.'

'Mr Iles often means well,' Harpur replied. Yes, he might have a look into what the letter said on his own. Iles would expect such improper secrecy of Harpur, and it was wrong to thwart the ACC.

'Why don't I introduce you to people?' Harpur asked Denise in bed when Kay Nivette had gone and the children were asleep.

'You do sometimes. It's people connected with work you don't introduce me to. You want us, you and me, to be separate from all that.'

He thought about this. She was right. 'Do you mind?'

'I don't think so,' she said. 'Probably I will as we go on together. I won't want to be compartmentalised.'

'No. You think we *will* go on together, then?'

'Of course.'

'That's nice,' he said. 'You used to say you thought you'd probably marry someone your own age but still keep in touch with me.'

'Did I? That was cheap.' For a while she went quiet. 'I looked at that woman and thought to myself I might have been carrying a message from the dead, too, not long ago. That's what she was doing, wasn't it? So I didn't worry about not getting familiar with her. I don't want to have to think like that.'

'No. Perhaps I do try to keep you apart from such things.'

'You didn't, did you? You gave me that letter for Iles.'

'But you got rid of it. I knew you would.'

'Liar. You were afraid.'

'Yes.'

'And when you were afraid you turned to me.'

'Yes.'

'That's how it should be,' she said.
'How do you get to be so wise so young?'
'I'm learning from you.' She moved against him.
'How did you get to be so horny so old?'
'I'm learning from you.'

Chapter Seventeen

Shale cycled down to the *Eton Boating Song*. The floating restaurant was moored in Spencer's Dock, nearly half a mile from the Invet, where they had found Slow unkindly wardrobed like that on the *Dion*. Shale had decided lately this was quite a worrying death, with ramifications. Ramifications was what you had to be on the watch for in leadership. Think of Eisenhower in history and worrying about the weather and tides for D-Day. This death might say something about Alfred. Of course, it had always been a bit of a risk keeping Alfie and Beau down to fifty grand, and especially Alfie. Probably Alfie had enough brain to work out there was a lot more earnings in the firms, although he never saw the main books, naturally. Shale tried to recall whether Ivis had seemed to know too much that night they looked for Slow on the *Dion*. Hadn't Alf seemed excited when about to open them wardrobe doors?

The Invet Basin and Spencer's were the only two docks now with water in them and not built over. Shale always felt upset when he saw how a great port had dwindled. This was a port playing at being a port now. The *Eton* was the only vessel in Spencer's, and she was not a vessel at all these days, just a once fine China clipper or something like that turned into a trough. He'd heard that when she worked her name was *Imperial Majesty*. God, the come-down. If they undone the ropes that held her to the dockside she'd most likely sink.

It was almost 2 a.m. and things aboard should be

starting to fold for the night. He wanted a quiet talk with the lad they had pushing stuff for them at the *Eton*, and there'd be a chance as trading tailed off. This might turn out a tricky bit of conversation but Shale thought he could probably organise it all right. Of course he fucking could. Was he going to be pissed about by some dealer? All right, so as dealers went Hector was tops, or Shale would not be on his way to talk to him now. Plus Hector knew weaponry. But Hector was still that, a dealer. He did bloody well, yes, as Ralphy said the other night at the banquet, but a pusher could not help doing well at the *Eton*, for God's sake – them big aristocratic hooters of all sexes looking for high sensation, dying to sniff up something elite and no problems paying.

Some of them people were what was called your genuine old money, meaning screwing peasants right back to Queen Victoria or even Rufus Ever-ready, and the loot invested so sweet with big dividends for snorts through the centuries. With these folk drugs was not just a habit they had picked up, it was passed on to them down the ages, like the family motto in Latin and paintings of ancestors. Naturally, Hector would want to hang on to this place for his market stall. Well, sad. Hector had what was known as a franchise at the *Eton*, and the thing about franchises was they got granted, and what got granted could be *de*granted and taken back. He was a fine deep person, Hector, and Shale felt sure he could make the slippery fucker understand eventually why he had to be pulled out urgent. This was a team matter.

Some people thought him stupid to wear cycle clips on his trousers even though the chain was covered by a guard, but his mother used to talk to him a lot about the importance of clips regardless. Often when he wanted to do an anonymous visit he would bike it. The Jaguar was too conspicuous, and even the two smaller cars were probably known. If you was top banana you got used to being recognised and all your things being recognised.

That bastard Denzil in the Jaguar probably going for Nivette like that – Jesus. In the fucking *Jaguar*. Probably? No probably. It had to be Denzil. He had a fancy for handguns and look at the way he was staring and palsied when he came back to the Agincourt.

Shale locked the bike to a disused loading crane near the *Eton* then took off his clips and put them in his jacket pocket. He had on a dark three-piece suit, black shoes, white shirt and a bow tie with gold unicorns on. A bit of formality seemed only right for the *Eton*. The suit was an old style he had bought second or third hand at Oxfam, great cut and cloth, with a bit of wear, naturally, but that was a plus. Upper-class folk would wear a good suit for years, and Shale thought it a mistake to go about in new stuff. The shirt was silk. Just the same, he felt sure some of them Eton sods in the *Eton* would look at him and the shirt and the county suit and know straight off that although he could afford eight nights out a week at the *Eton* he had never been anywhere near Eton, not even on a day trip, and his son, Laurent, would not get let in there, either. He knew they would know it and yet he did not know *how* they would know it. Obviously he knew they would know it as soon as he opened his mouth and spoke some sense, but Shale thought they would know it without that, just a glance. And it wasn't them gold unicorns, but just something general. He tried to comfort himself by asking how many of them had a business or even old money investments that could produce £600,000 a year untaxed and growing, but he still felt very hurt and a little bitter.

Class was a bastard. He had heard some MP on television, probably one who been to Eton, say unless a bottle of wine cost at least £40 it was not worth opening, and there was no proper claret under a hundred. Although Shale could pay to drink like that, he knew it would still not do the trick. Ralphy Ember thought he could crack the class walls because he wrote heavy letters to the Press and paid for his daughter at a French finishing school, but them boys louding it on the *Eton* would soon see through him and the made-to-measure shirts to the Ralphiness.

Shale went up the boarding ramp. There was a lovely long-time tradition on the *Eton* which the new owners had let return after quite a bit of negotiation with him and Ember. Ships were famous for ancient traditions, such as saluting what was called the quarter deck. This tradition on the *Eton* was different from that but had lasted for well over a year. It was that the pusher always sat at the same chair in the bar, with a glass of his or her favourite drink on the table near. The pusher was allowed to choose this drink, any drink at all, absolute liberty, when first starting to work the *Eton*, but then it had to stay the same. It was a procedure. This drink sent a sign the pusher was trading and ready for cus- tomers. The sign became well known, like the flag over Buckingham Palace when the Queen was home. A bril- liant old pusher called Eleri ap Vaughan had begun this drink tradition. She always showed a rum and black, though unfortunately this bright-baggage was slaugh- tered during a bad spell of company competition, and the lad who took her place got mercilessly killed, too. Shale could not recall what *his* drink had been, but something very personal. Those were such wasteful, bloody times and no wonder Iles went for peaceful co- existence. That's what Ember said it used to be called in the international scene when things were bad, the Reds and the West. Ralphy knew all sorts of words because he had started that university degree, never mind his age. Shale regarded preventing violence as his chief duty once the profits had come out decent.

When he looked into the bar Hector was handling a nice bit of selling, and Shale stayed politely back, wait- ing, watching the beautiful but very quick flash of twenties, then the package transferred, or even more than one. This was the thing about the *Eton* – the trading had to be discreet. All sorts came aboard here for the food and the feel they were on another Caribbean cruise, including old ladies and retired opticians and so on who did not know a thing about snorting but loved the atmos of portholes and masts and lifeboats and would be alarmed if they knew pushing was going on during, for instance, some rich slag's eightieth birthday dinner in the restaurant with speeches about her warm heart and that kind of pleasantness. The new owners were just like the one before and realised the drugs was a lovely vital extra for many who partied on the *Eton*, and they would party somewhere else if they could not get their supplies as well as the prize cookery. But the new owners did not want to offend the other customers, or patrons as they should be referred to. So, they would blind-eye the dealing as long as the dealing had a bit of tact to it, now you see it now you don't.

You could not of met anyone better at pusher's tact than Eleri ap Vaughan, and it was a real loss when she passed on in such conditions. Hector would never be so good, but not bad and getting better. A pity Shale had to pull him out. Hector Mills-Mills was his name, if you could believe that, but just the right prickish sound for the *Eton*. Although his drink was barley wine, you had to respect this choice, but it seemed a bit low for someone with a full-out fartarseing same-same name-name like that. Despite being called Hector he was white. Having the name Hector when white could help with racial equality, and Shale certainly did not mind that in our day and age.

This seemed to be the last deal tonight, and Mills-Mills finished his barley wine and stood up. He had seen Shale and they left the bar and walked the deck together. There were others out here chatting and strolling in friendly style after their meal, it could of been the Med. 'Manse, if anyone tells you times are still hard send them down to the *Eton* to see the business. It's a charm and getting more of a charm every day. This is only a Tuesday but I did nearly a thou and a half tonight. So much cash it's pushing my clothes shapeless, but one doesn't complain. Hardly!' He had on a beige lightweight suit which was not too bad, and, yes, you could see the lumpy heaps of notes in his pockets.

'It's grand, grand, Hector. I got to say you done grand here, which is why I want you to take a move up now.'

'Up? Oh, Manse, thanks, but – Up?' He had the right sort of face for the *Eton*, a butler's sort of face, long and bony. Also it was respectful but with quick small eyes and a very flat forehead that would do for pressing against a door when keyhole squinting. He did not use any of the stuff himself and never had as far as Shale knew. This was another reason Mansel had thought of him.

'We got some severe problems, Hector, I'm going to talk very frank to you.'

'As ever, Manse.'

'I believe in openness in a business. It always pays, and it is what I feel I owe.'

'Thanks, Manse.'

'You heard Slow disappeared, I expect.'

'Oh, Slow – chasing some star longcock, I should think. He'll be back when he's had satisfaction.'

'Well, I don't think he'll be back,' Shale said.

'He's done this kind of flit before, Manse. A couple of weeks, the money gets short, he's suddenly around again and busy.'

'He might not be coming back,' Shale said.

This time Mills-Mills heard it accurate. 'Slow's in the past?'

'I'd like you to take his sales area, Hector.'

Mills-Mills stumbled a step or two on the deck but did not fall, and an old couple nearby looked around hard for a moment, thinking he was drunk or drugged, most probably. Well, you could understand the poor sod's shock. This was a boy who had built a lovely, refined operation for himself on the *Eton* with some aid, and now he was told get back touting to social rubbish in student raves, public toilets and shop doorways. He would not be able to see Shale's point of view on this, not promptly.

'Manse, I'm grateful you should think of me, very, naturally, but I don't think I'm the sort for –'

'This is what's called a mask appointment,' Shale said.

They stood in the bows of the *Eton* looking out towards the dud dock, the string of boxy marina housing and the city beyond. It must of been great in the old days when this clipper was really clipping through an ocean to stare off towards the horizon from here over genuine waves knowing that what you had beneath the hatches would finish up in many a fine café and breakfast room with kidneys and so on – numerous blends from China before tea bags was even thought of. For people on this kind of ship in them days the sea would be a noble enemy and a road home, not just somewhere to drop inconvenient personnel like Slow and Finnane. The figurehead from the *Imperial Majesty* was still there at the front, a pork-faced girl with fair hair and giving for ever a gorgeous smile, like she knew how bucked the folk in Dover or Southampton or Hull would be when they seen the sails approaching from afar with enough cargo for buckets and buckets of tea.

'Mask?' Hector replied.

'This job I've got for you will look like something but it will be something else.'

They leaned over the side together gazing down at the docks water. Mills-Mills said: 'It's intriguing what you say, Manse, but things at the *Eton* need one's –'

'Alfie wants to put Luke Malthouse into Slow's spot.'

Mills-Mills nodded for a while, the narrow face going up and down like a busy chicken's. 'Luke's not a bad cove. A bit rough-and-ready, certainly, but plenty of salesmanship. When it comes to picking staff, Alf has a

remarkable skill. Probably Luke would be just the kind
of talent for –'

'I look at Alfie and I look at Malthouse,' Shale replied.
'I mean, Hec, I *look* at them.'

Mills-Mills stayed staring down at the water. 'Oh, like
that,' he said. Or it was more a kind of whisper. That old
couple were still about.

'Alfie got costs,' Shale said.

'I always thought Alfie was – I mean, you top banana,
obviously, and Alfie alongside in a position that –'

'Alfred been in many ways a grand friend as well as
a colleague, and it grieves me, truly grieves me, Hector,
to speak in any way dubious about him. But I look at
Alfie and I look at Malthouse. This would be bringing
Malthouse on not just in Slow's area but keeping his
own. This is sudden big expansion, Hector. Slow had
huge territory. This makes Malthouse more than twice
as big, almost three times. It's a power base. This is
something that could ruin all kinds of situations
which are nicely set up and nicely balanced for now.
Widespread.'

'Manse, are you saying the two of them would –?'

'Why do you think Slow had to tumble into the night
like that?'

'He saw something?'

'Slow's called Slow, yes, but maybe Slow was not so
slow,' Shale replied.

Mills-Mills went back to whispering. It was fright.
Shale did not blame him. Hector could feel himself
getting reeled in. 'Jesus, what have they done with Slow,
Manse?'

'In my position I'm always trying to glimpse the
future, control the future,' Shale replied. 'I got to see
beyond the day-to-day and look for the pattern of
things, known as strategic planning. I'm used to that,
luckily.'

'It's a high skill, Manse.'

'You say, what have they done with him? A mystery,

Hec. Total. At this time. I hear there might be another lad gone missing, also. Not a certainty, not at all, oh, no, but possible. This could be a political figure. This could be a political figure who was shagging Slow in a happy regular mode, nothing shoddy.'

'Political? What sort of political, Manse? My God, to wipe out someone like that.'

Shale stamped one foot gently on the desk, a plea for correctness. 'Nothing's definite. I don't say wiped out, Hec. Not at this time. He could turn up. Slow could turn up, as you said. They might just be honeymooning down the Riviera way or Acapulco. These things of the heart get very demanding with people, Hec. In its way inspiring. They just take off, regardless of commitments.'

'But you said Slow would not be coming back.'

'My *impression*, Hec. Nothing for sure, let me stress it again. At this time. As I see it, Alf and Malthouse spotted Slow had noticed their damned alliance. They'd be afraid of pillow talk – Slow and this political figure in bed, post coital and they're talking together in contentment before our political figure can get it up again and give Slow a further meaningful experience. This is how them two, Alfred and Malthouse, might see things. They can hear Slow lovey chatting to this political figure about what he observed recently relating to Alfie and Malthouse – this move towards takeover. That's what we're talking about, Hec. Destruction of what you could call a decent, steady way of life – this firm and maybe Ember's. Well, them two, Alf and Malthouse, are going to think to theirselves the political figure could pass on such information to other political figures. This political figure who's banging Slow is in touch with the MP here, who is in the Home Office, as you know. Now, what's the Home Office Minister going to make of it if he hears about a gorgeous, local peaceful arrangement suddenly smashed because Alf Ivis got cash worries and dirty ambitions? Alf would see that this Minister would be absolutely against any change of the way business is done here. A Home Office Minister got to preserve law and order, tidy serene trading on the streets et cetera. So, the simple answer, get rid of Slow, get rid of the political figure, also, before any messages can be passed on and up. I don't know whether them two lovers was done while they was actually intermingled, poor jerks – it's a messy thought – or whether they was took out separate. But what's known as the scenario is something like that, I really fear.'

'Terrible, Manse.'

'Exactly. I knew you'd see the perils could all come your way, too.'

'Me involved?' He turned to look straight at Shale, his back to the ship's side. His narrow face was narrower. Anxiety squashed him in a clamp. Probably there had not been many chats like this on the clipper in its tea days. 'Manse, I don't understand how I –'

'And then Denzil. You know my chauffeur? He've killed a cop. This was just for money. He can't think no further than that.'

'You don't mean Nivette?'

'I won't give no names at this stage, but a cop and a highish officer. You heard in the Press Nivette's dead, so I leave the deductions to you. What I got to think, Hec, is if I go at Denzil about this, trying to find out for certain, giving him a bit of pressure for the sake of truth and making him an alibi, he might turn ratty and move over to Alfie and Malthouse. Alfie's holding good funds which he could use some of to buy Denzil with. All at once I'd be on my own. Do you see it? Why I'm speaking to you now. Ivis gathers support, so I got to gather support myself.'

'I appreciate it, Manse. It's an honour – to be called on.'

'What we got is Alfred, Malthouse, Denzil, a secret crew. All of them know handguns, and Alf especially.'

'I heard he did Big Paul Legge. I mean, Manse, *Big Paul Legge.*'

'And maybe others. Who says he haven't killed this political figure?'

'Or even Slow.'

'Or even Slow. But I think mostly of this political figure. Alf would regard someone like that as big enough for him to take the trouble with. He can be arrogant. Would he want to live in a fucking lighthouse if he's not arrogant? He'd probably leave Slow to Luke. What I'm watching, Hector, is someone clearing the way for himself and Malthouse, his sidekick.'

Of course, Shale knew that what this fucker Mills-Mills would be thinking was, Who's going to win this one? If Alfred could turn the firm upside down so he comes out at the top with his mates, Mills-Mills wouldn't want to give them no offence by joining up with Shale. One of the most majestic skills in arselicking was make sure it was the right arse. Mills-Mills might look at Shale and think, Christ, this bugger's the past, and he's trying to lead me into the past with him. No, thanks.

Shale said: 'Oh, yes, he done Big Paul Legge, but that was an age ago, Hec. Alfie's speed's gone. He might be able to put a pistol against an injured lad's head and blow some death into him as a relief, but he can't cope with resistance now. Or, yes, maybe, maybe, someone non-gun, like Slow. We could handle Ivis, and all his back-up lads.'

'He's given someone a mercy shot?'

'What I want is a friend with great business achievements such as yourself, Hector, to stand by me,' Shale replied. 'Someone to block this Malthouse. That's the first job. But then, later, I'm going to lose Alfie one way and the other, aren't I? He's a traitor. He runs a conspiracy. I don't see how he can live, do you? Nor Malthouse and Denzil if they go with him. So I need someone to take Slow's territory, yes, and make sure

Malthouse don't get it, but I'll need in due course someone who can also take Malthouse's and then come in at
the summit and run this outfit with me, once we got rid
of the opposition. This is what I mean when I say a
record of fine business achievement. Plus, of course,
I believe you know quite a bit about the armament
side, too. You talk about Alfie and big Paul Legge, but
you've got some fine triumphs in that realm of things
yourself.'

'Well, Manse, I don't –'

'Boast. I know it. I like modesty, Hec. Or look at it
another way. Alfie and his crew do an approach to Ralph
Ember. All right, Ralphy's supposed to be my associate.
But this one is weak. Anything go a bit wrong and he's
in a fine panic and looking for the way out. So Alfie says
to him, Join up with me, Ralph, and all your worries will
fade away. He've got a piece of Ralphy's shirt, if there's
any pressure needed, wouldn't tell me where he's keeping it.'

'Shirt? What's his shirt have to do with it? A piece?
How?'

'And then when they got everything fixed between
them, where do you think you would be, Hec? If you
was still at the *Eton*, would they let you keep it? The
Eton is sure to be lined up as reward for one of Alfie's
louts.'

'I'd have to think about –'

'We can beat the bastards, Hec. I'm glad our conversation took place on the deck of this wonderful vessel, as
was. It gives a reminder about true values. That's what
you and I will be fighting for.' He gave Hector a thorough handshake, like Welcome Aboard.

Chapter Eighteen

Harpur was called to a special evening meeting at Mark Lane's home near Baron's Hill. The Chief would do this occasionally, particularly if he had slumped deep into nervous self-protection and wanted to shut out Iles from a discussion. At headquarters the Assistant Chief was always liable to sense when private talks were under way and stroll in on them. Iles believed Lane's morale so frail that it would be cruel to let him try some larger matters on his own, even if he wanted to, or above all if he wanted to.

Lane made the invitation by telephone himself: 'Do you think you could get here in an hour, Colin? It would be . . .' He did not seem able to close the sentence. His voice was sickeningly weak and pleaful, echoing tones Harpur had heard before when Lane was on the brink. They made Harpur grieve. There had been a time when Lane was a great street detective. Elevation had put him in a pit.

'Of course, I'll be there, sir,' he replied.

'Oh, God, new information. New and terrible. And then the funeral. Should I? Should I, Colin? Should any of us? I've reason to believe the Home Secretary herself might attend, unless I warn her of the – of the sensitivity of the matter. It is Home Office policy to identify more strongly with the police, and the funeral of an officer killed – an obvious occasion to demonstrate this. And then certainly Vesthal MP, who's a Minister in her department. Nivette lived in his constituency. Shall we all look fools? Have you thought, Colin, that Shale and Ralph Ember might choose to be there? They possibly regard Nivette as *theirs.*'

Yes, Harpur had thought of it.

'And do we know they are wrong? I mean *know* they are wrong?' Lane asked. 'There will be a certain guest here this evening.'

Harpur waited.

'Yes, a certain guest,' the Chief said. 'I expect you would expect that.'

Now and then, when Lane was near another mental crisis his speech grew clumsy.

'I'm sorry to bring you from your children so urgently, Colin, but there is a degree of urgency, in view of the funeral impending. I must decide. I shan't keep you from them for long, believe me. Sally would be so cross if I did.'

'That will be all right, sir.'

There was another pause and then a rustling sound. Lane must have handed the receiver to his wife. 'Chief needs you, Colin,' she said. 'Some speed?' Perhaps he had left the room.

'Right.'

'Things have amassed against him again, amassed and amassed,' she said. 'Oh, I do not believe any man could take so much without . . . without some, well, some slide towards despair. I think no less of Chief for that, believe me, Colin, but we must prevent the slide from once more becoming a disastrous plunge. This manor cannot afford it. Together we will accomplish his salvation, the three of us, you, myself and Chief. There is no need, absolutely no need, to inform Iles.'

'No, I understood that.'

'On no account should he be informed, Colin.'

'No, I understood that.'

Although Lane had learned to guard himself against the ACC now and then, Mrs Lane tried to do it continuously, and with brilliant venom. Harpur thought the Chief lucky to have her.

There was a pause. Then she said: 'Colin, may I add this: Chief is never sure how you stand vis-à-vis Iles. Whose camp you are in. I'm speaking very frankly, because matters are bad.'

'I don't think of the situation as opposing camps,' Harpur replied.

'No? Why not? ' She rang off. Harpur handed the receiver back to Denise to be replaced. They were in bed again. The children had gone to the rap caff about half an hour ago. Denise could be like this, inclined to stretches of great loving and sexual intensity during, say, a week or ten days. Then she would get drawn back to her life at the university and grow neglectful of him for a while, and longer than a while, weeks into months sometimes. She seemed unable to see that chances should be grabbed. She was young and thought there would always be chances, and she only half listened when Harpur tried to correct her. If you slept with a kid you put up with her gross optimism. Or perhaps she had different chances through that different life. The irregularity did not suit Harpur – could make him edgy and morose and promiscuous in what might be retaliation. He wanted to be indispensable to her. 'I feel used,' he would say.

'Well, you *are*. What you mean is, you want to be used *more*.'

'Some fucking book or lecturer or poem in French shoves me out of the way. Callous.'

'There are several damn good books around, and French poems.'

'What about lecturers?'

'Col, I could recite to you a fine French poem about a mother wolf and the way it silently accepts whatever turns up in life, no complaint.'

'It's when you *don't* turn up I complain.'

188

'Just your age. People get self-centred as they grow older.'

'I want to be at *your* centre.'

'Col, darling, you must know you'll always be among the first seven or eight of my priorities.'

'Which?'

'Eight.'

Tonight, he had ignored the bedside telephone when it first rang. At the time, they were into rough, sweet, escalating passion with the kind of for-ever implications he cherished and toiled for, and she would probably have been enraged if he let on he had even heard the bell. Her head flailed about under him on the pillow, except when he took a thorough handful of her hair on each side and held her hard fixed like in an old-fashioned interrogation, but so he could kiss her, a way of reminding Denise that he as he and only he was present. Their noses interlocked and front teeth banged together like dice in a shaker. You'd think she would be aware of him as him and only him, but he never counted on it. She had a middle finger hooked into his arsehole, which was a genial style of hers so he could not get off too soon, in her judgement. This device some women famously used to make a slow comer come and get things over, but she was after the opposite and it worked pretty well. Owner of an organised mind, Denise had charted what her requirements were. He liked that, as long as her requirements remained him.

She left her finger where it was as they subsided now and while he chatted to the Chief and Mrs Lane The phone had rung again. Harpur would have ignored it this time as well, but she had reached out with her available hand and picked up the receiver then held it near his face. He heard Lane's apologetic bleating and took the instrument from Denise and listened properly. 'Oh, Colin,' the Chief had begun, 'have I rung in the middle of some domestic episode? I have to admit, sometimes I do forget your special obligations there. You sound breathless. Sorry. I called earlier.'

'We must have been outside – bringing the washing in. I'm just folding my sheets.'

'Ah, and the children would have been out there helping. Family! They're grand.' And then Lane made his invitation, and his wife added her heartfelt commentary. Once or twice before she had called to Harpur for aid when the Chief was bad, or within sight of being bad. Although Harpur always wanted to help him and her, occasionally it was impossible. Lane sometimes did more than slide. As she said, he could plunge far into desolation, and Harpur did not know how to bring him back. There was no police training for this. In any case, Harpur often wondered whether desolation wasn't the right state to be in, for everyone, but especially senior police officers, and especially a very senior police officer pissed about by Iles.

After the call, Harpur detached himself and lay for a few minutes alongside Denise sucking her right shoulder. He loved the narrow neatness of her shoulders. She had not known much about the sexual pull of women's shoulders until he told her. It was in things like this that maturity gave him an advantage over her infantile stalkers at the college, if they *were* infantile: some of those sodding lecturers might not be that, and might know about shoulders, and everything else. Yes, sodding.

'You've got to go out,' she said. 'So *you* have priorities, too.'

'A funeral.'

'At night?'

'A police funeral.'

'At night?'

'I won't be long. You could stay over, couldn't you? The kids are bucked when you're here for breakfast.'

'How about you?'

'Yes, they're bucked when *I'm* here for breakfast, too.'

'That's not what I meant, prat, and you know it's not.'

'I love it when you're here for breakfast, too.'

'I love it, too,' she said. 'So, what is it about breakfast?'

'Institutionalises things. It's like permanence. We all feel it. As if you lived here.'

'Only "like", though. Only "as if".'

'I settle for what's offered, like that lady wolf.'

'It's your age. You're into the gratitude phase.'

'Yes,' he replied.

'Well, I'm grateful, too, Col. I like belonging here. Now and then. Now.' Denise turned on to her side. 'A short, snooze in a reasonably satisfied state and I'll cook them supper when they come in.'

He bent and kissed her on the temple. 'Thanks. Wash your hands first.'

'Actually the lady wolf gets killed, so forget her.'

Like Mansel Shale, the Chief lived in what had once been a Church of England rectory. Harpur had heard Shale speak with relish of this link between Lane and him, both successors in their different career paths to a distinguished tradition. Shale bought all the furniture with his rectory and had once told Harpur how it thrilled him to sit doing his trade accounts and person-nel plans at the wide mahogany desk where clergy through the years prepared sermons. A red Alfa Romeo Spider Lusso stood alongside Lane's Senator and his wife's VW Golf in the forecourt.

The Chief opened the door himself. He had on a green, short-sleeved sports shirt and flannels, a mis-erably jinxed effort to look relaxed. He was haggard and seemed bent over a little, the way people searched gut-ters for cigarette ends. He wore nothing on his feet. Like a dog scenting he pushed his sallow face towards Harpur. 'Finnane,' he said. 'Is this a name signifying anything significant to you, Colin?' He peered past Harpur, perhaps convinced he'd see Iles lurking some- where behind.

Sally Lane came into the large high hall and closed the drawing room door behind her. 'Tell him he must not give up, Colin. Tell him he is needed. Tell him that with help he can prevail.'

'Finnane,' Lane muttered. 'Is this a name signifying anything significant to you, Colin? Where is he? My God, what am I presiding over in this patch?'

'It's that damn woman,' Mrs Lane whispered. She nodded towards the drawing room. 'Chief is lost with her, lost. Beaten.'

'I want the diving team in the dock, Colin. I want it dragged. Make this immediate.'

'Yes, Chief, yes,' Mrs Lane whispered, holding his forearm comfortingly. She was a pain, she was an amaz- ing strength.

'Invet Basin, Colin,' Lane said. 'There are two names which might be significant, Bernard Finnane and Victor Goussard. I smell chaos. And the death of Nivette might be part of it. Oh, is almost certainly part of it. We are engulfed.' There was what Harpur took to be at the time and even when he thought of it afterwards a kind of sob. 'Engulfed. I have failed. I have seen my duty and have allowed myself to be diverted from it, like . . .'

Again Lane let the sentence die. Of course, Iles had his theory that everyone, everyone except himself, was pro- moted first beyond their level of competence, like St Peter. Had Iles been here he might have amiably asked the Chief if it was the disciple he had in mind.

'Chief is intolerably undecided about the funeral again, Colin.' Her face was long, cumbersome, stately. It had grandeur and fight. The three of them stood in a close group, speaking quietly so their words should not reach the drawing room. The Lanes had some big foul oil paintings hanging in the hall, country scenes with animals that did not look like animals and people in smocks and that sort of thing.

'My office must not be tainted,' Lane said. 'I – I – personally – I am nothing. But my office.'

'You are *not* nothing,' Mrs Lane cried. 'Oh, tell him is not nothing, Colin.'

'I know nobody who is less nothing,' Harpur replied. Jesus, did those negatives come out as what he meant?

'You and your office, your office and you, are one, Chief,' Mrs Lane declared, 'brilliantly mutual, wonderfully inter-supportive.' Her voice crackled with struggling belief in him.

'You'll ask me why search the Basin, Colin,' Lane said. 'Iles will ask me, and will seek to prevent it.' The Chief managed a tiny snarl: 'I do not care. I have my reasons. I'll persist. I am not accountable, except to those who placed me in my post.'

'Absolutely, darling,' Sally Lane said.

'I am entitled to exercise my judgement,' the Chief said.

'Certainly,' Sally Lane replied.

'I am *required* to exercise my judgement. It is my appointed role.'

'Come,' Mrs Lane said, and drew Lane towards the drawing room. 'Colin will help us with her, don't be afraid, Mark.' She opened the door to the big, light room and Harpur saw Angie Hyde of Coastal Waters Television. She was studying framed photographs of the Lanes' relatives which hung on one wall. 'Angela Hyde tells us she has already spoken to you, Colin,' Mrs Lane said.

'You see, I've had to go above you, Harpur. Things were not moving. I do not blame you. Perhaps it was beyond your remit. I think you'll understand.' And fuck off if you don't – that was the message.

'Mrs Hyde asked via our Press Office to see me direct, Colin,' Lane said with terrible weariness. 'And Lord Ambin – George Ambin, a friend – the retiring chairman

of CWTV – was on the phone, too. And so one arranged
. . .' He waved a hand to take in the room and the
rectory and the meeting.

'But Chief would never bypass you, Colin,' Sally Lane
said.

'Never,' Lane cried.

'Despite your – despite the familiarity you maintain
with Iles,' Mrs Lane said. 'Of course, Iles would never
listen to any recommendation from Lord Ambin, for
reasons we'll not discuss, but which have nothing to do
with work and much to do with Lady Ambin.'

'Never bypass you, Colin,' Lane cried.

'Hence this invitation to you,' Mrs Lane said. 'We
agreed it between us, Chief and I.'

'I want to act responsibly,' Angie Hyde said.

'George Ambin told Chief he was sure she would act
responsibly, though, of course, he has no actual power at
Coastal now,' Sally Lane said.

'This Finnane, Colin,' the Chief said. 'Angela's mentioned him to you, I understand. Oh, suddenly this
thing stretches into politics, into the Home Office itself.
And Mrs Hyde believes Richard Nivette's death is associated somehow, an element in a pattern.'

'Why?' Harpur asked.

'It seems obvious,' Angie Hyde replied.

'Why?' Harpur said.

'Because everything's coming apart,' Lane said.
'Symptom upon symptom. And what do we do? What
do *I* do? I let it.' Those small red nodules appeared again
for a moment on a couple of veins in the benign doughi-
ness of his face, his rare anger signs. No, Lane was not
much into anger. 'And yet I will *not* let things come
apart. Help me, Colin.' He turned to Angie Hyde. 'Colin
will help me. I know this, you see.' The red lights faded
and he smiled contentedly for a moment. Had he
glimpsed a sudden, lovely vision assuring the future?

'What pattern?' Harpur asked.

'There's a pattern,' Angie Hyde said. 'Bound to be.'

Mrs Lane poured drinks – sherries for herself, Lane and Hyde, gin and cider mixed for Harpur, in a half-pint glass.

The Chief said: 'Mrs Hyde has kindly promised to do nothing on the screen about all this for a week, Colin.'

'All what?' Harpur replied.

'The two men *are* missing,' Angie Hyde said. 'I've spoken to Finnane's family and to Slow Victor's friends. All right, no official notification yet, but they're gone.'

'Oh, what does it mean, Colin, what does it mean?' the Chief demanded. 'And then Nivette. Isn't attendance at his funeral unthinkable?'

'Mrs Hyde says she has seen Ralph Ember hanging about the Invet dock in the middle of the night.'

Jesus, the Chief's wife knew everything, as usual. She was an amazing strength, she was a menace. She must think of Lane as he once was, and longed to rebuild him.

'Yes, search, search,' Lane declared in a trembling whisper. 'You have looked through some ships with her, I gather, Colin.'

'Nothing,' Harpur replied.

'But beneath the water,' Lane said. 'Its secrets. We must. This could tell us so much.'

'It would prove you're doing something,' Angie Hyde said. 'We could show that on the screen, as part of my programme.'

'Nice for the programme,' Harpur replied.

'And then talk of some kind of coup in the firms,' Angie Hyde said. She swallowed the sherry. 'Things pile up. Do you know of this, Harpur – wars and rumours of wars? Of course you do, but you stay quiet, as ever.'

'You see, Colin?' Lane muttered. '"Wars and rumours of wars." That's a terrible, threatening phrase from one of the great historians, isn't it?'

'Well, the Gospels,' Harpur replied. 'It goes on, "be ye not troubled, the end shall not be yet."'

'Ah, a grand fundamentalist education.' But Lane *was*

troubled. 'Are we on the way back to carnage? All this supposed tranquillity, the Iles do-nothing policy – is it leading us inevitably to even more bloodshed? All-embracing bloodshed. What I always feared. Have we brought it on ourselves by passiveness, by irresolution? Indeed, has the bloodshed already begun? Finnane, Goussard, Nivette.' Lying almost flat in his armchair, he spoke this roll call of the dead slowly, like an indictment, an impeachment of himself. His eyes were closed. He had lost his consoling vision and seemed stunned by the prospects, the drink hanging untasted in his left hand.

Angie Hyde stood and grinned cheerfully at Sally Lane. 'I feel as if I might be intruding. You've all been very kind. My feeling is that something has certainly been achieved tonight. Matters will move forward now. Thank you, Mr Lane.' She walked to the door. The Chief waved, but remained where he was. Sally Lane showed her out.

When she came back she stood by the Chief's chair, one hand firmly stroking his sandy hair, willing him to refind his guts. His eyes were shut, still. 'Colin,' she said, 'this is not a happy situation – a certain degree of blackmail from her and her programme, clearly. What's it called? *Light*? *Light*! Yet she's correct. It *is* important that something should be done. I mean, not just for the sake of discovery, though that, obviously, is crucial. But for Chief's sake, too. It's vital he should still believe he can take action, and vital that he *should* take that action.' She spoke as if her husband were absent or could not understand – the way hospital doctors speak to each other across a hospital patient. Harpur found her impressive and awful. 'Vital that he should take this action, regardless of the views of Iles. He relies upon you to get this under way. We both rely on you to get this under way.'

'I don't believe there's anyone in Invet Basin,' he replied.

'We both rely on you to get this under way,' she said.

The Chief made another tiny wave in confirmation.

Harpur got it under way. Early in the afternoon next day he went down to watch the divers at work in the Basin. A small, changing crowd also watched, and Angie Hyde with her camera team, wasting money in the bright cause of truth.

Harpur had ordered the search first thing, wasting money in the cause of something else. Naturally he had ordered it. Hadn't he been given a direct instruction by the Chief, as well as by his wife? And it might turn out to be a mind-saving therapy for Lane, as she had suggested. The diving was the Chief's own decision, more or less. True, there had been influence from Angie Hyde, but none from Iles. This mattered above all when it came to guarding Lane's selfhood and morale. And it was not just that Iles had been kept ignorant of the Chief's intention: if consulted the ACC would almost definitely have opposed the search, so Lane had actually achieved a kind of defiance, a notional kind, which might be the safest kind against Iles. The ACC suspected everything that could disturb the settled business scene, and diving would possibly do that, by signalling a sudden move into police aggression. Plus, Iles knew from his lovely bought black girl, Honorée, that the dock was the wrong place. The bodies had been carted away.

Harpur knew this, also. But, although he had tried to discourage the diving, it was obviously too early to tell the Chief why or even *Mrs* Lane. Harpur sensed vast changes were on the way in the drugs game, yet could not make out what they were. And it was his fashion not to disclose what he knew until what he knew could be made to stick.

In fact, it was the way of *all* successful detectives, and especially not to disclose matters *up* the command system, where they would be reduced to shit through jumpiness and stupidity, or thieved for glory. The Chief was probably too honourable to try to steal credit, but these days he could be turned inept by nerves and haste: he yearned for a vast triumph before he retired or collapsed, and would often stumble in his hurry. On the other hand, Iles was never inept but would certainly pirate anyone else's discoveries in his own interests. And so as a rule Harpur told neither of them beyond what they had to be told, and often not that. Of course, Iles would not expect to be told and would have despised Harpur if he *had* told anything above crumbs and lies. Iles was the most naturally accomplished senior police officer Harpur had ever worked with and against.

He strolled around the edge of the Basin and drew near to Angie Hyde and her people. It was a hot afternoon and she had on lightweight blue slacks and a cream shirt, looking perhaps nicer than he recalled. 'This is all balls, isn't it?' she asked.

'Of course.'

'I had to get some action. Anything.'

'Well, it worked with the Chief.'

'It's not the Chief who matters, is it? Or his wife. They know zilch.'

'What *is* there to know?' he said.

'Whatever there is, you know it.'

'You'll get some good pictures. Plenty of light for *Light*.'

'No, no light. Pictures of what?'

'Divers' bubbles. And the Chief.'

Lane had just arrived driving himself in the Senator. He parked near the three laid-up D vessels and Hyde and the crew moved away to film and interview him. He was in uniform and looked almost tidy and resolute, even healthy. This was yet one more of those occasions he would regard as significant beyond itself and worth a personal visit. Harpur felt that fiddling around in the

Invet would probably not cause too much trouble, and anything which enthused the Chief was humane and therefore most likely worthwhile. As he began talking to Angie and the camera, Lane smiled, gestured economically and seemed to keep going all right. He would have the basic sense not to say much, and at least his wife was not present. None of the people watching, nor any of the audience who might eventually see this conversation on screen, would guess the Chief's fraying state, thank God. Harpur had heard they'd concealed the worst about Churchill following a stroke when Prime Minister after the war. It was like that. Perhaps Lane would come through his crisis OK. Harpur hated to think of him ambulanced off again and once more dosed into long, chemical ease.

But that could be on the menu for any of us. As he turned and gazed again at the segment of black water where the divers trawled now, Harpur had a vision of himself on a nursing home bed in . . . in how many years' time? . . . a vision of himself trying desperately to swim in search of one clear thought through all the dark opaqueness and shadows that would close upon the brain then. Beds could be so fine and so bloody final. Nobody would waggle a finger confidingly up his arse in those days, or nobody he wanted to. Divers and their hard, grubby game made him morose.

The Chief went to talk to the inspector in charge of the diving. Harpur did not join them. He could not talk hope, if finding bodies was hope. Lane might come over to speak to Harpur afterwards and afterwards would be soon enough.

Chapter Nineteen

Iles said: 'Between us we might be able to set things right, even so, Col. I've got a gem of an idea to put to you. Thanks so much for coming over. How did you decide in even your *paltry*, craven fucking brain, Harpur, to drop a superb creature like Honorée into peril?'

The Assistant Chief had his baby daughter, Fanny, in his arms and he occasionally bent forward and rubbed a cheek playfully, adoringly, against the child's and cooed comfortingly to it. The baby watched him but seemed entirely undisturbed by the closeness to Iles and now and then reached up smiling and tried for a hand hold on the short grey hair of his new style. 'This is a very lovely girl, Col. Honorée, I mean. *This* is a very lovely girl, too,' the ACC said, kissing Fanny's forehead lightly four or five times. 'Of course she is, she is. But Honorée . . . well, you've seen her, met her. The sweet warmth and so on. And clean. Drugs clean, that is, as well as the other, of course. It would really upset me to think of Honorée having to cut her price for the sake of a quicker fix.'

Iles moved some old newspapers and a colander to one end of the moquette settee and sat down with the child on his lap. A few cooked peas had been left in the colander and they came adrift now and slid on to a cushion. Iles scooped these up and presented them to the child to lick from his fingers. He beamed. 'Col, Col, these are some of the happiest sessions in my life – looking after Fanny at home. Some men kick up about

200

babysitting, refuse to do it. Myself, never. She can already call me dadda, you know.'

'I see you as a natural, sir.'

'You'll say they're not going to find any damn thing in the Invet, so why do I fret about the divers?' the ACC replied.

Harpur took a chair opposite him. 'The baby will have your colouring I think, sir.'

'Harpur – the least damage come to Honorée after the Invet trawl and you're at an end, obviously. I know you wouldn't expect to survive that, Col.'

'Your colouring and your wife's features,' Harpur replied.

'Col, I wouldn't say so in Sarah's presence because it would be unkind, but I really don't mind when she goes out alone sometimes and leaves the child and me. Well, who am I telling, for heaven's sake? You have children. You'll know the delight of communing.'

'Is Sarah at a concert, the theatre?'

'Along those lines, I'm told. They're entitled to their little freedoms, aren't they, Harpur?'

'I've always –'

'At least I know she's not having it off with you somewhere, like old times – because you're safe here, aren't you? Nowadays she is mystified at what she ever saw in you, Harpur. Utterly.' He began to shout as he usually did when on this topic and Fanny gazed with merry delight at the tautened shape of his mouth, its sudden blue-purple tinge, and the long flecks of tortured spit. 'We discuss it together often and try to find an explanation. And she's baffled at what she found attractive in Francis Garland, too. Well, especially Francis Garland.'

'Thank you, sir. As a matter of fact, I believe there's quite a play on at the Aspen that absolutely anyone's wife might wish to go to – *amour*, actors talking verse, death scenes with poison, the full thing.'

Iles leaned forward amiably over the child towards

Harpur: 'Col, what I want you to do is put up Honorée at your house for a little while, just until the main peril passes following this Invet betrayal.'

Harpur said: 'Well, sir, I –'

'Of course they're not going to find any fucking thing in the dock,' Iles said. 'Immaterial. It's what's perceived, isn't it?' The ACC became mild, patient, tutor-like. 'You know what I mean, perceived, Harpur? Perceived by whom, you'll ask. All right, perceived by Shale and Ivis and Panicking Ralphy. The word would get around as soon as our diving people arrived at the dock gates. So, what do Shale and so on perceive when they perceive these dry suits and wet suits slime-sifting in the Invet? They perceive someone must have seen something down the Invet at night lately. OK, the diving and dragging might not be to the point – is definitely *not* to the point – but it proclaims we, the police, know all is not right. How do we know? We know because there's been conversation. That's how these people will see things. A lot of folk have heard I'm fond of Honorée, am as it were in touch with her now and then. And they know where Honorée often operates and what she might have seen from her work station at the Invet. They deduce there has been chat between her and me and that there might be more chat, some of it ultimately via a witness box. They have it wrong, and the information comes from elsewhere. Where, incidentally, Col? Doesn't matter. That's how they perceive it and they'll perceive the need to stop any more revelations. How do they stop them? By removing Honorée. A doddle for someone like Ivis. Didn't he kill Big Paul Legge? And haven't they got rid of Slow Victor and Finnane? Haven't they?

'This is why I'm thrilled we can find her safe accommodation with you for a time, Col. You're the intelligent kind who would quite justifiably feel shame at having fingered her, and you would yearn to compensate. That big old dump you've got there in Arthur Street – plenty of space. You won't know she's even with you, Harpur. And neither will anyone else. Oh, I appreciate Mark Lane wouldn't think much of a DCS who gave lodgings to a tart, though I did hear of an officer sheltering a couple of threatened girls in some other Force. There'd be rules, and certainly no question of Honorée bringing toms home. And, even more certainly, not myself.' He chuckled for a while at the ludicrousness of this idea and the little girl chuckled for a while with him and dribbled on his shirt. 'Would I presume on a subordinate's property like that, for God's sake?'

'Dadda,' Fanny said, or something close.

'There!' Iles cried out exultantly.

'It's great to watch and hear, sir. People should see this. I mean, people who think of you as emotionally null.'

'Thanks, Col.'

Harpur was doing well for invitations lately – the Chief's drawing room last night, Iles's tonight at Rougement Place. The Chief's was cleaner. At one end of the ACC's room, piled across the floor, were books that had belonged to Harpur's wife, Megan. After her death he had given them to the ACC who did not mind a read now and then. Because they had been Megan's, the volumes could still bring a little flutter of sadness to Harpur, but he and his daughters had a down on books, and especially Megan's sort. There had been one title, *Edwin Drood*, or something like that, which really said it all as far as Harpur and the girls were concerned. Jill had hung on to a book on boxing and the Orton *Diaries*, but there had seemed no reason to keep the rest. Iles meant to get the books on to shelves eventually.

'When I say I like being left alone with the child, I mean nothing but the purest father-daughter relationship, Col.'

'Grand, sir.'

'Regrettably, so regrettably, one has to spell out such things these days, you know.'

'Not to me, sir.'

'Thank you, Col.'

'I understand.'

'Certainly. Father-daughters yourself. How *is* Hazel?' Iles asked. 'Growing up, growing up, I expect. Obviously, I expect dirty alliances between the Chief and yourself, Harpur. You've got your tiny future to consider.'

'Thank you, sir.'

'And so, the Invet search, deftly planned while I'm absent.' Fanny had fallen asleep. Iles took the child carefully to a large cot which stood near three heaps of books and placed her in it, then covered her with a blanket. He straightened and stood gazing down at the baby, his face vivid with pride and faith in many tomorrows. 'You're not going to let Honorée into your house, are you, you narrow, cowardly sod, Harpur? This damn undergraduate you've got there off and on and her jealousies. She wouldn't allow it. I've known people like you before.'

'What happened to them, sir?' Harpur asked.

'Oh, you'll ask why don't I have Honorée to stay here?' Iles replied.

'No, I wouldn't ask that, sir.'

The ACC stepped away from the cot and for a while walked hurriedly between two mirrors on different sides of the room, comparing how he looked in each and sighing with disbelief at both. Standing before the one near the fireplace he tried a profile pose and gave a small grunt of pain when he accidentally caught the full image of this re-reflected in the other glass. 'Oh, I know you only agreed to put men into the Invet so as to save Lane, Col,' he said. 'And, of course, I sympathise. The Chief's a wreck, but he's a *noble* wreck, and he's *our* wreck, the way the Church of England is ours. You're right, he needs divers to keep him afloat. I hope I'd never deny we have a holy duty to guard his last bits of sanity.'

Iles was wearing the trousers of one of his magnificent navy suits and a white cut-away collar shirt and sporty tie. He had been in London at a meeting of the police rugby committee when the Invet diving operation began or it probably never *would* have begun. The jacket of his suit was hanging on the back of a dining chair and he went and put it on. 'We must go and see Honorée is all right, Col. Now. I have a terrible anxiety about her. Thank you, thank you, for sharing it.'

'Sir, I can arrange some very discreet protection for her if you're –'

'I must see her personally, Col. This is something I – Oh, clearly I'm not actually responsible for putting this unparalleled kid at hazard. That's you, you pathetic crud, you and Mark Frailwit. But I *feel* responsible for the errors of those dependent on me – you and him. I'm like that. At Staff College I was known as "Desmond the Scapegoat". My reports there said I was so incapable of passing the buck I'd never reach the highest rank.'

'Go and see her where, sir?' Harpur asked.

'I don't know how much cash we've got between us, Col,' Iles replied. He put some notes from his wallet on the table. Harpur added fifty. Iles took a fat pink china piggy bank from the mantelpiece and shattered it with one blow of his fist. The pig was full of twenties and tens. 'I slip contributions in for Fanny's marriage portion,' the ACC said. 'That can wait.' He put the savings money with the rest and then sat down at the table and counted all the funds. It came to £380. 'This will be a help for the dear girl,' he said. 'Honorée, I mean.'

'We can't leave the baby, sir.'

'Of course we can't. What kind of parent would do that, for heaven's sake?'

'But perhaps Sarah will be here soon. The play will have ended now.'

'Yes, perhaps. Perhaps.' Iles crossed the room to the cot and lifted Fanny out, wrapped in the blanket. She whimpered a short protest, but that was all. He handed her to Harpur. 'I'll drive,' the ACC said. 'You and Fanny in the back for safety.'

The ACC took them down to the Valencia Esplanade area and they cruised slowly in the big official Rover but could not find Honorée among the girls working along the Esplanade itself nor in Dring Place. Iles drove to Invet Basin and parked near the derelict warehouse. He and Harpur left the car and went to search among Honorée's favourite rubble. The baby nestled warmly against Harpur's chest. Iles had a flashlight, but even so Harpur found it difficult to avoid stumbling over debris while cradling the child. She affected his balance and his view of the ground. Honorée was not there. They returned to Valencia Esplanade and Iles pulled in along-side one of the girls so Harpur could ask about Honorée through the passenger window. Fanny stirred at the voices but did not wake up.

'Oh, lovely, Mr Harpur,' the girl said. 'She's really like you.'

'Honorée? Is she working tonight?'

'Away in a car with a client, or clients,' the girl said.

'Jesus, which car?' Iles asked. 'Which client? Or clients?'

'Just a car. Just a client. Or clients.'

'Did you get the number?' Iles replied.

'Of the car or the clients? Anyway, she should be back by now,' the girl said. 'She'll want one more trick tonight at least.'

'There she is,' Harpur said. Honorée hadn't seen the Rover and was walking with a man away from them over a piece of waste ground towards the shadow of an old bit of wall. At once Harpur and Iles left the car and went after her. In a moment, Iles called her name and she turned, waved and smiled delightedly. She was in a long white dress with a navy or black shawl around her shoulders and even in the dark looked brilliant.

'Des,' she called, 'here's a bright surprise.' She would

have walked back towards Iles, Harpur and the baby but the man with her gripped Honorée's arm suddenly and held her. Although she struggled, he would not let go. He was tall, heavily made, in his late twenties, nobody Harpur recognised.

'I seen her first,' he told Harpur and Iles. 'It's agreed. Terms.'

The ACC said: 'Go along now, laddy, would you?'

'You what you relic?'

'Vice patrol,' Iles replied.

'You what? With a baby?'

'Go along now, laddy,' the ACC replied.

For a second it looked as if the man would attack Iles. His arms and hands twitched. But then he seemed to sense this might not pay, although Iles was only a bit above half his size. Harpur had seen people back off like this before with Iles. They seemed able to spot the ferocity in the ACC, and his tuned street skills. The punter released Honorée. 'I can't fight men in charge of a baby,' he said.

'Of course you can't,' Iles replied. 'That's why we always bring her.'

They walked back to the car with Honorée and climbed aboard, Honorée in the front alongside Iles. The ACC said: 'Harpur thinks you should get out of town at once. I hate the idea. It will be hellish to know you're not around. But Harpur's the nitty-gritty man. I can't argue with that kind of experience. We're going to drive you to the station. Harpur's come up with the standard subsidy for girls in this situation, £380 for rail fare and a room somewhere else for a while. Say Liverpool or Manchester where there's plenty of work. Get on whichever train comes first. Best you don't hang about at the station. Well, when I say the standard subsidy, it's standard *plus*. Col's actually put some of his own money in. It's because he's so ashamed at having endangered you. So you must agree to go, Honorée. Don't make Harpur's pain worse by rejecting the generosity. I know you won't.'

'But when shall I see you again, Des?'

'Soon. She can come back soon, can't she, Harpur? Go quickly, there's a dear. He's afraid for you.'

'And you? Are *you* afraid for me?' she asked. 'I knew it was bad when I saw the baby. It's *your* baby, isn't it, Des? Harpur's just sort of nannying. You're telling me in your sly way you're still a family man, regardless.'

'Harpur does have all kinds of flairs. Of *course* I fear for you. You know it. But what I'm telling you, Honorée, love, is that people will come hunting you, and Harpur can't look after you as well, born nanny though he is.'

He held out the money to her and after a few seconds she took it. 'Yes, I do know you care, Des. I'll phone and say where I am so you can come and bring me back.'

'Yes do, do. Say you're the Association of Chief Police Officers secretariat.'

She leaned over to the back of the car and kissed the child on its woollen hat. 'If it's a parting, though – well, couldn't you drive up on to this patch of ground here. A few minutes. Mr Harpur and the baby will take a little walk. Just to show you haven't gone *all* family values, Des.'

'*Could* you and Fanny take a little walk, Col?' Iles said. 'You two have hit it off, anyone can see. People around here are going to think of you as much more human after this. You could do with that, Harpur.'

Chapter Twenty

Now and then when Ralph Ember felt the galloping approach of senior panic he would force himself to sit down at the table and compose one of his letters to the Press about a truly worthwhile topic, something deep into the human condition. Often this would calm him. He began a letter tonight, and it was working beautifully – as it always worked beautifully – until that duo, Ivis and Luke Malthouse, walked into the club. Well, more *paraded* in, so cocky, Johnny back from the war. Before this Ember had never thought of any pair as being a duo, but that's how these two seemed, a duo. They were looking for him, anyone could tell, eyes everywhere. Jesus, he had left the Bodyguard .38 in his room upstairs. He never expected trouble on his own ground, The Monty.

Although Ember was crouched over the stationery when they first entered, he at once sensed something wrong and looked up before either of them spoke. Always Ember struggled to keep The Monty wholly separate from his other business commitments, such as the trading links with people like Manse Shale and Ivis. Only a few years before Ember bought it, The Monty had been a well-thought-of place for professional folk like accountants and solicitors, even stockbrokers, and he longed to get that reputation back despite the present all-sorts membership. One day he would definitely manage a real clean-out at the club, an upgrading. He had kept all the mahogany and brass fittings for quality, and it was disgusting to see Alf and Malthouse stroll into this setting, so damn relaxed, expecting a welcome.

Ember was behind the bar at the little desk he used for paperwork and had about half a letter to the *Echo* editor completed in pen. He loved a real nib. The downstrokes gave character. Malthouse waved as they crossed the floor past the pool tables, very hearty and amiable, and said, 'Ralphy, you crafty old sod, what you up to there – hatching some way to dodge the fucking Inland Rev, so good luck to you? If the Inland Rev ever got near R. Ember, ha-ha-ha?'

'Excuse me, but could we have a rather pressing word, Ralph?' Ivis said.

'We'll take some of that special Armagnac you pamper your fucking self with,' Malthouse said. 'Jump about a bit, Ralphy. You got customers.' He leaned across the bar and pulled the first sheet of Ember's letter towards him and read it. 'Parks? *Parks*? You writing about parks? What you got with parks then, Ralphy?'

'Just a civic project,' Ember replied.

'You want them to grow weed in the parks?' Malthouse asked. 'Always, always fresh ideas from Ralphy!'

'Ralph's interested in all kinds of general matters,' Ivis said. 'This is another side of him, Luke. Ralph's very much an all-round person.'

Ember reclaimed the piece of paper from Malthouse. These Press contributions made Ralph feel solid, at peace, part of the municipal fabric. He would become an established and respected voice. But as soon as he'd seen Ivis and Malthouse just now, he felt a sweat panic start across his back and thighs. Restart. It was an on-off night. Panics could come and go like that sometimes. He had only begun the letter because he felt unnerved by rough events lately: that know-all and nosy TV woman at the Invet, then the slaughter of Richard Nivette, and now police diving at the docks. Before he started to write he had been wondering in terror whether it was time to get out, right out, perhaps to France or even further. This terror ebbed nicely soon after he picked up his pen and thought parks. Now, it was back.

'You heard they're down in the fucking Basin, have you, Ralphy?' Malthouse said.

'The Invet?' he asked, giving it astonishment.

'You knew?' Alfie replied. 'No need to fret, Ralph. Well, I don't need to tell you. They're way off, wouldn't you say?' He had a small laugh. Ember did not like it. Never laugh at the police. Didn't they have a long time to remind you of it?

Malthouse said: 'There been some talk, some pointers, that's obvious. Not talk that got things right, as Alfie says, but talk just the same. We're not saying talk from you, Ralphy. Not necessarily from you at all, in fact most probably *not* from you because they're in the wrong fucking place, and if you'd give them talk they'd be in the right place. But there *have* been talk. We'd hate to think it was talk from you, Ralphy.'

We? These two were all at once a team then? Lately it had grown hard to keep track of new alliances, some so unbelievable.

Ivis said: 'We think probably a tart. There's an ethnic kid Iles likes who uses buildings at the Basin. She might have seen something.'

'Jesus,' Ember replied.

'Yes, it could be serious,' Ivis said. 'The girl's not around suddenly.'

'Plus there'd be a customer,' Malthouse said. 'We're looking for him. Iles does it in the car or her room, so not Iles.'

'As you'll gather, Ralph, this is a confidential visit, very much so,' Ivis said. He looked about the bar. 'A strategy visit. Could we get a bit more privacy?'

'You're going to really like this plan Alf got, Ralphy,' Malthouse said. 'Oh, you're in it. You *really* figure. This is the future. People got faith in you, Ralphy, regardless.'

Ember did not know if he could walk or even stand yet. His feet felt clothy. Twice he had touched his jaw scar to check it was still dry. He did not want to leave his desk and the letter. The letter was identity, stature. Always he signed his Press contributions, Ralph W. Ember. He yearned to believe this was an utterly different being from the Ralph Ember in the distribution trade, never mind how distinguished a member of that trade he had certainly become. And, of course, absolutely no links existed between Ralph W. and the person he knew some grossly referred to as Panicking Ralph, or even Panicking Ralphy. That's what this slob Malthouse would probably call him on the quiet. There was a kind of protective wall around Ralph W., and Ember meant to make it stouter and higher from now on.

These Press letters had passion and were from his authentic self. Tonight he had been writing his proposal for a health-giving line of parks in new housing developments, so one could walk virtually right across the city without leaving greenery. He'd do a sketch which the *Echo* could probably reproduce. And these green spaces would be properly supervised so they did not degenerate into waste dumps or whore grounds or drug-pushing centres like Fulmar Gardens. Never would he suggest it himself, but eventually, perhaps, one of these amenities could be called The Ralph W. Ember Flower Park. He dearly wanted it known that his contributions to this city went beyond helping build its brilliant, famous non-violent drugs traffic. This hope and the act of writing had soothed and strengthened him tonight and, as he got the good phrases together, he had been thinking what a wonderfully different kind of experience it was from tipping sinkered bodies into the sea and scouring the dockside for a shirt fragment. But suddenly now these two totally unsafe people were on his premises bringing all the shadows back and reminding him the police were not behaving to pattern.

'You heard what he been doing, have you?' Malthouse asked.

'Who?' Ember said.

'Who?' Malthouse gave a muted whistle and shook his thin head a couple of times. 'Fucking who, he says, Alfred. Shale, of course. Manse Shale.'

'It's delicate,' Ivis replied. 'Luke is blunt and quite justifiably angry, Ralph, but things are delicate.'

'You heard of Hector Mills-Mills?' Malthouse asked.

'At the *Eton*?' Ember replied. 'Of course.'

'Yea, at the *Eton*. At the *Eton today*,' Malthouse said. 'But tomorrow? The day after? Manse is bringing the bugger on.'

'Nobody would want to disturb the *Eton*,' Ember replied.

'Oh, nobody wouldn't want to, wouldn't nobody?' Malthouse said. 'You sure, Ralphy? You in touch, Ralphy? You got your head down writing about parks so much, you got no time to think of Hector Mills-Mills.'

Ember hated this kind of conversation in the club, and not just because it might be overheard. He found it unsuitable for The Monty, that's all – The Monty as he wished to think of it, and as he would make sure it actually was one day. This was rough-house conversation. He glanced about. Nobody seemed near enough to eavesdrop. A party along the bar had bets on two girls playing very efficient pool, and there was some cheering and barracking. Ember would stop all that crudeness in the new Monty. Although he did not believe the club could ever be entirely like the Athenaeum or Boodle's in London, he wanted to outlaw noisiness and the kind of coarse language from the men whenever these girls leaned over the table to play shots.

Ember stood and did not feel too bad. He took a bottle of Kressmann Armagnac and some glasses from the shelf and the bar. The three of them went to a table which Ember always thought of as the conference spot

213

in The Monty. It was a largish table and away from the main crush of people, unless the club grew unusually busy. On the wall nearby hung the blown-up framed photograph taken when the club's 1990 summer outing set out to France. The party looked joyful and mild at this stage, though during the trip a Parisian tart was kidnapped for thirty-six hours by Caspar Nottage and Bespoke Vincent, and two pimps given nasty injuries in the fight when they came looking for her. This was the troubling thing about The Monty at present – it could be variable in social calibre.

They took chairs and Ember poured. 'The first person Alf decided he had to see as soon as we got a view of this situation, Ralphy, was Ralphy,' Malthouse said. 'This is the kind of reputation you got.'

'And yet it's by no means a meeting that one rushed into, Ralph. The implications are too grave. I was very aware that you and Manse have a fine and established understanding. May I ask you to think of this little get-together as a search for advice only?'

'Them was the very words he used, Ralphy, I can swear it – a "get-together", that's all. Like informal? It's to ask what you might think of matters, from your experience. Absolutely no fucking commitment. Nothing heavy. Alfie would not do it, would not expect it, at this point.'

Ember said: 'In an arrangement like ours – the one between Mansel and myself, as principals – in that kind of arrangement there will always be little shifts of direction and emphasis. And discussion of the current state of things will always be relevant.'

'Manse will fucking ditch you two,' Malthouse replied. 'He's going to ditch me as well, of course, but what am I – just shit status, not what you call a principal, Ralphy, only a trooper out there? All right, Alfie's not a principal either, not exactly, but he's top management, no question. Or middle, anyway. So, it's as grave for him as for you, Ralphy, if Manse decides he don't want you aboard no more, either of you. Or probably don't want you alive no more, knowing dear Manse and his gun tendency.'

'Things do grow *confrontational*, Ralph – from Manse's side, I mean. Forgive the word, but it's one I can't escape, given recent developments.'

'Alfred tells me he got a piece of your shirt, Ralphy, name tag, the lot. That could of been found in the Invet by this swarm, and then where are you? You're so lucky Alf's sitting on that garment slice. He'll hold that for you. Alfred's method is the method of reasonableness. He's known for it. There was Big Paul Legge, but that was forced on Alf, almost self-defence as I hear and a long time ago, anyway. Alf prefers this sort of solution – a civilised drink in your lovely club that you got a right to be proud of, Ralphy. Whoever done your polishing should get the OBE.'

'I've been uneasy over certain recent developments,' Ember replied.

'Of course you have,' Malthouse said. 'Like Alfie says, confrontational. You're known for that wonderful coolness, that same reasonableness Alfred himself got so much of, and if these recent developments been making *you* uneasy they got to be serious.'

'This is what I mean – confrontational,' Ivis said.

'Alf could give you a list of them developments, yet there's no real need, is there, because you could make a list yourself, Ralphy. Which is why you're uneasy, as you call it – a great, cool word. Many would be scared shitless, I tell you. This is leadership in you, Ralphy. What we'd expect as par for the course.'

'A list starting with Finnane and maybe even with Slow, then going to Nivette and lastly Hector Mills-Mills,' Ivis said.

'Finnane definitely,' Ember replied. 'I don't know about Nivette.'

'Don't fucking know about him?' Malthouse yelled. Someone along the bar turned and stared, but probably nobody ever stared at Malthouse for long, except, say, Iles. Malthouse was not the sort for staring at. 'Who do you think done him, then?' he asked.

'Most likely Denzil,' Ember answered.

'Most likely? *I'd* say most likely. Who else is likely?' Malthouse asked. 'Done by Denzil – like *performed* – but whose orders?'

'You believe it was Mansel?' Ember replied. 'Oh, I thought Denzil going solo, the way he does. Maybe looking for bribe cash.'

'You're generous, Ralphy – known for it,' Malthouse said. 'Generous to Mansel. That's nice, loyal – he's an associate. But is it balls? That's what got to be asked at this point.'

'With respect, this is why I say confrontational, Ralph. This looks to me like Manse deciding something on an impulse and sending Denzil, without reference to you or anyone else. It's as if he was telling us he'd do things the way he wants and we'd better put up with it. Am I wrong to say confrontational?'

'Not in my book you're not, Alf,' Malthouse replied.

'And the way he wants it is raw violence. Why? I'm baffled. Can Desmond Iles ignore the death of an officer? This is the kind of extremism we've striven to avoid for the sake of peace on the streets and an accommodation. And now suddenly this – a break-out into chaos.'

Ember said: 'Oh, I still don't –'

'Giving you the finger,' Malthouse replied, 'the two of you, not to mention the rest of us. If that is not confrontation I never seen confrontation.'

'But worst of all, Hector Mills-Mills,' Ivis said.

'Diabolical,' Malthouse said.

'I don't think I exaggerate when I say provocative, Ralph. An affront.'

It was a hot night but both Ivis and Malthouse had on dark heavyweight suits. Ember insisted on a good dress standard for The Monty and there was a notice in the

216

vestibule demanding jackets and ties for men and no jeans or shorts for men or women. He did not like these two coming here, but he was glad that at least they accepted the rules. Ivis had probably told Luke to get into something decent. With the suit Malthouse wore a white shirt and broad blue and amber tie. He had a wide, undomestic face and scars alongside his right eye. He reminded Ember of diplomats from the old Iron Curtain countries you used to see acting inflexible on TV in the Cold War.

'I think you'll recall, Ralph, that at our last board meeting I proposed Luke should take over Slow's trading beat. To me it seemed the obvious answer to an annoying little problem, acceptable to all.'

'But Manse brings in this fucker Mills-Mills instead,' Malthouse said.

Ivis held up one hand. 'Please, Luke.'

'Squeezing me out after I don't know how much steady work for him,' Malthouse said. 'Bringing in this Mills-Mills who got no salesmanship, no pressure to him, because he don't need them, dealing just with sellers' market toff layabouts at the *Eton*.'

'This was a message from Manse to me – to us all,' Ivis said. 'It was a message saying, in my view, that he, Mansel Shale, had his own scenario for the two firms, and Mills-Mills was part of it, a vital part, not Luke. And why not Luke? Because Manse has protégé plans for Mills-Mills, plainly.'

'This is not just about Slow's beat, Ralphy. You, in person, you're in peril here, regardless of eminence and your club and long-time fine friendship with Manse. This is bringing that Mills-Mills on, so –'

'I've said this meeting is only to seek advice, Ralph, and it is,' Ivis remarked. 'If I may, I'd like to ask you how you see this rejection of my candidate, Luke, and the advancement of Mills-Mills.'

'Don't tell us this haven't got big implications,'

Malthouse said. 'That's what Alfred spotted as soon as he had a whisper about Mills-Mills – implications.'

Ember wished for a disturbance in the club, so he could be drawn away and stay away until these two left. But things stayed quiet. The girls had finished their pool game and there was not even any shouting now. 'I'd need to talk to Manse,' he replied. 'I'd need to know his views, from himself. Manse has usually thought matters through.'

'He'll destroy everything, Ralphy,' Malthouse said. 'He got to be stopped now, but now.'

Malthouse was a piece of wildlife who might eventually turn himself civilised in ten or twenty years' time, if he kept out of jail and made enough money to buy some idleness and decency. The suit, shirt and tie could not do it for him yet. The suit, shirt and tie looked like exhibit labels saying 'Thug, off duty.' This was a lad it would be best not to get too close to, as enemy or mate. Ember saw that this pair were here tonight to recruit an ally against Shale, and the idea pushed him once more hard towards panic. Against *Shale*. Did they really think they could take on Manse, even with Ember's help? He would agree that Shale had become a liability and something needed to be done, but what Ember wanted to do was run – Eurorun at least, and possibly beyond – Australia? Cape Town? – yes, anyway, run, not try to shove Manse under and replace him.

Ivis said: 'Finnane, Nivette, the end of safety on the streets, the jeopardising of the *Eton* franchise – can any business, any combination of businesses, no matter how successful – can any business endure such wounds – self-inflicted, possibly deranged, wounds?'

Malthouse leaned across the table and gripped Ember's wrist for a moment. 'Ralphy, that's a word I know Alfred don't want to use, that term, "deranged", which is why he kept it until the very end. Alf and Manse, they had a sweet business relationship and I know Alf have always respected him and would not want to call him a fucking fruit cake now. But how else we going to see it, such behaviour? Mad. Haven't he got to be removed, Ralphy? It's a duty. A lot of ordinary good folk depend on these businesses and is it right to let him smash them? Remember that movie on TV with Humphrey Bogart the navy captain going to pieces so the officers got to take over to save the ship even though it could be mutiny? That's how I see it now. We want you in with us, Ralphy. It got to be. Don't think we're saying this just because we got a piece of your shirt, name tag et cetera. Probably that don't matter at all. No, this is about knowing we *need* you. Your fucking flair. This is Alfie coming here to say if we cut the life out of Mansel and maybe Denzil and Mills-Mills also we'll want you with us after to help run the future and help prove to Iles that there are still decent lads organising the businesses, lads he knows, lads with a fine place in the community through them letters and parks and this grand club, lads who can go on giving him that lovely peace on the streets, which is the result of good policing and good business management. You're valuable, Ralphy. Couldn't be more.'

'He won't mind my saying it, Ralph, but Luke always pushes to the ultimate, it's his way,' Ivis said. 'Myself, I don't think we'd definitely need to take Manse himself out, or even Denzil. I've no wish for a massacre. But Mills-Mills dead – that would let Manse know what we're thinking. Even after all this, Manse would still have something to give our firms. He has talents, nobody disputes it. And, as Luke says, he's been a mentor to me. I have feelings for him. He could stay in the business, but at a very dropped level, obviously.'

'I don't like it,' Malthouse replied. 'You think Shale's going to let himself get pulled down to office boy?'

'It will have to be quick, Ralph,' Ivis said.

'Now they've done a search of the Invet it will be fine to put Manse down in there – all right, Mills-Mills, then – we slip him to the bottom of the Basin because the search is going to say the Invet's clean as clean,' Malthouse suggested. 'I like looking on the plus side.'

'I don't understand how you come to have this fragment of shirt, supposing it really is mine,' Ember replied. His voice went damn fragile for part of this, but he managed some aggression, too.

'Really yours?' Malthouse said. 'You Ralph W. Ember? That's what I heard, Ralphy. Ralph W. Ember is what the tag says. That tub of genius, Beau Derek, make it available?'

'Just by accident,' Ivis replied. 'Gathered up just by accident with some of the other gear.'

'And kept,' Ember said.

'Oh, yes, kept,' Malthouse replied. 'We got it safe, don't fret. This is the kind of thing that should be stored well out of sight of awkward folk, if possible. This is not something to be found by them divers, nor to get somehow mixed in with say Mills-Mills' body wherever we put it. That would be real fucking carelessness.'

Chapter Twenty-One

'Oh, God,' Denise said. 'We've had something like this before, haven't we, Col? The ghost of Keithy Vine? Someone's tapping a window.'

Harpur was still far gone in half-sleep alongside her and could not manage an answer yet, supposing there *was* an answer to something like that. He had another question to deal with: in his dream a girl he thought he recognised from Valencia Esplanade – white, small, slight, with a lisp, not Honorée – had asked Harpur enviously, 'Are you carrying Desmond Iles's child?'

'Can you hear it?' Denise said.

'People do call here late at night sometimes,' he muttered.

'Jesus,' she said, 'insight. Dig your brain out from wherever it's buried and tell me who exactly it is that's calling tonight.'

'You talk lovely long-winded sentences the moment you're awake. It's education.' Harpur sought black-out for a second longer, tried to mould with the sheets, then made himself sit up. A while ago there used to be an informant called Keith Vine who would visit late for secrecy's sake, but Vine was violently dead. 'If it doesn't stop I'll go down in a minute,' he said.

'Are you expecting anyone?' she asked.

'I'm a police officer. My address is in the phone book. Many people need help. It could be said I'm *always* expecting someone.'

'I know, Saint Col of Arthur Street. Are you expecting anyone?'

'It might be the Chief. He gets nervy in the dark.'

'I was here last time he and his wife came at night, remember? They knocked the front door. This is not the front door. It's like Vine.'

'It's stopped,' he said.

Denise was lying on her stomach with her head raised to listen. She stayed silent for a while. 'Yes,' she said. 'Gone. So, if this is that someone needing a police officer's help at midnight he-she can get lost.'

They were under only a sheet and Harpur rolled it down and rested the side of his face on her bare behind, one of his favourite places of rest.

'Don't go to sleep there,' she said. 'I feel trapped.'

'You are.'

'I hear talking,' she replied.

'No.'

'You're only using one ear.'

Someone pushed open the bedroom door without knocking and switched on the light. Jill, in a floor-length, obsolete Manchester United football shirt, said: 'A voice to see you, dad. It's a fink voice I'd recognise better on the phone, but I decided to let him in all the same because of urgency.'

Harpur, looking up from his spot, could make out the huge frame of a man on the unlit landing behind her. 'Jack?' he said. 'Jack, *here*?'

'I had to see you in a hurry, Col,' Lamb replied. 'I explained to your daughter. You need to get moving.'

Jill came forward and stood close to the bed, but looking away. When Harpur lifted his head off Denise, Jill pulled the sheet up over her. 'You told me to be polite to him so I've been polite to him,' she said. 'We had a discussion while I was deciding if I'd keep him out. He mentioned some bits to do with finking I hadn't thought about before this. Quite sensible bits.'

'Good,' Harpur said. 'I've tried myself.'

'I still hate it,' Jill replied. 'But he doesn't look what I think a fink ought to be like. Not slimy. He's too big – and nice. And he doesn't look like he's bought.'

'As if,' Harpur replied.

'He doesn't look as if he's bought,' Jill said. 'Grammar *now?*'

'It's through sleeping with Denise. No, he's not bought.' Or not the way Jill meant.

'He's dressed like he could buy *you*.'

'As if,' Harpur replied. 'Yes, probably. All of us.'

'In a way it was Fate that I heard him and you didn't,' she said. 'So, I get to talk face to face in depth. It's made a change in me.'

'I couldn't make a change in you,' Harpur replied.

'Fate's bigger,' she said. 'Are you naked, dad? Do you want to get out of bed to go on an emergency but feel shy? It's all right by me. I don't know about Mr Lamb. You're not still in a state of arousal, are you? I expect you're thinking of Lot's daughters in the Bible, when they looked upon their father's nakedness. But that means a lot more than what it says, you know.'

'Ah.' Harpur climbed out of bed and dressed. 'Yet you had to cover Denise.'

Jill said: 'Different. I'll leave you now and in the morning I'll tell Hazel that as finks go Mr Lamb is all right. I don't know if she'll wear it, mind. She's more set in her ways through age.'

'Try,' Harpur replied.

Lamb shifted out of the doorway to let her go back to her bedroom. She paused and shook hands with him. 'Sorry about the past,' she said. 'The rudeness and so on. I was such a child.'

Denise turned over and hunched herself up for sleep. 'You'll be going out,' she said.

'He must,' Lamb replied. 'Quickly.'

'I'll do breakfast,' Denise said.

'I'll be back by then,' Harpur said.

'Will he?' Denise asked Jack.

'He might be,' Lamb replied.

She turned on to her stomach again and lifted her head, the lizard-in-wait pose, her breasts more or less concealed. 'What's that mean? It's dangerous?'

'Complicated,' Lamb said. 'It might take a while.'

'Complicated equals dangerous?' she asked.

'Not necessarily,' Lamb replied.

'But?' she asked.

'Complicated,' Lamb said.

'So what is it?' Denise asked. 'Security says you never come to his house. Why now?'

'Not a phone matter,' Lamb replied. 'And no time for anything else.'

'Can he just pull you out of bed like this, Col?' she snarled. 'Is he . . . well, is he *entitled*?'

'Oh, yes,' Harpur said.

'You owe?' she asked.

'I owe. He owes. That's why he's here. How things work. It's not in police training manuals, but that's how things work.'

She folded back down in the bed. 'Magic circle. I'm outside it.'

'So complicated,' Lamb replied.

'Fuck off both of you,' she said.

'I'll go with him, if you're afraid,' Lamb replied.

'Would that be good, Col? Are you armed? Of course you're not. Is *he*?'

In Lamb's car, Jack said: 'I won't be able to come close, Col.'

'To what?'

'God, you're lucky to have someone like me,' Lamb replied. 'The widest of wide views.'

'The Chief's the same. It turns him sickly.'

'I worry about Mills-Mills,' Lamb replied.

'About Hector? We're on our way to the *Eton*?'

'I'd have gone direct. But can I act alone?'

'Act?' Harpur said.

'Ivis and Luke Malthouse have been talking very rough about Mills-Mills tonight.'

'How do you know, Jack?'

It was the kind of question Lamb always ignored. Tipsters never answered on sources. Harpur asked as a routine only. But tonight Jack said: 'I get whispers from a pool-playing girl I've been kind to once or twice and who knows the general scene.'

'Pool? Ivis and Malthouse talking business at The Monty? Ember won't like that.'

'Ivis, Malthouse, Ralph,' Lamb replied.

'No Shale?'

'Ivis, Malthouse, Ralph. You know Shale's been in negotiations with Mills-Mills?'

'Negotiations?' Harpur replied.

'Christ, you *don't* know. As a detective what do you detect, Col? You're *so* lucky to have me. The widest of wide views. Manse was down the *Eton* the other night.'

'Your pool-playing lady there, too?'

'If Shale is strolling the deck of the *Eton* colloquing everyone knows. Except you.' Lamb was driving one of the smallest Citroëns, his great shoulders hunched around the wheel like dogs with a hare. It was dark but Harpur had the impression of big solemnity in Jack's face. Oh, Christ, that meant he would offer his gospel of grassing again. Lamb was the world's greatest informant, but always felt he had to explain why he did it. 'Hector Mills-Mills is nothing to me, just a high-table pusher,' Jack said. 'But Manse Shale – he's a customer. He's bought pictures, you know.'

'I've seen them at his place. Ginger-headed women in purple dresses.'

'Pre-Raphaelite, yes. I feel a link with folk I deal with. Art's a personal thing, Col.'

Yes, personal between Jack and Harpur, too. 'You want paintings to go to a good home, like kittens,' Harpur said. 'Shale told me those artists were a brotherhood. He liked that. It's the same for you and him, is it?'

'I don't go blabbing about everything I hear, do I, Col?' Lamb replied. 'There's many a matter I could tell you about and don't.'

'You have a lot of loyalties, Jack, all sacred.'

'I'm not some non-stop dirty fink.'

'Even Jill admits that now,' Harpur said.

'This is Ivis and Malthouse trying a coup on Shale. Maybe Ember's come in on it, too, tonight.'

'Didn't the pool ears hear that?'

'They'll start with Mills-Mills, I'd guess. Isolate Manse, then dispose of him. That upsets me, and so I tell you. I don't mean only the art connection. When I say "the wider view" you'll see now what I'm getting at, Col. You're looking at the overthrow of a system.'

'Iles won't like it, either.'

'Alfie, Ralph, Malthouse, Beau running the firms – can you visualise it, Col? Honestly? Four nothings. We'd have London, Manchester, Liverpool crews all deciding they could come in and blast them out of the way. Carnage again.'

'You think like Iles on some things and like the Chief on others. I'll get you a peaked cap and whistle and you can take over here.'

They drove on to the docks. Lamb said: 'We've got a tail.'

'Since when?'

'Not long after your house. I wasn't sure in the traffic but it's still with us, lying well back.'

Harpur did not turn to look. 'What car?'

'Panda.'

'It could be Denise.' Now he did turn, then waved. She flashed. 'Denise frets. She's young, but she frets. And she can't be passive, has to intercede.'

'This is a girl who thinks a hell of a lot of you, Col.'

'Off and on.'

'Nobody should expect more than that,' Lamb replied.

'Yes, I do.'

'You'll get hurt then.'

'I do,' Harpur said.

'But you're lucky it can still happen at your age – very late thirties now?'

'Lucky to get hurt?'

'Sure,' Lamb replied. 'You're alive emotionally – pain, joy, frustration, satisfaction, they're all pluses at your era.'

'Is that right?'

'No, it's shit,' Lamb replied. 'But I'm trying to make your life sound tolerable. This is a noble girl. She'll leave her bed for you and go into the unknown.'

'Here's the unknown now,' Harpur replied. 'Yes, stay back.'

Lamb parked on the far side of some rail trucks, out of sight of the *Eton*.

'They wouldn't do him on the boat, Jack. Too public.'

'Of course not. As he leaves. Other people from the *Eton* have been picked up and finished like that. Just hope it's been a busy night and he's still there. Sometimes he shuts down his spot and goes home early.'

Harpur looked around the quayside. 'I don't see anyone waiting.'

'You wouldn't, would you? If *you* could see them, Mills-Mills could see them and wouldn't come down the gangplank. People who work the *Eton* know about hazard.'

Denise pulled in alongside them and waited in her car gazing ahead. Harpur left the Citroën and she got out of the Panda then. 'We're going on the *Eton*, are we?' she asked.

'Me. I'*m* going on the *Eton*. You wait with Jack.'

'What is it?'

'Just a check,' he said.

'Right, I'll come.'

'Not necessary.'

'I'll come,' she said. 'I'm here now, so I'll come. There might be trouble.'

'Denise, love, there won't be, and what could you do if there was?'

'What can *you* do?'

'You're not dressed for it. This is a select place.' She was in jeans and denim jacket over a T-shirt with *The Beautiful And Damned Unavailable* on it in red letters, some sort of book joke, he thought, but couldn't ask, obviously.

She began to walk swiftly ahead of him towards the restaurant. He caught up. Bouncers on the deck would see him approach, of course, and get on their two-ways to make sure no dealing could be seen by the time he reached the bar. Only Mansel Shale was in there when he and Denise arrived, and Shale was about to go. There seemed few people aboard. Mills-Mills' trading spot looked as though it had been shut down a while ago, the table cleaned over and the ashtray empty.

'Manse,' Harpur said, 'here's a treat.'

'I've only just arrived,' Shale replied.

'And now you're leaving.'

'Don't go because of us,' Denise said. 'Please. It's only a check.'

'This is your . . . this is your friend, is it, Mr Harpur?'

'His friend, yes,' Denise replied.

'Nice,' Shale said.

'It is, generally,' Denise said. 'I get all kind of nights out.'

'You're very late,' Shale said.

'But so are you,' Denise replied. 'Why are *we* so late, Col?'

228

'I wanted a word with Mills-Mills,' Harpur said.

'Mills-Mills? Is that a person?' Denise asked.

'Why?' Shale replied.

'Did *you* come down for a word with him?' Harpur asked.

'With Mills-Mills?' Shale replied.

'Who is he?' Denise asked.

'You've missed him, have you, Manse? Like us. Are you going over to his place now?'

'To Mills-Mills' place? Why, Mr Harpur?'

'To see he's all right.'

'*Is* he all right, Col?' Denise asked.

'Well, if you're worried about Mills-Mills we could go to his flat if you like,' Shale said.

'Yes, I'm worried,' Harpur replied.

When Shale, Denise and Harpur appeared at the top of the gangplank, Shale's Jaguar with Denzil at the wheel emerged from behind an ancient shack on the dockside and came over to pick Shale up. Shale held the rear door open for Denise and Harpur. 'I'm here in my friend's car,' Harpur said. 'We'll follow.'

'Denzil will drive you to her vehicle.'

'I saw two cars arrive,' Denzil said.

'Really?' Harpur replied.

'Yes, really.'

They drove to the Panda. Jack and his Citroën had gone. The Jaguar led to a street not far from where Harpur lived. Denzil locked the car and came with them. They tried the bell of a first-floor flat in a big old converted terraced house. There was no reply.

'This could be disturbing, couldn't it?' Harpur asked.

'Why?' Denise said. 'Perhaps he's got a girl somewhere.'

'Perhaps he has,' Harpur replied. 'Has he, Manse?'

'Mills-Mills? I wouldn't know much about his private life. But it looks as if you'll have to come back to the

Eton tomorrow if you want to see him.' He glanced at his watch. 'Or I should say later today.'

'You've got a funeral for the dead cop soon, Harpur, haven't you?' Denzil asked. 'Tragedy.'

'Yes, a funeral. He *would* be dead, wouldn't he?' Harpur replied.

Chapter Twenty-Two

Ralph Ember drove out to have another look at the place where Alf Ivis lived. This was not long after dawn, about 4.30 on a misty, warm summer morning, a morning that spoke backbone to him. He felt all right. Sometimes, when he decided to do something, *really* decided, he could reach this state, absolutely above dreads. At such moments he knew his filthy nickname to be unjust. There was nothing Panicking about *this* Ralph. He saw himself as solid, capable, an early bird on a worm hunt. The stillness heartened him. The undisturbed air gave nourishment, sweetly backdropped his poise.

He had slept for just over two hours after that meeting at The Monty with Ivis and Malthouse. Margaret grunted and opened an eye when he got up and Ember said he could not remember switching on the club alarms and felt troubled. He would have to check. 'If anyone's going to break in they'll have done it by now,' she said. 'It's day, isn't it?'

'I can't rest in bed.'

That much was true. He had shut his eyes only – not really slept – while his mind worked and took him through to the decision. Ember did not resent Margaret lying there mind-dead, know-all and womanly like that, making comments. She could not be told what Ivis and Malthouse were planning, and how did you explain to a wife that the dynasty might depend on an old bit of shirt used as a floor cloth? The way Ember saw things, a man should take aboard most of the main cares of a marriage, particularly when he was a business head. It would be damned inconsiderate to burden Margaret with all that matter of the Invet and concrete fence posts, or with the grim possibility that Alf Ivis and even Malthouse might have to be killed. That is, have to be killed by him, Ember, alone, personally. Beau Derek would be useless. Beau? Brilliant at some skills but a joke in any wipe-out situation. He would say so himself, sort of boast of it, the eternal scruffy idler.

In fact, the need to remove Ivis and Malthouse was a lot more than a possibility, supposing Ember decided to stay and not withdraw with his family overseas. He could read Alfie, and had read him so thoroughly last night. Ivis, that born second-string, was ready to try his grand career move. This had been on blazing show in his face. Usually, those meat and two veg features registered not much at all, but they were vivid with ambition this time, his eyes a conqueror's. He had set himself up in that mad lighthouse so perhaps ambition and a lust for status had always been around, but he kept them leashed until Shale's turn to Hector Mills-Mills edged Ivis now into hurt revolt.

Alf would get rid of Hector as the immediate threat and then probably dispose of the betrayer Shale. Once Ivis committed himself to doing Mills-Mills he would be bound to do Manse. Hector might be already dead. Those two had come to The Monty last night looking for Ember's backing. He had not offered it, not actually spoken approval. But he had not objected, either. They would interpret that the way they wanted to, as a nod, an Ember nod, and as such supremely influential – the nod of a renowned chieftain. *Yes, remove Mills-Mills, then Mills-Mills' patron, Shale.* They would not draw Ralph into the actual executions, of course, rating him as beyond labourer's work. But, after they had dealt with Manse, Ivis would need Ember for a while to soothe Iles and other police. Ralph gave continuity and weight. These were invaluable strengths for any business, but

especially one that depended on so many subtle under-
standings. Those two struggling freaks, Alfie and Luke,
had actually admitted it, described why they wanted
Ralph with them. He was their Platinum Card.

Not for ever, though. Once Alfie had the new outfit
established he would come to regard Ember as just
another likely menace to his position. Anyone could
forecast that. It was classic. Ivis wanted dominance,
solodom. Malthouse would prop him and protect him,
but never be allowed true power, the way Ivis had never
been allowed true power by Manse. Like all the jumped-
up, Alfie would be terrified of any partner with real
stature, Ember included, Ember above all. It was everywhere in history – conspirators came together to win
control, and then butchered one another out of rivalry
and fear. Look at almost any new African state. Look at
Stalin and Trotsky. Look at those murderous leadership
battles on the Left after the French Revolution. Look at
that trio who took over from Julius Caesar. Ember had
picked up many stark lessons from his mature student
degree course, in suspension for now because of business demands. And the main lesson he saw in all of it
was, Act early. Or 'Do it to them before they do it to
you,' as the desk sergeant used to say in *Hill Street Blues*.
Until tonight he had never applied this teaching to his
own life, and when he did the idea immediately caused
him a rush of dizziness, even lying by Margaret in bed,
hopelessly awaiting sleep. Simultaneously, he had
begun a heavy, panic sweat down his back and arms.
Just the same, that blunt text, Act early, had stayed, and,
once he had settled with himself that this was how he
would play things, Ralph calmed, grew strong almost
and determined.

He dressed properly in a suit, white shirt and silver-
dot amber tie, and shoulder-holstered the neat Bodyguard, which he had brought home with him. He
strapped a small jemmy to his left forearm, enough to
do a window. How many years since he last carried a

jemmy? What did he feel about it now? Rejuvenated? Or appalled at the slide? He would have liked to wear something looser than the suit jacket but this afternoon he and Margaret had a vital appointment with their daughter Fay's headmistress about subject choices for the girl's future years, and it comforted Ralph to clothe himself for that rather than for a probably violent visit to Alf's. These days, overseeing his daughter's education seemed far more part of a worthwhile life than breaking into Ivis's den and maybe breaking into Ivis. The girl attended the kind of private school where parents did wear formal outfits to see the head. Would Ralph W. Ember send his girl to any other?

He parked a long way from the lighthouse. It was on a piece of headland outside the city and remote enough for the sound of a vehicle to be noticed so early. In the past it must have helped guide ships into the docks. He did not know how that was done now. The reefs were still out there. Moving pretty fast and slightly crouched, he approached on foot across fields. Larks rose from their ground nests ahead of him and hung in the warm air belting out music. To him they sounded like victory. He still felt good, sweatless, his legs brilliant, heart steady, no banging at his ribs. The SAS would be trained to this kind of dawn surprise over rough ground, and he was in a tradition.

He had no plan. That did not matter. He disliked plans. They were always liable to go wrong and if they did and you could not adapt you were lost. He had known such disasters in security van raids and bank jobs, and only through cleverness and a special gifted speed had he survived and profited when others had not. Today, best to see how things went and look for openings. He might do no more than remind himself of the layout here. And then he could come back, perhaps at night, and see to Alfie, maybe on his way in or out. People were relaxed and least on guard near their homes, even a home like this.

Of course, Ember had been here before, when they assembled for their visit to the Invet. The bedrooms occupied the base and first floor of the lighthouse tower and the living rooms were in a long single-storey building that joined it and once contained the foghorn. This was just the sort of place you could imagine some big-ideas serf like Alfie going for.

Ember felt sorry for his family. Well, yes, he felt sorry for his family and would feel more sorry still for his family afterwards. Ember had a heart as well as a hard brain. But Alf was not the only one with a family to think about. His mistake was to reach out for what he could never be entitled to or capable of keeping. In his stupid search for this he did not care who was damaged. So, he must expect come-back. Whatever happened Ember would try not to harm Ivis's wife and children, except obviously for the emotional harm that could come through mourning Ivis. Alfie would be dear to them regardless. There were three children, weren't there, a girl and two younger boys? Oh, God, let them and their mother keep clear. Ember touched the Bodyguard through his jacket and then his jaw scar. For a moment his legs grew shaky. He loathed himself for these signs of weakness. SAS? He was idiotic. Would the SAS fall into such doubts when almost at a target, for God's sake? He stopped briefly, shielded by a hedge, and took long breaths. He could smell the grass and vegetation and perhaps the salt of the sea. The mixture had to be helpful. He was part of this landscape, wasn't he?

But he wondered whether he should have brought Beau. Although it was true he would be only a liability at a killing, Beau knew breaking and entering and still did it now and then. Hadn't Ember sent him to look over Nivette's place for the money? An ex-lighthouse would not worry Beau. In a way, Beau *ought* to be here. It was his damn carelessness that had given Ivis the shirt fragment. Beau should have been compelled to search for it now in the lighthouse and make up for that error. Alf might have the piece in a safe, which would require someone with Beau's skills to open. But Ralph did not really expect a safe. The inside of Alfie's place was so low quality it looked as if he could hardly afford furniture let alone expensive extras.

Ember moved forward. His legs would do it. Of course they would. This was *his* mission. He was Ralph Ember or Ralph W. Ember, and these names signified. Panics could be no part of him. One reason he had not included Beau was that he felt he should handle the whole operation himself. He needed to know he could still act when he was threatened, could still smash an enemy and look after his own and his family's future, as well as the future of a friendly career underling like Beau. One of Ember's central values was belief in the family, and no matter what he did outside marriage that belief never weakened. This was one reason he would be going with Margaret to see the head teacher today.

He opened a gate and went into the lighthouse yard. The Land Rover was at one end, though without its roof rack now. Alf must fear the vehicle had been seen at the dock or later and that the rack might give a lead. Taking a couple of careful steps at a time and putting his feet down very gently on the terrace Ember moved to a window in the single-storey building. There were curtains but they had not been drawn. Out here that would be unnecessary. It was the same at Low Pastures. Ember had read that upper-class families in country houses thought it suburban to hide behind curtains. Neighbours could not nose because there weren't any. Ember looked in. They had used this room briefly when preparing their Invet trip. It was grimly furnished with sixties and seventies stuff Ivis must have bought from house clearance shops. Ember remembered a couple of sadly thin and faded carpets on the boarded floor. He had heard Shale joke about them once behind Ivis's back and say he felt scared something incurable would creep up his legs from these carpets and finish him.

As his eyes methodically surveyed the room now Ember realised he was hoping to see his bit of shirt somewhere on view, and a thought had slipped into his head that if he could spot this he would force a window, take the fragment and disappear. Immediately, he felt ashamed of such stupidity and weakness. Something so valuable would not be on display. In any case, there should be more to the job than a cleaning cloth. Pathetic to imagine this operation could be so simple.

He rolled back his sleeve, released the jemmy, forced the window and climbed in. He restrapped the jemmy and undid his jacket so he could reach the holster easily and unbuttoned it. For a couple of seconds he stood near the window and listened. Nobody, not even Beau, could force a latch quietly. So, did he hope Ivis had heard and would come looking? If Alf entered through that far door from the tower end he would be nicely framed and with enough light behind him. But, of course, Alf would never do anything so crude. This was a man who had killed Big Paul Legge. More likely he would go out into the yard and come at Ember from behind, firing through the window. Swiftly, Ralph turned to look and dropped again into a half crouch so none of him would be above the window sill. He had been able to keep his breathing in here subdued until now, but suddenly he was sucking hard at the air in shock and fright.

He made himself move from the window, not just because of the danger there but to convince himself his legs would still do it. On the other side of the room he began to work systematically through the two drawers of an orange-brown bulge-fronted sideboard, looking for his piece of shirt. It was important to be systematic, as important as being able to walk. Both showed he was nowhere near breakdown. No, it was more: both showed this lone project could turn out one of Ralph's most splendid triumphs, and that was to say plenty, damn it.

In the upper drawer he found tea cloths and table napkins and a case of fish knives and forks, the kind of thing friends and relatives of Alf might give as a wedding present. When he began on the second drawer he had to lift out some old copies of *Punch* and a collection of newspaper supplements about the history of the Royal Navy. As he removed the last batch of these supplements he suddenly found himself reading his own name, Ralph W. Ember. For a moment his only reaction was irritation at having anything that had belonged to him inside this foul piece of furniture no distance from fish knives. Next, though, he realised that a part of the triumph he had promised himself was here already, happening. He smiled and could have cheered. Tenderly he lifted the monogrammed piece of shirt out of the drawer, kissed it twice, and put it folded into his jacket pocket. He replaced the printed material and closed the drawer. Of course that was only a formality. Alfie would see the forced window, know at once what it was about and go to look in the drawer. It was the sort of primitive hiding place you would expect from someone as low calibre as Alfie. He did not know about real thinking and decision-making. How could he? That was why his attempt to clamber to the top was so foolish and presumptuous and doomed.

Yes, doomed. Suddenly it struck Ember that he could not really leave here without killing Alfie. The shirt triumph *was* a triumph, but . . . Once Ivis found the place had been entered and the piece of cloth gone he would naturally realise who had taken it and be on instant special guard against Ember. The kind of surprise night ambush that Ralph had visualised would become impossible. In fact, Alfie might not wait for the next move by Ember. It would be clear that once Ralph had the shirt piece he might betray them to Shale. Perhaps Ivis and Malthouse would come gunning for

Ember, and Ivis knew about gunning. There was Big Paul Legge, and there was Finnane in the bottom of the boat. Ember began a sweat and felt his shoulders start to lock. He put out a hand to prop himself on the sideboard. He was going to have to wait here or in the yard and knock over Alfie this morning. *This morning.* That had always been an option. Now, though, it was not an option. A requirement. Had he done something he had always excelled at *not* doing, left himself without an exit? He was appalled.

But, of course, there *was* an exit. He could get back out through the window and run. And run. He could even use the front door and run. And run. Whichever way he took, the running was the thing. All right, Ivis would know he had been there and might come after him with Malthouse. Ember could run again, though – out of the country. That had been in his mind, anyway, and discussed occasionally at home. Fay loved the idea of settling in France and possibly joining Venetia at her school near Poitiers. This might be better for her, anyway. Didn't it enrage Ember that Fay's school here had dropped Latin and Greek and was giving pupils the Classics only in translation? 'Soundbite Aeschylus' he called it. Ember had protested and lost, but would certainly mention it again at the meeting with the headmistress today. Things were not like that in Venetia's school. Everywhere in this country, compromise and shoddiness. If he knew the languages himself he would have taught Fay at home. Obviously he could leave the jemmy and probably the gun in his car before going to meet the headmistress, especially if the gun had been fired and smelled of cordite. Like most people, he had a range of very different roles. He was a parent, an undergraduate on sabbatical, a civic figure and a competitive businessman forced now and then into extreme actions.

True, a move abroad could not be done in an orderly way now, because he must get himself, Margaret and

Fay away fast. The Monty and Low Pastures would have to be shut down and sold in his absence. Not ideal, but not impossible. Yes, run for God's sake. It was mad to let a damn piece of shirt dictate his programme. God, the stupid arrogance of having his name sewn in like that, so exact – Ralph-fucking-W.-Ember, in case there turned out to be another Ralph Ember and identification was disputed.

And then as he leaned there dazed near Alf's sideboard he became aware of something new. Oh, Jesus, he thought he heard movement from the far end of the room, possibly on the stairs of the lighthouse tower. The sounds were careful, like someone stalking, or like a woman or child very nervously but very bravely coming to investigate a sound. Yes, the jemmying had been heard. It was idiotic not to have brought Beau. He could have found a way in without any breakage. Ember put aside his thought that this could be Alf's wife or one of the children, somebody harmless. It would be Ivis himself, no question. Alf had placed himself at the head of a very dangerous plot and would be alert to trouble even while he slept. Of course he would be armed. Ralph looked towards the window and wondered whether he could get to it in time. Now, it was Ember who would be framed as a target if Ivis appeared while Ralph climbed out. God, he did not want to die falling back into a ramshackle room like this and on to one of those carpets.

Just the same, he must attempt to get across the floor and to the window. He could not risk the front door now. He might meet Alfie in the hallway. Gradually he relinquished his hold on the sideboard and made himself stand unsupported. He could do it. He turned his body slowly towards the window and tried to move. But his legs would not function, not even for those half-dozen steps. His fucking feeble treacherous legs in their fine Cachape and Drew tailoring refused to answer. They were wet with at least sweat and numbed by terror. He waited a little while, still listening and staring off and on up the room towards the door, and then again attempted to walk. Paralysis as before. There would be no running, not out of here, not to Europe or South Africa, either.

Instead, Ember folded down against the sideboard and as quietly as he could pulled an easy chair on its uneven castors in front of him as a shield. He brought out the pistol. Could he hold it steady? He raised the gun and jammed his arm against the sideboard to stop it waving about, that grand, helpful, pathetically cheap, vile sideboard.

The sounds on the stairs were a lot nearer. The foot-steps still seemed very light. At his basic rank Ivis would be into all the basic skills and one of the basic skills was how to tread gently in a manhunt. Ember covered the doorway and by a couple of small, sharp shakes of his head struggled to clear the vatfuls of scalp sweat from his eyes. His legs felt slightly better. That could happen sometimes when action seemed very close. How could he have successfully exited so often otherwise? But it was too late to exit now.

'Disappointed is I think the word,' he told Fay's head-mistress. 'Yes, disappointed. I said to Margaret when I first heard of the proposal that if a school like this can't give pupils a full classical grounding I don't see what hope there is for the subject. I don't believe there has been a similar falling off in European schools. Well, I *know* there has not. Our other daughter, Venetia, is completing her education near Poitiers, and I'm happy to say is learning both Latin and Greek, and when I say Latin and Greek I mean the languages themselves, not texts in translation.'

'This is one of Ralph's enthusiasms,' Margaret Ember stated.

Ember said: 'It's well known that many of our greatest

figures in public life had a proper training in the Classics and were subsequently able to apply the discipline they acquired in those studies to the demands of business, politics and, yes, statesmanship. Think of Harold Macmillan. He could deal with all those problems – Christine Keeler, winds of change – because far back he had read Homer and so on in the true tongue.' He gave a small wave with his left hand to dismiss the topic. 'But enough said. That battle has been lost and objections are pointless.' It was nice to have easy use of his arm now the jemmy was no longer strapped there.

'May I raise one point, Mr and Mrs Ember?' the headmistress replied. 'Fay has spoken now and then of the possibility that you might all move to France. I wonder whether that is still under consideration? Or do I deduce from your kindly calling here today that there is now no likelihood of such a change and that Fay will complete her schooling with us?'

'France has certainly been a possibility,' Ember said, 'hasn't it, Margaret? Why I mentioned Poitiers. But, no, we don't now see that as on the cards in the near future. There have been changes in circumstances, business circumstances, which have caused a rethink. We will stay, and Fay will remain here.'

'Good,' the headmistress replied. 'Forgive me, do, for cross-questioning you in that way, but we have such pressure for places in the upper forms. I need to know accurately how our numbers will look in the coming years. People remain unhappy with the comprehensive schooling system and at the same time might not want to send their children away to boarding school – the separation involved and, indeed, the expense. And so they turn to us.' She paused, as though deciding something. 'I mention what follows only because of the dreadful fortuitous relevance to our discussion today on the pressure for places.' Ember saw she wanted to soften him up with some little secret after his remarks about the Classics, and also wanted to prove how sought-after the school was even so. She leaned forward over her desk. 'In confidence, I can tell you that we had recently a very pressing inquiry about a place here for his daughter from the man reported on today's lunchtime news to have been shot to death in his own home – the famous converted lighthouse, I mean.'

'Awful,' Margaret said.

'Ivis,' the headmistress said. 'Alfred Ivis. Yes, only a few days ago he came to see me.' She had been speaking quietly but lowered her voice further. 'I gather some possible gang war aspect, so perhaps I won't be altogether sorry if in the changed family conditions the daughter does not arrive. One has to be so careful, as you can imagine. Parents such as yourselves might be quite anxious if they thought their daughter was a fellow pupil with a child from such a background.' She sat back, reddened a little. It suited her. She was young for the job, fresh-skinned, slim, her hair almost blonde. Ember felt she might turn out fuckable at some stage during Fay's schooling. 'Does that sound harsh, snobbish?' she asked. 'Nonetheless, it *is* a consideration. And especially as the gangs concerned would appear to be trading in drugs. There are enough problems of that kind around for youngsters without creating new risks by admitting such a child.'

'Ivis, yes,' Ember replied. 'I did hear about that incident. Drugs, you say? I think I've bumped into him once or twice. I must say he struck me as an ordinary sort of small businessman. Boating equipment?'

'Oh, they often have what is called "a front", Mr Ember – some totally respectable company to conceal their real interests,' she explained.

'As a matter of fact he did not seem to me to be doing very well,' Ember replied. 'I'm surprised he –'

'I think he expected some kind of rapid improvement in his prospects which would enable him to consider private education now for the girl and two sons. One has to wonder whether that expected improvement is in some manner related to his death. These terrible drug "turf wars" as they are called are always ultimately about money, aren't they?'

'I hate to think of his daughter being excluded from the school because of such a tragic event,' Ember replied.

'That's a commendably liberal view, if I may say,' the headmistress replied, 'but I'm not sure it would be shared by all our parents. This girl might well have been in Fay's class. Of an age, I believe.'

'Ralph *is* liberal about that kind of thing,' Margaret said.

'I'm afraid this is a case of "the sins of the fathers" as the Old Testament puts it,' the head replied.

'Yes, well one of the subjects Margaret and I would certainly like Fay to continue with is Religious Knowledge. In a time of very uncertain values Bible studies can provide a real moral foundation for children. And not simply for children. I myself was doing a degree down the road until I had to take a year or two out and I found a basic course in Religious Knowledge a wonderful guide and . . . yes, and consolation.'

Chapter Twenty-Three

The Chief wanted to see where Alf Ivis was shot and he drove Iles and Harpur to the lighthouse in the Senator and parked next to Alfie's Land Rover. They would go on from there to Richard Nivette's funeral. Lane and the ACC wore their pale blue dress uniforms. Harpur was in a suit. Ivis's body had been removed and his family were gone to stay with relatives. The lighthouse was under guard. None of the bloodstaining had been cleaned up and the entry window still hung open.

They stood in the long living room and Iles said: 'Given time, I believe Alfie might have made this place attractive. He had flair, though you needed patience to find it. And the money would have come in if Col's right and Ivis plus Luke Malthouse were expecting to displace Shale.'

'But how can we know that?' Lane demanded.

'Harpur knows. We don't ask how, sir. Harpur communes.'

'Do we say Shale shot Ivis, then – pre-empting?' Lane asked.

'He's alibied again, sir,' Harpur replied. 'Well alibied according to Francis Garland. So's the chauffeur this time.'

Iles was looking at the blood streaks down the door frame and wall alongside. 'On the whole, I'm not opposed to a death like this,' he told them over his shoulder. 'It could settle things. Conditions will revert to balance.'

'Balance?' the Chief said. 'What does that mean, Desmond?'

'Oh, you know my obsession, sir – peace, that's all,' Iles replied.

'And is this peace?' Lane asked, pointing at the stains.

'Peace along the highways and byways, sir. There's something neat and private about a hit in a muted foghorn room, don't you think?'

'But *was* it private?' the Chief cried. 'A child involved, I think.'

'One of Ivis's children, only, sir,' Iles said. 'If your father's Alfie you have to expect some snottiness in your life. But the rough stuff is kept within the family, you see. Yes, sir, private.'

Harpur crouched near the sideboard and looked towards the door. 'Where the shot came from, probably,' he told Lane. 'Ivis's twelve-year-old daughter tells us she thought she heard something in one of the living rooms and came downstairs from the first floor in the tower to look. She stood in the doorway here and saw the window had been forced and a chair moved. She's a bright kid and didn't let on she'd noticed anything wrong but turned and went back into the tower and woke her father. He and Mrs Ivis sleep on the ground floor. Alf immediately got out of bed and went to a drawer in the dressing table, presumably to get the automatic he had in his hand when we found him, unfired. Ivis was naked and the girl says she turned away, out of modesty, I expect. Some young girls are like that. Not my own, but some. She was going to lead to the foghorn room, show him what she'd spotted. Alf probably didn't want the girl risking herself again and rushed to stop her – to pull her back and get ahead of her. And he did, but it meant he was framed in the living-room doorway and a fine target for someone in position here, partly screened by the chair. Obviously, Alf would never have done anything so careless if it

246

hadn't been for the child. As soon as he'd been shot, the girl bent down to try to help him, was talking to him, pleading with him not to die, she says. She pulled off her nightdress and attempted to plug the hole in his chest with it.'

'So much sad nakedness,' Iles said.

'My God,' the Chief replied.

Harpur stood up and crossed the room. 'We assume the gunman left by this window and ran while she was preoccupied. She says she did not see or hear anyone go.'

Iles joined Harpur at the window and stared out. 'I've spoken flippantly, harshly about that little girl,' the ACC said. 'There are times when I'm the shit of shits, Col.'

'Many have noticed that, sir,' Harpur replied.

They drove to the funeral and waited in the car outside the church for the arrival of the Home Secretary and the local MPs, including Finnane's. Iles was due to give at least a Bible reading and possibly an address about Nivette during the service. It was the kind of thing Lane himself should have performed, but he had deputed the job to the ACC. Harpur was not sure why. It could be that Lane still felt unsure about Nivette's loyalty and drew back from this final open endorsement over the body. He had ultimately agreed to come and had agreed to advise the politicians to come, and perhaps that was his limit. Or it might be that Lane felt too worked up to take on the responsibility at such an emotional gathering. This could easily be: Harpur had seen him pass the same sort of duty to the ACC at the funeral of a young murdered girl not long ago. Iles stayed nerveless, and the only hazard was that once in the pulpit he might commandeer the service and keep the vicar out. This had almost happened at the murdered girl's funeral, and *would* have happened if Harpur had not first tried to remove the ACC physically from the pulpit and, when this failed, had disconnected the pulpit microphone and led the congregation in a hymn to drown Iles's special sermon.

Today's funeral was in a handsome old Norman church, squat and grey, not far from the rendezvous blockhouse on the foreshore. Harpur often wondered what effect police funerals had on the public, even one in such a fine setting. Did people feel sympathetic and outraged when they saw the ceremony on television and reported in the Press? Or did it make them troubled and afraid because the police had suffered yet another loss and would never defeat evil nor learn how to defend the good?

'My God, Desmond,' Lane cried suddenly, 'these two men approaching – Shale and Ralph Ember, aren't they? Aren't they? It's what I feared. They *have* decided to attend in their damned arrogance. We'll be cheek by jowl with villains in there. The Home Secretary will be cheek by jowl with villains. This is a statement. They're telling me, telling the Home Secretary, that Nivette belonged to *them*. Didn't I forecast as much? Didn't I, Desmond, Colin?' His voice had gone to less than a whisper.

'They're doing their civic bit, that's all, sir,' Iles replied. 'Ralph W. Ember sees himself as part of the city's authentic fabric. He wants to be publicly associated with mourning for a butchered representative of law and order. And if Ralphy goes, Shale has to as well, matching him. They'll be seen on telly. Angie Hyde and her gang are about. Magnificent suits, both. Ember's could even be Cachape and Drew. They've made an effort. They'd know that if they're going to be cheek by jowling with you and the Home Secretary, sir, they had better be dressed for it. Manse is strong on decorum.'

Lane reached down and started the engine. 'We withdraw,' he said. 'We cannot be a party to their crowing. We must intercept the Home Secretary.'

Iles, in the front with the Chief, leaned across and switched off. 'We can't leave, sir,' he gently explained.

'We've been filmed arriving by Hyde. It would look like an insult to Nivette's family. It *would* be an insult to Nivette's family.'

'Colin, what's your view?' Lane asked, turning, his voice still weak. He did not attempt to restart the car.

Harpur said: 'I think we –'

'They're not fucking crowing, sir,' Iles said. 'Did you see their faces? That wasn't grief for Nivette. They're scared, that's all, poor dears. Ivis is dead but Malthouse isn't, and liable to be unforgiving. This will trouble Mansel. On top of that, they seem to have lost their star – Hector Mills-Mills from the *Eton*.'

'Who says Mills-Mills is gone?' the Chief asked.

'Who do you think, sir?' Iles replied. 'And quite possibly there's no trust between these two any longer, Ralph and Manse. It's because they're in such a bad way and can't let each other get even a step ahead that they're both here today. They have to show themselves to the world as solid business folk, because they're not any longer. They've been severely frightened, sir, and will behave with even more restraint and responsibility from now on. For a while. We've been handed a victory.'

'Victory? You mean they will continue to run their businesses?'

'With tact and temperately.'

'But this I cannot tolerate,' Lane cried. 'This is –'

Iles said: 'It might even be Ralphy who did Ivis. Ember would see the long-term dangers in someone wanting dictator's powers. Ralph can summon up all kind of surprising talents. Well, why he's where he is. How he affords Cachape and Drew. He could have done us a good turn, sir. He'd like that.'

'We're discussing a murder, Desmond,' the Chief said.

'Ralph's a real thinker,' Iles replied, 'and he'd probably be able to stop his arm shaking for long enough with support.'

'Here's the Home Secretary and her minders et cetera,' Harpur said.

'They've been filmed, too,' Iles said. 'We must back her, sir.' Iles opened the passenger door and stepped out so the Home Secretary could see him. She stood waiting for the three men to join her. In a moment Lane took the keys from the ignition and he and Harpur also left the car. The Home Secretary with her group entered the packed church and they were all led to reserved pews immediately behind Mrs Nivette and other members of the family. Harpur sat between the Chief and Iles. 'Try and keep that lovely font of weakness upright on his seat and quiet while I'm in the pulpit, will you, Col?' Iles said, nodding towards Lane while the Chief was bent in prayer. The coffin came up the central aisle carried by officers who had known Nivette and the service began.

They sang two hymns and the vicar spoke two prayers. Then he called upon Iles. The pulpit was high, reached by half a dozen spiral steps. To Harpur it looked a spot alarmingly easy to defend. Iles would be able to kick direct into the head and face of anyone who tried to get him if he took over again. Harpur picked up a prayer cushion which could be used as shield against the ACC's black lace-ups and fists and noted where the plug for the mike was. Momentarily Iles posed, looking down at the casket then out over the congregation. The high gloss pulpit brilliantly set off his splendid uniform, his cropped grey hair and endlessly unreadable, bony impatient face. Harpur heard the Chief groan and mutter, 'Oh, God, why have I let him?'

Iles began to speak something from Isaiah in a big round voice: ' "Who is this that cometh from Edom, with dyed garments from Bozrah? this that is glorious in his apparel, travelling in the greatness of his strength?" ' The ACC had been leaning forward over the edge of the pulpit to offer this question but paused and straightened up for a moment, perhaps to let people reply or take in the glory of his apparel and sense the greatness of his strength. He continued: '"I that speak in righteousness, mighty to save. I have trodden the winepress alone; and of the people there was none with me."'

He stopped again and again stood back, very upright, very alone in his battle for the right, the right arrangement on the streets. '"I will tread them in mine anger, and trample them in my fury; and their blood shall be sprinkled upon my garments, and I will stain all my raiment. For the day of vengeance is in my heart, and the year of my redeemed is come. And I looked, and there was none to help; and I wondered that there was none to uphold: therefore mine own arm brought salvation unto me; and my fury, it upheld me. And I will tread down the people in mine anger, and make them drunk in my fury, and I will bring down their strength to the earth."'

Iles had intoned the grand slaughterous words from memory, as he did in that previous funeral, but he closed the Bible now and pushed it aside. 'Vengeance? Righteous fury? Brisk ideas, and ideas perhaps we all feel today as we think of Richard Nivette and his grieving family. Vengeance? Righteous fury? Yes, we shall try to exercise these against whomever has done this to Richard. He was our man and a good man. All his colleagues know this, from the Chief Constable down. Oh, yes, from the Chief Constable down.' He gave a small unhostile bow towards Lane.

'But perhaps things were simpler in the day of the prophet,' Iles said. 'He wanted ·to exercise his vengeance, his righteous fury madly in all directions. We have a trickier prospect these days. We have a city to run – or a country to run, in the case of the Home Secretary who sits among us this afternoon. We have to compromise, to do deals, to recognise that there are factors we cannot wholly change, only make the best of.'

'Never,' the Chief gasped.

'We have to look for the lesser of eternally competing evils.'

'No,' the Chief muttered. 'Stop him, Colin.'

'We cannot, like Isaiah, give rein to –'

'Can you look after *me*?'

Harpur turned abruptly to see where this new, urgent voice came from. A slightly built man of around thirty in shirt-sleeves had stood in the middle of a pew towards the rear of the church and was staring at Iles and pointing like an accusation with the index finger of his right hand. The Chief had turned, too. 'What is it, Colin?' he asked. 'What? At a *funeral*?'

The man in shirt-sleeves shouted: 'In this church, and only here, I feel safe because it *is* a church and holy and because I knew from the Press a Government Minister is here and the Chief Constable. I believe the Government can protect me. I trust the Chief Constable.'

'I hope we all do that, laddy,' Iles replied.

'I don't trust *you*.'

'Some do,' Iles replied.

'Your people have been looking for me, hunting for me, dragnetting for me. I did not feel safe because I do not trust you or them. And avowed villains have been looking for me also.'

Iles gave ten seconds' thought and smiled a comradely smile: 'You're the friend who was with *my* friend Honorée at the Invet on the night in question?'

The vicar, standing at the foot of the stairs to the pulpit, cried suddenly: 'This must cease.'

'I came here because I knew I would be secure, could speak at last,' the man declared. 'And only here and with witnesses. The Press have seen me now, perhaps TV. I cannot be victimised or made to disappear.'

'What did you see at the Invet?' Iles asked encouragingly. 'You were well placed, I gather. Your view would surely be fuller than Honorée's.'

'No, this must not continue,' the vicar said and began

to climb the steps. He did not seem to think of dis-connecting Iles.

'Oh, God, Colin, save him,' the Chief said. 'Save the vicar.'

'I saw nothing, nothing,' the man said, 'but you send people to find me, try to finger me, put descriptions around, open me up to terrible danger. Is it because I was with your girl?' He had been yelling at Iles down almost the whole length of the church in a harsh, unfor-giving voice, but now suddenly began to whine. 'Hon-estly, I wouldn't have gone with her if I'd known you felt possessive about Honorée, Mr Iles. Please, Home Secretary, Chief Constable, make him show me mercy.'

'I think no ill of you,' Iles replied. 'Honorée and I are not like that – narrow, negative. But what did you see, boy?'

'Nothing.'

'Oh, nonsense,' Iles said. 'Some gal, though, isn't she?'

'You're more understanding than I thought.'

'At Staff College I was known as "Heart-of-gold Iles". So, what did you see?'

'The side of a vehicle.'

'What vehicle?'

'A Land Rover or Range Rover. Nobody, only the vehicle.'

The vicar took the ACC's arm and tugged. Harpur stood and stepped into the aisle holding the prayer cushion, ready to intervene if Iles threw the clergyman down the steps and jumped on him. But the ACC only smiled once more, this time humbly to the vicar, then gave way without trouble and came back to his seat. The vicar returned to the pulpit and the service resumed. Harpur sat down again. During the final, triumphant resurrection hymn, Iles turned to Harpur and said: 'So, the Land Rover. We can put it all on to Alfie, can we, Col? Slow Victor, Finnane, perhaps even Nivette.'

Angie Hyde would safely run her programme now. 'Almost all,' Harpur replied.

'Quite so. I mean, who did Alfie? Oh, yes, probably Ralph. But does it matter much?'

'I don't think Ivis killed Nivette.'

'No, perhaps not Nivette,' Iles replied.

'You'll be able to tell Honorée she can come back now, sir,' Harpur replied.

'I'm a bit hurt that she would go for such a run-of-the-mill object after me, Col.'

In the church porch, as they followed the body out, Mrs Nivette came and spoke to Iles: 'Thank you,' she said and touched his arm. 'I have the idea that it was you who persuaded the Chief to attend and even the Home Secretary. That was so important to me. And I know you'll find who killed Richard.'

Very briefly the ACC put an arm around her shoulders and hugged her. 'Kay, your husband was a good, good man,' he said. 'The Chief's a good man, but now and then confused. His wife sees a great deal in him. Some wives are like that about their husbands. Not all. Not all, are they, Col? Harpur knows about men's wives, you see, Kay, don't you, Harpur?'

Iles's voice had begun to whirl and rattle around the little porch and some spit flew. The Home Secretary and her people moved urgently away from him.

Harpur said: 'The interruption in the church –'

'Didn't matter,' Mrs Nivette replied. 'Perhaps there was useful information.'

'What happened to that little laddy?' Iles said, looking about. 'One does feel a kind of bond with him, with anyone who trusts the Chief.'